More Praise for *Hanging Up*

"*Hanging Up* is not merely hilarious—though it is that. It also gets you in that place where family ties bind and hurt."

—Betty Rollin

"Ephron writes with truth and insight into the conflicting emotions that plague all families, and to do that while maintaining a witty equilibrium is one heck of a balancing act."

—*Dayton Daily News*

"A funny, touching, often penetrating exploration of individual and family strengths and vulnerabilities."

—*Booklist*

Ballantine Books

NEW YORK

HANGING UP

DELIA

EPHRON

Copyright © 1995 by Delia Ephron

All rights reserved under International and Pan-American
Copyright Conventions. Published in the United States
by Ballantine Books, a division of Random House, Inc.,
New York, and distributed in Canada by Random House
of Canada Limited, Toronto.

http://www.randomhouse.com

This edition published by arrangement with G.P. Putnam's Sons.

Library of Congress Catalog Card Number: 95-96197

ISBN: 0-345-40444-0

Cover design and illustration by Honi Werner

Manufactured in the United States of America
First Ballantine Books Edition: June 1996
10 9 8 7 6 5 4 3 2 1

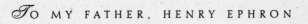

TO MY FATHER, HENRY EPHRON

1911–1992

HANGING UP

I always knew my mother had no friends because she never talked on the telephone. During the day, when the phone rang, the cleaning lady would answer, saying, "Mozell residence." Or my father would pick up, yelling, "I've got it." Or else my sisters and I would fight for the receiver, grabbing it out of each other's hands. If Georgia answered and then just dropped the receiver, leaving it dangling about an inch above the floor, the call was for me. It was never for my mother.

My father planned their social life. "The Irvings on Friday," or whoever, he would say, bounding into the room after hanging up. Social life turned him on. He was like a dog pulling at its leash, waiting for the moment when he could bolt out to dinner, see friends. My mother lay on the couch doing the crossword. "The Irvings on Friday"—sometimes he had to say it three times to get her attention.

Every day, when she returned from teaching, my mother did the *New York Times* crossword puzzle. We were the only family I knew in Los Angeles who took *The New York Times,* and we took it because my mother said, "It's the only crossword puzzle worth doing." She lay there, her head propped up on throw pillows, her stocking feet neatly crossed, and worked her way straight through from one across to sixty-two down.

The crossword seemed to be the thing she lived for, and it was the main constant in our daily lives, until the fights.

That's what my sisters and I called them: the fights. As if the frequent arguments between my parents were bouts in a ring.

They started in the fall of 1966, when I was a sophomore at Uni High School in West Los Angeles, the same high school where my mother taught literature—*A Tale of Two Cities, My Ántonia, The Stranger*. She finished teaching at two, I didn't get out until three-thirty, and I would go into the living room to let her know I was home. She always said the same thing, "If you're hungry, have an apple," working her pen on the crossword without pause. But one day when I came home she was staring at her feet, the puzzle lay undone on her stomach. Her shoes were on, and they were not the usual brown pumps that she wore each day with her shirtwaist dresses. They were red high heels with open toes. As I watched, she raised one leg and turned her slender foot to and fro, wiggling her toes and then admiring the open back with the strap across.

"Hi, Mom," I said.

She sat up and slipped the shoes off. "Slingbacks," she said. "Do you like them?"

"No."

"No?" She smiled at me. "Well, I do." She got up and walked over to a mirror and did something else I had never seen: She turned up the collar on her shirtwaist dress.

"That looks dumb," I said.

She ignored my comment, smoothing her hair over her ears.

My mother wore her dark wavy hair cut almost as short as a boy's, and slicked back off her face, a style she referred to as "no nonsense." Her only concession to vanity, until the slingback heels appeared, was the bright pink lipstick she freshened every hour or so.

I kept an eye on those shoes. They disappeared into the closet for the rest of the week, although her collars stayed up, and she even added a scarf, a jaunty silk thing that she tied around her neck western style in a little knot, letting the short ends lap over her collar.

Then, on Saturday morning, she tipped her hand.

Maddy, my younger sister, who was ten, was lying on the floor in the family room watching *The Flintstones*. I was perched on the pantry counter clocking the first of many daily hours of conversation on the telephone with my boyfriend. His name was Stuart, but I called him Sonny and he called me Cher because, like Sonny and Cher, we fancied ourselves sparring partners. "What are you doing?" he would say. "Who wants to know?" was my quick comeback. We thought this was hot stuff. Anyway, Georgia, four years older than I, was in Massachusetts, a sophomore in college, and it was just another peaceful weekend morning—my parents drinking coffee, the lazy Susan stacked with bagels, lox, and cream cheese—when my mother, reading the newspaper, said, "Those damn loggers."

The swinging door was open and I could see my parents in the breakfast room. Even though I was deep in Stuartland, I heard the comment and noticed that my father, who was spinning the lazy Susan in search of a second helping of lox, halted a second.

A few nights later, instead of going to his weekly poker game, he followed her to a motel and nearly broke down the door.

They fought regularly after this. Night after night, they relived the moment—my father's eureka at the breakfast table, my mother's fury and humiliation at being caught in bed with Tom Winston, the biology teacher, who, we learned from the fights, was a very active member of the Sierra Club.

He had red hair and he was huge. "His body is as big as a double bed," Georgia said ominously when Maddy and I took the telephone into the hall closet and, hunkering under the coats, called to let her know what had happened.

"Was he your teacher?" I asked.

"Yes. He taught me to dissect frogs. How can Mom have sex with someone who knows that much about your insides?"

Maddy yanked the phone away from me. "Come home, Georgia."

I pulled it back. "She can't, Maddy. Do you want her to flunk out?"

I tried to imagine what I would look like if Tom Winston were my father. Would I be as big as an ostrich, forced to buy my clothes at the tall women's shop instead of wearing my neat size seven? Maybe I wouldn't have black hair with curls springing in all directions but thick, well-behaved tangerine-colored locks that kept a clear part in one-o'clock position. Would I have blue eyes instead of brown—blue eyes with, oh God, pinkish lashes like his?

Every day I invented reasons—told to no one but myself —why I had to walk by the science lab. I sneaked a look, barely taking in a blur of microscopes and Tom Winston's white lab coat. I never saw my mother with him (something I craved and dreaded), and Tom Winston never looked at me. He traveled through the halls as if on cross-country skis, making gigantic strides, and if by accident we passed, he didn't jerk or slow down. There wasn't even a flicker in his eyes that we had a connection.

I checked out the lab every day right through June, and then, on the first day of my junior year, I took another sur-reptitious stroll past. Where was Tom Winston?

I waited until after French class, pretending to take a long time collecting my books. When I was the only one left in the room with Monsieur Lecard, I said very casually, "Oh"—the "oh" was important, it showed that this thought had just popped into my head—"Oh, I was walking by the science lab and I noticed there's a new teacher. What happened to Mr. Winston?"

"En français," said Monsieur Lecard.

"Où est Monsieur Winston?" I said, starting to sweat, thinking that my mother was going to appear, just waltz in from her English class at that very moment.

"Il est à Big Bear."

Big Bear? I called Georgia at college. "He moved to Big Bear. Do you think they're through? Where's that?"

"It's this grungy little town in the mountains. I went

there by accident once when I was going to Lake Arrowhead. It has a bowling alley."

"Los Angeles has bowling alleys."

"That's not what I mean." I could hear her disgust. "I mean that's all there is. At night people come out of their log cabins and go bowling. Guess what, I'm engaged."

"Hey, congratulations."

"Georgia's engaged," I said to my mom when she came in from the garden, where she was inspecting the rosebushes. My mother frequently inspected the roses after she did the puzzle. Then she gave the gardener instructions. When I was older, I wondered why she had so much to say. Joe and I have rosebushes, and the only thing we do is cut them back and spray them. Cut and spray. Cut and spray. Maybe she was having an affair with the gardener too. "She's going to call tonight and tell us all about him."

"It won't last," said my mom. She opened the cabinet, took out a bottle of scotch, and poured herself a glass. It was four in the afternoon and she did it as if she were having orange juice. I watched, eating Oreos, as she dropped in two ice cubes.

"Are you looking at something?" she asked.

"Uh, no. Want an Oreo?" I offered the bag.

"Don't be smart, Eve."

"I'm not."

My mother considered, poking the ice cubes down with her finger. I thought she was thinking about me, but then she turned, looked out the window, and began slowly sipping her drink as if I weren't there at all.

She had never been much of a cook. Her idea of dinner was broiled meat (chicken, lamb chops, or steak), baked potatoes, and a Birds Eye frozen vegetable. But at least she used to arrange the food on platters and let my dad serve. These days she loaded up our plates in the kitchen, and while we ate, she disappeared into the den and poured another scotch.

I tried to keep my father occupied. "How's the writing going?" It was something I'd heard one of his poker friends ask him.

"Fine." My father stared at the door, in my mother's direction.

I kicked Maddy.

"Mrs. Weber plays favorites, she really does," Maddy yakked. "She won't put me in the front row of the Pilgrim tableau. I'm going to complain to the principal."

"She can't complain about that, can she, Dad?"

My father flung his fork across the room and we were struck dumb. He went into the den. And they started screaming at each other.

Our house, like all the houses on the street, sat on an ivy-covered hill, which sloped down to the sidewalk. Once, really late at night during the fights, my mom threw herself off the front steps. It was as if she were doing a gigantic belly flop off a diving board. She landed with a smack in the ivy and lay there facedown. Maddy and I watched, amazed, our faces pressed against an upstairs window, making little breath circles on the pane, with our mouths hung open. After a few minutes, our mother stood up and came back inside. Had she expected us to rush out? Or had she been waiting for something to happen, something like death, and when it didn't, had she just returned to the house to scream some more?

When Georgia came home for Christmas, she, Maddy, and I went out for ice cream. We sat in a row—Georgia eating pistachio, Maddy peppermint stick, and me chocolate chip—and I told Georgia all about Mom's feeble attempt at suicide.

"Death from ivy asphyxiation." Georgia laughed, then snorted by accident, sending us into hysterics. Normally she was utterly composed. She kept still, her arms very close to her body, and although she wasn't tall, she seemed to be looking down at everyone, even when she was sitting. She licked her ice cream in an exquisitely well-mannered way. It remained a perfect round mound that got smaller and smaller. It never dripped.

I couldn't keep up with my ice cream. It melted onto the back of my hand, which I licked, getting some on my chin. Once, when I flipped my hand out to the side to emphasize some comment or other, the scoop flew out of the cone and across the store. I always talked with my hands. Georgia could pull the eye just sitting. I must have known I had to work harder for attention, because whatever I said was accompanied by a streak of hand patter.

"Really," I said, my hands doing their usual dance, "we watched from the window. Mom was in her fancy pink robe, facedown in ivy."

"Maybe next time she'll impale herself on the rosebushes," said Georgia.

"Or take an overdose of daisies."

"I know, I know." Maddy threw her hand up high.

"Yes, Miss Madeline Mozell," said Georgia, imitating Mom's teacher voice. "Do you have a suggestion to make to the class on how our mother, Patricia Mozell, might commit suicide?"

"She'll run around the science lab until she drops. Around and around and around and around."

"Like *The Red Shoes*," said Georgia.

"Her red shoes?" I asked.

"No. It's this movie where a girl puts on ballet shoes and can't stop dancing until she dies."

"Kerplop," said Maddy. She threw her arms up and flopped down on the floor, dead. "Kerplop, kerplop, kerplop"—she died over and over, all around the ice cream store.

One night, while Mom and Dad fought, Maddy and I sneaked out. I had just passed my driver's test, and braving the freeway for the first time, I drove us to the airport. "People always hang out waiting for planes," I told Maddy. "No one will notice us. They'll think we're meeting our parents." After an hour or so of traipsing from one arrival gate to another, we called Georgia collect.

"We're at the airport because of the fights. We don't want to go home. What should we do?"

Georgia instructed us. "Go to a motel. There's a gray one with white iron railings at the corner of Sepulveda and Washington. Not the one across from it with the sign that says 'Our rooms are tops.' You'll think it's better, but it's not."

Georgia always knew how to advise us so we wouldn't make a mistake. She even anticipated our anxieties. "You can register in your own name, they won't ask you any questions, but do you have fifteen dollars? That's what the room will cost."

"Maybe this is where Mom went with him," Maddy said after we checked in.

We stood in the center of the room, not knowing what to do, although there were only two choices, bed or television. "We should sleep in our clothes," I said.

"Is it safe here?" Maddy wondered. She sat on the tiniest inch of bed, looking down at it warily, then over at me.

"I'll tell you what, if you get scared, just say 'Aroo.'"

"What's that mean?" Maddy scooted back against the wooden headboard.

"It doesn't mean anything. Aroo." I marched over to the TV and turned it on.

"Aroo." Maddy pulled the blankets out from under herself and tucked her feet in. "Aroo, aroo, aroo." She snuggled down and put her head on the pillow.

I got into her bed, although we had never slept in the same bed before. "Move over." I kicked her.

"Aroo." She kicked me back.

We left the TV on all night.

In the morning we tried to put the bed back exactly as we'd found it. The sheets were barely rumpled. We had each slept in one position, or else it seemed that way, but we folded and smoothed the pillows so they were again shaped like Tootsie Rolls, and tucked the spread over them, working together, feeling very competent, a team.

"When they find out where we were, they'll feel awful," I told Maddy on the way home. "If they're mad, I'm leaving forever." I slammed my hand against the front door, pushing it in, and moved aggressively ahead of her. She trailed a car's length behind as we hunted around, finally locating our parents in the kitchen. My father said, "Hi, you hungry?" My mother glanced over from where she was squeezing oranges for juice, and kept squeezing.

A year and a half later, when I left for college, my parents came to the airport and we all pretended to be a family. Mom bought me magazines and Dad stood at the departure gate with his arm around her. The plane was announced and Maddy jumped on me, piggy-back.

She was thirteen now, taller than I was, and long and gangly. Her legs went on forever, and disappeared into her baggy shorts like firehouse poles that go right through the ceiling. She wrapped her legs around my waist and her arms around my neck. "Maddy, let go." It was like being locked in a vise.

"Aroo," she squeaked.

Not fair. I shook her loose. "Bye, Dad. Bye, Mom. I'll miss you." Big lie. I got in line and didn't look back.

During my first two years of college, my mother never phoned. But my father did. There was a pay phone in my dorm that served the entire floor. It was in a wooden booth with glass doors and a seat inside, and I spent more time in that booth talking to my father than the girl next door to me spent gabbing with her fiancé. I began to anticipate my father's calls. "For Eve," whoever answered would shout. I approached the phone with trepidation, picking up the receiver and listening to see whether the call was long-distance. You could hear long-distance then. It was an empty sound, like air in a tunnel. If that sound was there, I knew who it probably was.

"Hello. Just checking in," he'd say.

"What's new?" I'd say.

"We had a fight last night. Your mother's driving me crazy."

I called Georgia to complain. "Do you believe they're still at it?"

"Refresh my memory," said Georgia, who was now in New York City, working as a girl Friday at *Mademoiselle* magazine.

"What?"

"Mom had one affair, right?"

"As far as we know."

"Well, I don't mean to state the obvious, but it's hardly a big deal."

"Maybe she can't get over him, Georgia."

"Over that lab rat? Over a man who smells of formaldehyde? I don't think so. Anyway, doesn't our father start the fights?"

"Not exactly. She drinks, which provokes him. Besides, it's all her fault for having an affair in the first place."

"Eve, there are hundreds of people in the country right now having open marriages, swinging, the works, and he is carrying on about one petite affair. You know, when Richard and I get married—"

"Who's Richard?"

"You'll love him. If he talks. But he doesn't talk that much in public."

"Where does he talk?"

"At work—he's a lawyer. Or with me."

"Is this serious, or is it like that engagement you had in college? Mom predicted it wouldn't last."

"This is serious. We're eloping next summer. I can't have our parents at the wedding. Who knows what they'll do."

I spent the summer when Georgia eloped as a camp counselor in Maine. No sooner had I dumped my luggage back in my dorm room than the pay phone rang. I picked it up.

"She won't go to school," my father said. This was new: He didn't say hello. He left the front off the conversation.

"What? She's dropping out? Put her on, Dad."

"Not Maddy, your mother. She says she doesn't give a shit about Sydney Carton. She's locked herself in the bathroom with a bottle of scotch." He hung up.

This was also new: No good-bye. He left the end off the conversation.

The next day, I answered again. And again I heard long-distance. Then crying. Well, not crying, sniffling. Very large sniffles.

"Dad, what is it, what happened?" I closed the phone booth door.

Still nothing but major intakes of breath.

"Are you all right?" I started breathing heavily too, inadvertently, in unison. I could see Joanne, the girl with the fiancé, coming down the hall to use the phone. Minutes went by. She stared at me so I couldn't help but notice that she was waiting.

"Dad?"

No answer.

Joanne used her diamond ring to knock on the door. I twisted in my seat so I wouldn't have to see her.

"She's gone," my dad said finally.

"Mom's gone?"

"Yeah."

Fine, I thought. Great, she's gone. Thank God. No more drinking, no more fights. "Dad, don't worry. I'm sure she'll be back."

"She ran off with that redwood."

"What?"

He hung up.

She ran off with that redwood. She ran off with that redwood. His words played over and over in my brain. Joanne rapped her rock against the glass again and glared at me. *She ran off with that redwood.* I stuck my tongue out at Joanne and yanked open the door.

I didn't sleep that night. The next day, I couldn't focus on anything. I had invented a system, five minutes of study, five minutes of daydreaming, which allowed me to relive necking each weekend with my boyfriend, Mark. But as I sat at my desk trying to study, then trying to think about Mark, my mind kept veering off to Mom and Tom Winston. Had she pined for him for five years, or had she been seeing him secretly the whole time? Did they meet at exits off the freeway all along the route from Westwood to Big Bear, or did they have a favorite rendezvous, a favorite room? Did he pin her on the bed the way he pinned those little frogs when he cut them open?

"It's for you," Joanne yelled. "Telephone."

Maybe it's Mom. Maybe she's calling so I'll know where she is.

I took the receiver and, holding it away from my head, stood outside the booth and listened. There it was again, but dimly, the long-distance sound, plus noise, horns, traffic. "Hello?"

"Evie?"

I slammed the phone against my ear. "Maddy, where are you?"

"In Malibu. In a parking lot. Guess what? I'm moving in with Isaac."

"What do you mean? You can't move in with Isaac. You're only fifteen. What about school?"

"I don't have to live at home to go to school. God, I knew you'd say that." Her words turned into a wail. "Just leave me alone, all right? You don't have to live with a drunk."

"But I thought Mom moved out. Dad called last night. He said she left."

Now she was crying. Gulping sobs. Big fat teenage tears. "Not Mom, dummy. Dad. Look, I'll be at Isaac's. He doesn't have a phone. Bye."

Dad? What was she talking about?

Two

The door is unlocked from
the inside, an orderly opens it, and Angie wheels my father in.

This place is not old, really, just battered. The painted plaster

walls have scrape marks on them, probably from wheelchairs.

The wooden trim around the doorways and windows, that

homey touch signifying extra care and concern, is gouged,

and the walnut stain is scratched and thin. "UCLA Geriatric/

Psychiatric"—the words are discreetly printed on a rectangular plastic plaque next to the door, which the orderly relocks after us.

The wheelchair squeaks on the linoleum as we go down the hall. We pass first an old-fashioned telephone booth built into the wall—it is nearly identical to the one in my college dorm years ago—then a room filled with rows of chairs. Assorted chairs in assorted colors, but mostly they have metal legs and metal arms, with cushioned vinyl seats and vinyl pads on the armrests. Old people are sitting in some of them. They are facing a television set, which is on. Straight ahead is something I will begin to call the cage. It's an office that has a small opening fitted with a protective grate, like the kind in front of bank teller windows in dangerous neighborhoods. The nurses hang out here. There is glass on the sides so they can see out into the patient rooms that surround them.

My father twists around to look at Angie. It's a strain for him to turn because he's so fat. He takes up all the space in the chair, and when he turns, his shirt strains, almost to popping open. "What's Claire doing here?" he growls.

"I'm not Claire, I'm Angie."

"You know Angie," I say. "She works at the Home, where you live. She's helping me bring you here."

Angie wheels him into a dining room. An older man in glasses and a woman, both in medical whites, come into the room, closing the door behind us.

The woman introduces herself. "I'm Dr. Kelly," she says. She looks like a high school cheerleader. That young and wholesome. "This is Rob Bateson."

"I'm the social worker," he says cheerfully. "Why don't we sit down?" He gestures toward the nearest Formica table.

Angie wheels my father to the table and then stands back, waiting for the rest of us.

"I'll sit next to my father," I announce. This is an unnecessary statement. In the almost twenty-five years since my mother left, my sisters and I have taken turns calling the doctor about him, putting him in loony bins, drying him out, buying him clothes. And when more than one of us are present, we even take turns sitting next to him. But today, at UCLA Geriatric/Psychiatric, my father's final incarceration, there is no one here but me.

I hear a squeal as Dr. Kelly jumps, throws my father a dirty look, then catches herself. She smooths the back of her pants, where he obviously has just pinched, then takes a chair, sits, and smiles calmly.

I'll be out of here in a half-hour, I comfort myself. This is a trick my son has taught me, the way he gets through classes he hates.

They start asking my father questions. Your name? "Lou Mozell." Age? "Thirty-nine," he says.

"Eighty-one," I say, smiling.

Where were you born? "The Bronx." College?

"Harvard," says my father. "I graduated with honors." They write all this down dutifully.

"What month is it?" My father has no idea. "What day of the week?" He looks up at the ceiling, studying it as if there were something to see.

"Look," I say, "this is ridiculous. My father lives in a Home. Every day is the same. How does he know whether it's Monday or Wednesday? And this is Los Angeles. The sky's always blue. Even I don't know what month it is half the time."

"These questions have been tested," Dr. Kelly says, an edge to her voice.

"Well, they don't make any sense."

Meanwhile my father is refusing to say anything.

"Will you write your name, Mr. Mozell?" She offers a pen and her clipboard.

He obliges.

"Would you write a sentence?"

He does that too. She shows me the clipboard.

He has written, "It's too late."

Oh, wow. I actually have this dumb high school reaction. Oh, wow. Heavy. And in my mind, I am already on the phone to my sisters. " 'It's too late.' That's what he wrote. Do you believe that?"

"Why don't we show you to your room," Dr. Kelly says to my father.

"Are you leaving me here?" he asks me. His hands, which have been lying listlessly in his lap, fly up and seize the arms of his wheelchair.

"You're going to stay here for a week or two." Maybe more, I don't say. "You're having memory problems, Dad. They'll run some tests."

"You bitch. You and Claire. You put me here before. You're in cahoots." My father flings a backslap at me but misses by a mile.

"That's not Claire, that's Angie, and you've never been here before." I say this quietly, but I can feel my face flush.

Angie springs up. "I'll take him." She spins the wheelchair around. "I'm taking you to your room, Mr. Mozell," she declares, as Rob Bateson jumps to open the door for them. "Bitch," my father shouts as she steers him out, and Bateson closes the door behind them.

There is silence. A moment of respect for the departed.

"My father didn't go to Harvard."

Dr. Kelly laughs, then immediately crosses out the entry on her form. "Where did he go?"

"He went to, oh, what's that school, you know, it's in New York City, what is it, ohh—"

"Columbia?" says Bateson.

"No, no, downtown."

Bateson and Kelly look at each other, stumped. Dr. Kelly actually winds some of her long sandy hair around her finger while she thinks. "New York University," she offers tentatively.

"Right. He went to NYU. I can't believe I didn't remember that. I do know this is the month of May and it's somewhere between the fourteenth and the twentieth, right?"

No one laughs. Bateson leans toward me across the table. "Are you close to your father?" he asks.

I hate this question. It's none of their business. Their business is to find out what's wrong with his brain this time. Their business is to adjust his medication so he functions. He just needs a new cocktail. He's gone off his rocker before. He's gone off many times. I will answer this question dispassionately. I will show that an inquiry about my feelings for my father triggers nothing. "I look out for my father but I am not close to him," I say firmly. I smile to show that this cool answer is not only the truth, but easy.

☎

"He wrote, 'It's too late.' Do you believe that?"

"Really," says Georgia.

It's impossible to convey Georgia's affection for the word "really." She caresses it. She packs in multiple meanings: astonishment, disbelief, sometimes disgust, suspicion, pleasure, maybe even thrill, plus curiosity. All understated. She owns "really." Also "possibly," just because she knows exactly how to emphasize it.

"Do you think our father could possibly have meant what he wrote?" she asks me.

"You mean, can you be brain-damaged and cosmic all at once? I think so."

"But what did he actually mean by it? Too late for what?"

It occurs to me I don't know what he meant. "I guess help. It's too late for help, right? But then it could be too late for anything to change, or for anything to happen, or just, too late."

She says nothing. I assume she is mulling this over, but maybe she is just editing some copy on the computer while she talks to me on the phone. Sometimes Georgia switches off right in the middle of a conversation—she starts doing something else or thinking about something else. I have to work to get her back.

"He pinched Dr. Kelly. On the tush."

"Really," says Georgia.

Maddy shrieks when I tell her about the pinching. "What a riot."

"It wasn't a riot, believe me. You weren't there."

"You told me I could go away. You said you'd take him to . . . what's this place called?"

"UCLA Geriatric/Psychiatric."

"Is it like a hospital?"

"More like a loony bin really, sort of a cross. Anyway, I don't care that you aren't here."

"It's my only vacation. We work ten hours a day, five days a week."

"Maddy, it's okay."

But she's on a roll. "We work fifty-two weeks a year, Eve. Fifty-two weeks!" I think about putting the receiver on the table. If you check out of a conversation with Maddy and then return several minutes later, you are usually in the same place. The identical thing happens if you watch the soap opera she's on and then don't see it again until two weeks later. "The only reason I can go on vacation now is that Juliana is supposed to be in the Bahamas so her boss can have an affair with the temp."

"Who's Juliana?"

"My character? Eve, don't you even know that? God, don't you ever watch the show?"

"Of course I do. I just didn't realize what you were saying, Maddy, it's no big deal."

"You know it's not easy to get to the phone here. It's not easy to get to anything in Montana. You can drive forty-five minutes just to buy milk."

I call Georgia back. "Maddy says it's a forty-five-minute drive to buy milk in Montana."

This is one of my favorite things—to serve as a conduit between my sisters. What is the joy in hearing something absurd from one if I can't pass it on to the other? But this time I'm just using Maddy's comment for an excuse, so I can unload more to Georgia.

"Imagine Dad pinching that doctor. It's so sad, repulsive, I don't know. I think he winked too. Is that all that's left to you when you're old? Eating and flirting?"

"He's a pathetic old man," says Georgia. I am certain I hear her shudder.

"That's for sure. Dr. Kelly looked like Doogie Howser's younger sister."

"Well, Eve, she obviously wasn't the doctor. Obviously, obviously. She's a resident. What you have to do tomorrow is call and speak to the doctor. The real doctor. Find out who's in charge of the whole place and insist that he or she speak to you directly. You know it makes a huge difference whether you're speaking to the top or the bottom."

"Maybe you should call."

"Darling, I would, but you're right there. I'm in New York, so if they have to call me back, it's long-distance, which is a big thing to doctors, I have no idea why. Besides, I'm totally backed up on this tenth-anniversary edition. I keep thinking, On the one hand, I am so lucky my magazine has lasted ten years, on the other hand, why am I putting out a special edition, it's a nightmare."

I am hit suddenly with an exhaustion I get only when I converse with my sisters. I feel as if my mouth and ears are going to fall off my head. "I've got to go," I say. "I'll call you tomorrow." I hang up. The phone rings. "Hello?"

"Mom?"

"Hi, Jesse, where are you?"

"It's not my fault."

"What?"

"It was an accident."

☎

"Goddamnit." I burst into Joe's study. "Jesse had another car accident."

"Is he all right?" Joe spins around in his desk chair, knocking into phone books from different cities, stacked like building blocks around him.

"He's all right."

To make room to sit, I shove over a bunch of radio tapes that are littering his couch. "He's on his way home. He had to tie his car door closed with rope. His insurance is going to go through the roof, but maybe we can convince the driver not to notify his insurance company. Would you take care of this?"

"I'm going out of town next week," he reminds me.

"So you have time. Besides, they have phones in Iowa."

Joe just looks at me. He knows and I know that I am going to make this call. We've been married too long to have a conversation we've had sixty times before and already know the ending of.

I hear a car and peek through the blinds to see Jesse pulling up to the curb. He slides over to the passenger side and gets out. He strolls to the door, his shoulders moving back and forth enough to cause, with each step, the slightest ripple of muscle across his T-shirt.

"I'm home," he yells, but not too loudly. There's a bit of dread in his voice.

"Come in here. We're in Dad's study." I hear the refrigerator open and close, and then Jesse appears, swigging water from a large plastic bottle.

"What happened?" Joe asks.

Jesse slaps a hand against his head and lets his mouth hang open a second to let us know he's been through hell. "I was sitting there, okay, just opening the door, when this guy comes around a curve at about, I swear, sixty."

Joe slips his fingers under his glasses and rubs his eyes. He's tired in anticipation of this discussion. "You were parked?" he says wearily.

"Yeah, I was parked. That guy should look where he's going. Thanks to him, I couldn't take Ifer home."

"Who's Ifer?"

"Only my best friend, Dad. God."

"Ifer is Jennifer, but there are so many Jennifers in the class that she calls herself Ifer. I told you, you forgot." This is something I do to Joe when I am feeling cranky. Make him feel guilty for not remembering all the fascinating things I tell him.

"Why doesn't she call herself Jenny?" asks Joe.

"Ifer is Kasmian," says Jesse.

Joe's glasses land back on his nose and his eyes snap open. He knows he's just heard something that is going to turn out to be satisfyingly off-kilter. He's no longer interested in the car accident. Too mundane. Jesse's fine, he's sitting right in front of him. But Ifer could turn out to be as intriguing as the woman in Iowa he's going to interview who bakes six-foot-tall cakes. "So Ifer is a Kasmian name?" he says.

Jesse uses a tone of voice that means that you are ignorant but he will condescend to enlighten you. "In the Kasmian religion, Dad, four letters is good luck. 'Luck' is four letters, get it?"

"I hope these Kasmians aren't nuts like those people who drank that drink in some South American country," I say. "What was it? It starts with a large letter."

"Kool-Aid," says Joe.

"I didn't remember Kool-Aid? My God."

"Kasmians drink only Coke. Four letters, get it?" says Jesse. "This guy owes us. He could have killed me."

I take a few breaths, just for punctuation. "Look, the important thing is that you're fine. That your leg wasn't outside the car or anything." This is the important thing, and it's not that I don't know it, but I say it for only one reason: So I feel entitled to say the next thing, which I feel guilty about. "But it's your fault."

Jesse slams the bottle down. "The guy came around a blind curve. I can't see behind a blind curve, can I? I am really having a hard day. I don't need this. It's not my fault I can't see a guy coming around a blind curve going eighty."

"Did he take the door off the car?" I ask. The phone rings. I pick it up. "Hello?"

"Georgie Porgie won a Pulitzer."

"That's great."

"Your sister's something, isn't she?"

"Yeah, she's great, Dad."

He hangs up. I hang up.

"Georgia won the Pulitzer again. How can he call? I don't think he has a phone in his room. The only phone I saw was a pay phone."

"Did you give him quarters?" asks Joe.

"Are you kidding? Why would I do that? To torture myself?" I turn to Jesse. "I had a hard day too. I had to put your grandfather into the geriatric/psychiatric facility at UCLA."

"Oh yeah, how come?" Jesse collapses in a chair. His long legs stick straight out into the room; he's waiting to trip someone so he can insist it's not his fault.

"He's having memory problems."

"He's always had memory problems. He doesn't even know my name."

Joe laughs.

"It's not funny, Joe." Now I'm angry with them both. "He's having other problems too. He hit someone, he's been screaming just out of the blue whenever he feels like it. He can't walk—his balance is off. They think his medication's out of whack. You could both be a little compassionate."

"I have no compassion for your father, and you know why," says Joe.

"Why?" Jesse asks.

"None of your business," I say. "So Jesse, did he take the door off the car?"

"No."

"Well, if he didn't take the door off the car, he couldn't have been going eighty."

"Just 'cause your door stays on the car has nothing to do with speed. It has to do with the weight of the car that hits you."

Is this true? I have no idea. Even though, as far as I can tell, schools these days don't even teach you what a pronoun is, Jesse claims to know everything. He knows whether dogs can be said to commit suicide, under what conditions planes can take off at LAX, whether astigmatism will one day be curable by laser. I give up trying to prove my point. "Did you get the guy's insurance information? I hope you got his phone number too."

Jesse holds out his hand. A name and a number are written on his palm in black ink.

"Jesse, that's so careless. Suppose you got water on that? We'd never be able to reach him."

"He'd find us."

"That's not the point."

"He *would* find us. Unfortunately," says Joe. "Do Kasmians have a place of worship?"

"They light candles in their rooms," Jesse tells him.

"Can we talk about this accident, please?"

Joe and Jesse both look at me—their heads swivel exactly the same way and stop at exactly the same tilt to the right. They look as if they have paused mid-beat in a song they perform in unison, like the Temptations. They are both vertical in the extreme, and whenever they walk or eat or just move around, their arms and legs go from straight lines to angles. Only, Joe wears glasses—round horn-rimmed glasses. With those comical circles on either side of his narrow nose and the rest of him hanger thin, he has the appearance of a very friendly figure painting reduced to its geometric essence. They both wait for me to talk, Joe tolerantly, Jesse with his familiar scowl.

"It's important to contact this guy before he contacts you so—"

"So what, Mom?"

"So you have a plan, so it doesn't get out of hand."

"Do your mom a favor," says Joe. "Copy that information off your palm onto a piece of paper and leave it on her desk."

Jesse gets up slowly, stretching, so we notice him ascend to his six-foot height. He saunters out.

I wait until I hear Jesse on the stairs. I don't want him to hear me. "What?" Joe says, knowing something's coming.

"You shouldn't make fun of my father, especially now."

"Don't expect me to have feelings you don't have." He shrugs. "Besides, this is just another round."

"It is not. For God's sake, Joe, why don't you clean up in here? Look at these tapes. And there are newspapers and telephone books all over the place."

"I like it messy. Then I know where everything is. Eve, stop worrying. Your father just phoned, so obviously he's fine."

"Then why can't he walk? And he kept calling Angie Claire. He knows Angie."

"You just couldn't remember Kool-Aid."

"That's hardly the same thing." I start picking newspapers up off the floor, grabbing them two-fisted, each one a big deal. "Look, this place is a complete mess. Suppose we have a fire or something? This room would go off like a rocket. And then the house."

Joe takes the stack of papers from me and puts them back

on the floor, carefully, even ceremoniously, as if they were not old newspapers but an elaborate silver service for tea.

"Joe, he's dying."

"You wish."

"Yes, I do. Is there anything wrong with that?"

Three

When I went home for Christmas after my parents had separated and Maddy had moved out, Maddy picked me up at the airport with her boyfriend, Isaac.

Her hair, long and parted in the middle, left just a sliver of her face showing, and looked as if it should come with a cord so it could be drawn open like a curtain.

When we hugged, her hair got in my mouth. "Where's Dad?"

"Probably playing tennis. Stay with Isaac and me. Only ten of us are living there."

"No, I'll go home."

"Well, don't expect me to go in. I'm not going in."

Maddy and Isaac were dressed identically, in jeans with silver studs running down them and jean jackets with American flags sewn on the back. She had a tank top underneath and he had his bare chest. Below each of their jacket collars was an embroidered red heart with embroidered tears falling from it. "We're still in mourning," she explained, reaching over and fluffing my hair.

"Don't." I knocked her hand away.

"It's wilder than ever," she said.

"I know." I squished my curls against my head.

"Your hair's the same color as Mom's," she said wistfully.

"Don't remind me."

"Why don't you let it grow? Live a little, Eve."

I changed the subject. "Why are you in mourning? Who died?"

"Jimi Hendrix, who else?" Maddy boomed this and did not seem to mind that half the airport turned to look. She called ahead to Isaac. "Eve's really nice, she's just ignorant." Then she spoke only slightly lower: "Jimi was Isaac's soul mate."

"Right on," said Isaac.

"I embroidered the hearts."

"Very pretty," I said.

"I'll teach you," said Maddy. "It's really fun."

We walked through the airport, Maddy clumping along on thick platform shoes, Isaac's head bobbing, as if there was music in it and he was keeping time. "Isaac's a musical genius," she said. "He's like hot, I'm not kidding." She tugged playfully on his ponytail.

"Get lost," said Isaac.

"What's your instrument?" I asked him.

"He can play everything, bass guitar, keyboard . . ." Maddy thought a second. "Bass guitar, keyboard." She put a period at the end this time. "They've got this group—Isaac, Aaron, Kevin, Presto." She ticked the names off on her fingers. "I'm going to be the lead singer, and we're going to make a demo tape. Do you think Georgia would know anyone who could help us get, you know, arrested?"

"Why Georgia? Madeline, don't you think you should live at home?"

She ignored that. " 'Cause Georgia works at *Mademoiselle*. Even though they only do stories on dumbos like Karen Carpenter, I thought maybe . . ."

"Are you going to school?"

She laughed. "When I want. Listen, Eve, we've got this groovy song that Isaac wrote. 'Born Too Late for Woodstock.' We just missed it, you know." Her voice was pained. "If Woodstock had been this year, we would have been there. Isaac's got some dirt from it. He bought it at this head shop. You'll see it—it's on the dashboard."

"I don't know, ask her."

"Ask who?"

"Georgia, if she can help you. That's mine." I pointed at my suitcase rolling toward me on the conveyor belt. Isaac didn't move so I pulled it off myself.

"The car's right over there." Maddy indicated the lot directly across. Isaac preceded us, his head still bobbing. "Isn't he cute?" she whispered. I nodded. She squeezed my arm. "Do you believe your little sister's going to be a rock star?"

We rode home in a car with a peace sign dangling from

the rearview mirror over a mayonnaise jar filled with dirt. Isaac stayed in the car while Maddy helped me get my suitcase out of the trunk.

"Don't ask me to go in, okay, Eve? I can't stand it."

"Why?"

"It's creepy. He's creepy." She pulled one foot up behind her and stood there like a flamingo.

"Get going, Maddy. Don't worry, I'll talk to you tomorrow."

"Peace," she shouted as they took off.

The house looked the same, except for the rosebushes. They hadn't been cut back. The stalks were long, with the remains of dead blooms on the ends, pathetic yellow centers with a petal or two hanging off.

I tried the door. It was unlocked. "Dad?"

"Hey, Evie, I'm out back."

I left my suitcase in the entrance hall and walked through the living room to the garden behind. My father jumped up from the patio table. "Evie, baby." He pulled a handkerchief out of the pocket of his tennis shorts and mopped his eyes. "I always cry," he explained to the woman who was sitting with him.

"It's true," I said. "He used to cry when I came home from Brownies."

"Or from camp," he said. His mouth wiggled as he tried to get control, stiffen it up. He tucked his handkerchief back in his pocket and hugged me. "This is my Evie," he said proudly.

"Well, don't I know it," said the woman.

"You do?" I said doubtfully.

"I knew she wouldn't recognize you. Want a hint?" my father crowed.

"Sure, but what happened to your nose?"

My father touched the bridge of his nose, where there was a big scab. "I hit myself serving." He paused. "But at least I got it in."

"Well, that's what matters, isn't it?" I smiled at the woman.

"Mouthwash," said my father.

"Oh my God, Esther."

She was the receptionist at our dentist's. She'd been the receptionist forever. Her hair, an assortment of browns that would be very attractive on a puppy but was unlikely on a person, was piled on top of her head in large loopy curls, and she had frosted orange polish on very long nails. I had always viewed them with wonder while she filled in the card for my next appointment.

"I'm so sorry about your mom. It's tragic," said Esther.

"What hap—" I saw my father put his finger to his lips, shush. I corrected, "Oh, thank you, that's very kind."

"Myself, I hate to fly." She fixed some of her stray hair in place with a bobby pin. "I think it was so brave of you to get in that airplane to come home for Christmas. If that happened to someone in my family, I'd stick to cars."

I noticed a pitcher of iced tea on the table. With real lemons floating in it. That's great. Mom left, and Dad finally learned to make something: iced tea. He even made it with loving care, which is more than Mom ever did.

Esther poked around in her purse and pulled out a little round compact. She peered into the mirror, remade her lips, and snapped the compact shut. "I'm going to buzz off now and let you two gab. Would you like me to leave the tea and just take my pitcher home?"

"You brought that over?"

"I did." Esther arranged the ruffles around her neckline.

"Leave it here," said my dad. "You know where the refrigerator is."

"I certainly do."

She was not anything like my mother. My mother was not coy, did not wear ruffles, and would never make the words "I certainly do" into a sexual innuendo. At least I didn't think so. But every time Mom brought Tom Winston a beer—that's what I imagined a large, meaty science teacher drank—maybe she sat in his lap and blew the foam off for him.

My mother wasn't here anymore. That was clear from the neglected roses. But her leaving made everything about her behavior when she was here mystifying. Not only didn't I know who she was now, I didn't know who she was then.

Before disappearing into the house, Esther waved goodbye by holding her hand up next to her shoulder and flapping her fingers.

"Great gal," my dad whispered.

"Are you dating her?"

"Yeah, she's a great lay."

"Dad, please, I don't want to hear about that, all right?"

"Sure, kid. Let's go sit with the bullet."

On the mantel in the living room was a gold-colored bullet standing straight up like the Empire State Building. John Wayne had presented it to my father when he wrote a movie called *Luck Runs Out*, in which Wayne played a sheriff who had to track a killer named Lucky. The year was 1956. I was five years old, and I met John Wayne on the set. There was a fake saloon and five cancan girls. "Your father's a great writer," Big John had said, and he patted me on the head. I always insisted I had no memory of this, because my father had told the story so many times it made me perverse, actually made me perverse by age ten, but I did remember. I had looked up at this tall man. I remembered his red neckerchief and stubble—little black hairs sprouting like grass on his cheeks and chin. I remembered knowing that this was supposed to be a really important moment. I had said, "Howdy," which had made him laugh three times, "Ha, ha, ha."

My father didn't write movies anymore. After several westerns, he switched to television, and worked on a sitcom called *Ghosttown,* which sounded like a western but wasn't. Supernatural shows were in, like *Bewitched* and *I Dream of Jeannie,* and his show was similar. It was about this town where a husband lived with the ghost of his dead wife, and you knew when she was around because you could see the couch cushions in their house getting punched and puffed, and a vacuum cleaner moving back and forth across the carpet.

My father settled in on the living room couch and put his feet up on the coffee table. I couldn't decide where to sit. The logical place, the chair directly across, was where Mom had always situated herself when we had company. I noticed one of my father's tennis shoes was untied. "How's school?" he asked.

"Fine. What did you tell Esther about Mom?" A picture on the wall was lopsided. I straightened it.

"Oh, nothing. I just said she went down in that crash over Denver."

"What crash over Denver?"

"Kid, you heard it here first. People always think they remember plane crashes, even when they didn't take place. Or maybe they did. You think we know about every plane crash?"

"But Mom's not dead."

"She's in Big Bear, it's the same thing."

I laughed.

"See, I can make you laugh, can't I? Your old man's still got it."

"Have you seen Maddy lately?" I asked, knowing the answer.

"Your sister's a bitch. I'm her father. I can say it."

☎

"It doesn't seem too horrible here." I was in my room that night unpacking while I talked on the phone to Georgia. "The only thing in the refrigerator is iced tea, which he didn't make, and packets of soy sauce, but I don't see why Maddy had to move out. She probably wanted an excuse." It was nine in L.A., midnight in New York. I could hear Georgia yawn. "Why don't you and Richard come out for Christmas?"

"What? Next week?" She sounded incredulous. "First of all, Richard works nonstop. Lawyers kill themselves. Besides, coming there could be a disaster for me. I've been assigned to Makeup. At *Mademoiselle*, Makeup is the fast track. Remember my friend Ursula? She went to the dentist, and when she came back, she'd been transferred to Health, a dead end."

I could hear Georgia moving around as we talked. "What are you doing?"

"Getting out my clothes for tomorrow."

Georgia always made a "flat man" on the floor, putting her clothes in the shape of a body. She even placed earrings approximately where the earlobes would be. "Do you wear base?" she asked.

"No."

"That's good. I thought it was bad, but it turns out to be

good. You want to show your natural skin color as much as possible even if it's blotchy. Yellow covers red, did you know that?"

"I had no idea. What does it mean?"

"It means if you have a big red nose, you put yellow makeup on it. You know what your nose is like when you have a cold, Evie."

I checked my nose in the mirror. It was a nice pinkish white. When I was eleven and Georgia was fifteen, she had informed me that my skin was the color of a scallop—an insult with so much power I think about it every time I see my reflection. In truth, my skin is my best feature: clear, fair, delicate. "It's like porcelain," I had shouted back at her. This was a description I had picked up from a romance novel. But she was right about my nose: it did turn bright red when I was sniffly.

"You're not going to believe this, but Dad's dating Esther with the nails from Dr. Seymour's."

"Esther?" Georgia was appalled. "After Mom, he's dating Esther?"

"I know." We contemplated the comedown of it. "Does Mom miss us?"

"I doubt it. Do you miss her?"

"No. I don't know," I said. "I feel like something's wrong."

"In the house?"

"Maybe. No, with me."

"You might need analysis." Through the phone I heard a doorbell. "That must be Richard," said Georgia. "He doesn't have his key. Bye."

"Bye."

I sat cross-legged on the bed with the phone in front of me. It was silent in the house, more dead than quiet. I couldn't hear the TV, which my father almost never turned off now. I wondered if I should buy a Christmas tree tomorrow and get out all the ornaments. That would be so weird.

I spotted my tennis racquet propped against the wall. The wooden kind nobody has anymore. I got off the bed and picked it up. I switched my grip a few times from forehand to backhand.

I did a service swing: dropped the racquet down, then lifted it high, a big stretch, dropped it behind my back and circled, then up again, and snapped it down. Wrist action. I repeated this a second time, trying to make the racquet hit my nose. I couldn't. My father got the strangest injuries. His accidents were impossible to replicate. There was a knock on the door. "Eve?"

"Yeah, Dad."

He came in, in his blue pajamas, and stood there, filling up the space. I could smell scotch. He smelled like Mom. "What are you doing?"

"Nothing."

"Want to go for a ride?"

"Not really. Why don't you call Esther?" He swayed gently from side to side. "What about your friends?" I threw out a few names, people he and Mom had seen regularly.

"That's couple stuff." His eyes became watery. "I can't sleep without her."

"Yeah." I started thinking about my dorm room, wishing myself there. "Where do you want to go?"

"Does it matter?" The odor of scotch was really strong. I considered not breathing. Get out, Dad, get out, please. "Let's just drive, okay, Evie?"

"Okay, get dressed. I'll meet you downstairs."

I drove around Los Angeles while he slept stretched across the backseat, snoring loudly. Listening to these noisy wheezes over and over and over, I felt like a victim of this water torture Georgia had told me about in which a man had to lie under a leaky faucet and after a while just waiting for the next drop to fall drove him mad. I tried to blot Dad out by reciting poems that I'd memorized in the fifth grade. "Ay, tear her tattered ensign down!" "The outlook wasn't brilliant for the Mudville Nine that day." As I tried to blanket my brain with them, my father snorted, a sound so sudden and gigantic that he woke up sputtering. He took a moment to orient himself. I watched in the rearview mirror while he jerked his head, looking out one window, then the other, before crashing back down on the seat. And the snores began anew.

Eventually I drove home and parked in the driveway. It took me a while to get out because I tried to open the car door silently so I wouldn't wake him. Probably nothing could have awakened him, but I didn't want to find out.

These drives became a routine.

I stopped sleeping and lay in bed each night waiting to hear his footsteps on the stairs. I didn't want to fall asleep. I didn't want him to surprise me.

"Move in with us," said Maddy, who was calling from her neighborhood taco stand. I was lying in bed with the phone receiver tucked between the pillow and my ear.

"I can't."

"Why?"

"He's so lonely. It would hurt his feelings." I was listening for his footsteps then, dreading to hear them. "Where did all his friends go? Did he dump them or vice versa?"

"Probably vice versa. He's a drunk, Evie. He drinks scotch. Who drinks that anymore? Isaac says Dad should smoke dope. Then he wouldn't be a drunk, he'd just be out of it."

"Goddamn Mom. This is all her fault. If she'd stayed, this would never have happened to him. Not that she cares about anyone but herself."

"She cares about me," said Maddy.

"Oh, right."

"I see her every couple of weeks."

"What?" I sat up in bed. "Did she phone you? She didn't phone me."

"She gave me her address when she left. She's not much for the phone."

"You have her address? Does Georgia have it too?"

"No, only me."

"Who cares, anyway. I don't want to see her. I have no interest in it."

The next day I called Big Bear information.

"I have a Thomas Winston on Coot Street, would that be it?"

I guessed a number. "One thirty-five?"

"No, twenty-six," said the operator.

I started driving south on the San Diego Freeway, then cut east to the San Bernardino. With each mile the ground got flatter, the buildings uglier, and when it seemed that the world could get no duller, civilization stopped, and the only things on either side of the road were cactus and tumbleweed. The turn for Big Bear was modestly marked with a wooden sign. As I negotiated the winding road up the mountain and into a forest of pines, I felt more and more ridiculous. I passed motels—built of whole logs, just as Georgia had promised—with names like Hitching Post Inn. I couldn't turn back, I'd come too far, but I felt as if, on a lark, I was heading for Dodge City.

At elevation four thousand feet there were patches of snow between the trees. I didn't even have a sweater with me, and my radio now was picking up only one station, which played country-western music. I stopped for gas but didn't want to ask the man how far it was to Big Bear. He might guess why I was there, and I would be found out: girl needing to see mother. In the gas station office I browsed among the maps. There was a street map of Big Bear, not officially printed but something that had been run off on a mimeograph machine. I chose it in what I imagined was an off-handed way, so the guy who was paying no attention to me wouldn't notice.

Driving the twisty road was beginning to make me carsick, when the road suddenly straightened and I passed into town—almost through it, actually: Big Bear General Store, the Bear Claw Diner, a bowling alley, many more motels. All the buildings on the left had a shiny blue lake as a backdrop.

At the edge of the main drag was Spruce Street, which headed away from the lake up the mountain. At the first curve I found Coot—not a proper street really, but a gravel road with houses turning up every so often. One was a trailer; some were prefabricated shacks with water tanks and stacks of wood in the front yard. But then I hit Twenty-six. The number was painted in whitewash on a pile of rocks by the driveway. The same type of gray rocks, only much larger, formed the foundation of the house, which, like almost everything else, was constructed of logs.

It wasn't a one-room cabin like Abe Lincoln's. It had a big wide porch and even a second story, although the second story was much smaller than the first. But it was as different from our home in Westwood as a little grass shack in Hawaii would be. Dad always called our place a *"Father Knows Best* house"—graceful but sturdy, two stories, gray with a white door and white wood trim around the big bay windows, which proudly offered a peek at the comfort within: wall-to-wall carpeting, upholstered couches and armchairs in sensible rectangular arrangements.

I started to get out and then realized that the lumps of brown that I had mistaken for more tumbleweed were squirrels. At home we had one squirrel per block, but this place had squirrel armies. I was terrified to leave the car. I sat there trapped, occupying myself by trying to figure out how to explain my arrival. I couldn't say that I was passing by. That was ludicrous. Suppose I said that I was on my way back from Palm Springs and detoured on a whim? That seemed okay, I thought, as a pickup truck pulled into the driveway and my mother got out. She walked around to the passenger side and opened the door. Oh my God, she has a kid. I had this panic that she might, in three months, have produced a five-year-old. Instead two dogs bounded out. Golden retrievers, I guessed, but then I didn't know dogs.

"Mom?"

"Eve, is that you?" she said in a way that sounded pleasantly surprised. The dogs barked, chasing off the squirrels.

As I followed her into the house, I rubbed my bare arms for warmth. She was wearing a jacket stuffed like a pillow, a kind I'd never seen before, and she'd exchanged her shirtwaists and pumps for jeans and heavy brown laced boots. She tramped, placed her feet down solidly with evident pleasure. My mother's identity is all tied up in her shoes, I thought, watching her whack the soles with a piece of kindling to clean off the snow and mud before she opened the front door. I just wiped my feet on the mat and felt, as I did so, that I was maintaining allegiance to Westwood and my father.

I tried to get past the entry but the dogs kept sniffing me. "I'll put them out. Muffin, Daisy." My mother snapped her fingers. The dogs immediately trotted after her into the kitchen, leaving me alone in Frontierland.

The floor of the living room was wood, something never seen in my neighborhood, and scattered here and there were small multicolored circular rugs. There was a huge stone fireplace. The pine cones on the mantel seemed less like decoration and more like a scientific display of forest vegetation. The furniture was made of branches tied together and bent into shape, with the barest concession to comfort—flat corduroy cushions. A plump throw pillow sitting by itself against the back of the twig couch frame was embroidered with these words: "Take nothing but pictures. Leave nothing but footsteps." There was a framed photo of Mom with Tom Winston, standing by the lake. He had his huge pale arm around her, and she, barely visible, looked like a plant tucked into the crevice of a very large rock.

"Would you like coffee?" she called out.

I looked at the photo. I couldn't answer. She appeared in the doorway. "Do you drink coffee now?" I shook my head. "How about orange juice?" I nodded yes.

She waved me into the kitchen. It had no conveniences. There weren't even cabinets, just shelves with pots and pans and a jumble of canned goods piled on them. The tile on the counters was chipped. Out of an ancient refrigerator she took a carton of juice, then handed it to me with a glass. This was what she would have done at home, let me decide how much I wanted. As I poured, she put the kettle on and opened a jar of Sanka. "She's switched from scotch to Sanka," I prepared to tell Georgia.

I stood there holding the juice carton. It seemed too forward for me to stick it back in the refrigerator. The carton got heavier and, in my mind, more prominent. Finally I placed it on the counter. While my mother spooned some Sanka into a mug, I examined my glass, running my fingers over the design of dancing balloons which was almost worn off.

"So how's college?" my mother asked.

I burst into tears. She stood there watching. She did not come over and put her arms around me. She just waited. Eventually I stopped crying long enough to ask for a tissue. She disappeared into another room and returned with a box. I wiped my eyes. "Come home, Mom, you have to."

The water in the kettle started to boil, sending a scream into the room. My mother poured hot water into her cup. "Why don't we sit in the living room," she said.

She pointed to a rocker as if it were the most comfortable spot, and seated herself opposite on the couch, her back squarely against that embroidered pillow. She looked the same, really, her hair just longer, curling now around her ears. Probably there wasn't a decent place in Big Bear to have your hair cut. The pink lipstick hadn't changed. So if I poured her back into her old clothes . . . "Why did you leave, Mom?"

She dusted some imaginary spot off the corduroy while she considered. "I turned forty-five."

"That's not a reason."

"You'll see," she said seriously.

I glanced at the picture of her and Tom again. I didn't mean to, but . . . once I had a toothache, the tooth really hurt if I touched it, yet I couldn't help myself. I kept poking my tongue there to see if it still ached.

"We were looking for aeries," she said.

"Huh?"

"When that picture was taken, we were looking for aeries."

"What's that?"

"Eagles' nests. I knew the word only from the crossword. It's always used, I guess because it has so many vowels. Who thought I'd ever see one?" She laughed, almost embarrassed.

"Are you still drinking?" I startled myself with this question, but my mother didn't blink.

"Tom said he wouldn't be with me if I drank."

Tom set conditions? He actually told her something like, "I won't be with you unless you . . ." That made their relationship so ordinary it was finally real. My mother was going to spend her life in this log cabin with these dogs, these twig chairs, this man.

"What about me? What about me and Maddy and Georgia?"

"Darling, look at you. You're fine." She sat back and crossed her legs. She didn't seem disconcerted. Or guilty. She took a sip of Sanka. "Let me think how to put this."

"Yes?" Now I was in no danger of ever crying again.

"Motherhood doesn't turn out to be a reason." That idea sat in the air for a while.

"For what?" I asked.

"What I mean is"—she considered again—"I'm not one of those women who needed to be a mother. When I was growing up, all girls wanted to be, so I did too, only—" She leaned forward as if she was about to blurt out a whole paragraph, set a record for revealing herself. Then she changed her mind. All she added was, "I'm being honest."

"Thank you."

"I do not believe you thanked her," Georgia told me later. "You do need analysis."

"You have your father's brown eyes," my mother said. "Have I ever told you that?"

"Lots of times. Should I pluck them out?"

"Eve, don't get smart." She was mad, drawing the line, brooking no backtalk. For a second, she was my mother.

Then she said, "Tom makes me happy."

I stood up. "Well, good, great. Look, I was just stopping

by because I was on my way home from Palm Springs and Maddy gave me your address. I'd better get back."

"Are you sure you can't stay? Tom will be home soon. I'd like you to get to know him."

"I really can't."

"Would you like to come by for Christmas?"

"I'm spending Christmas with Dad. We're going to do it the way we always have." I took my purse. "I'll see you," I said, moving toward the door. As soon as I was out, I saw the squirrels. I picked up the piece of wood that Mom had beaten her boots with, and tossed it into the yard. The squirrels scattered and I ran to the car.

When I got home, I practically fell on the telephone. "She doesn't need to be my mother, fine. I don't need to be her daughter." That was the first thing I told Georgia; then I ran her through the entire encounter. "It's like she's turned into an earth mother, minus the mother part."

"Thank God she waited until we grew up," said Georgia. "Suppose we had to live there?"

"Look, I'm not going to tell Maddy. Oh, maybe I will, I don't know."

As soon as I hung up with Georgia, Maddy called. "But didn't you think it was beautiful there?" she asked.

"What are you talking about, it's nowhere. And the squirrel situation is completely out of control. They probably have a million cases of rabies a year."

"But did you notice the sky? If you're there at night, it sparkles."

"It sparkles," I said sarcastically. "I'm sure you didn't make that up yourself. Did Mom say that, or Tom?"

"You're impossible." Maddy hung up on me.

I went downstairs and into Dad's study. He was in his tennis outfit, which he now wore during the day even when he wasn't playing, and he'd swiveled his chair around to stare out the window. A yellow legal pad lay in his lap. "Are you still working?"

He showed me the pad was blank.

"Let's buy a Christmas tree."

He bounced up, as if he'd been ejected. "Great idea, Evie."

He drove, which was a switch. "There's a big lot on Third and Fairfax," he said. "I noticed it last week."

It felt luxurious to sit in the passenger seat, to have him know where he was going, to be able to fiddle with the radio dial. I hunted for some Christmas music.

"Let's get a big tree." My father slammed his hand against the steering wheel defiantly. "Like always."

He was humming along to "Rudolph the Red-Nosed Reindeer" when we pulled into the lot. "I see it," he announced. "I've got my eye on one already."

"But who will make the turkey?" I asked.

"Esther," said my father. "We'll invite Esther."

So Dad, Esther, and I had Christmas dinner together. My dad looked snappy in suit, tie, the works. Esther had a wide red ribbon wrapped around her hair and tied into a bow. "I'm your gift," she told my dad. She presented me with a roasted turkey.

While Esther prepared the rest of dinner, Dad and I loaded the tree with ornaments. The history of our family was on the tree; at least the public history. The angel Maddy and I used to fight over. The garlands Mom was partial to. The clay elf Georgia had made in Girl Scouts. The clear glass ornaments with wreaths inside, our pride and joy. "Put those where they show," my dad said happily, knowing it was something he'd said all the years before.

We ate turkey, sweet potatoes, creamed onions, and string

beans. Esther was a better cook than my mother—not much of a stretch—but she informed us that she had broken a nail while opening the can of cranberry sauce, and had left the nail on the windowsill. "Remind me to take it home," she said.

By dropping by her place to apologize for my behavior, I had managed to talk Maddy into paying a visit. She gave us all, even Dad, homemade bead necklaces, and he reciprocated by giving her money to install a telephone.

Later my father turned up the Christmas music really loud. You could hear "Joy to the World" in every corner of the house. "I forgot about celebrating," he said. "I forgot all about it." He closed his eyes for a moment and let the music wash over him. "Evie?"

"What?"

"When you don't celebrate, you might as well be dead."

"Hardly, Dad."

"Hey, wait a second." My father chucked me on the chin. The gesture was so cliché-paternal it might have come from a sitcom, maybe even the one he wrote. "I don't say too many smart things anymore, sweetie pie, so when I do, listen up."

☎

On the basis of his behavior on Christmas Day and the fact that, between Christmas and New Year's, I had to drive him around only twice in the middle of the night, I informed my sisters that he was simply brokenhearted, our old dad was somewhere inside the droopy outer shell and would be back eventually. But this didn't mean I wasn't ecstatic to return to school. "Just drop me at the airport," I told him.

"You sure?"

"Yeah, absolutely."

When we arrived at the terminal, my father pulled my suitcase out of the trunk and stood there, his handkerchief out, ready to catch his tears. I kissed him lightly on the cheek.

"We have something special, don't we, Evie?" A sad smile trembled out.

I grabbed my suitcase. "Bye, Dad." I backed up fast. "Bye," I shouted louder, although he wasn't far away.

I wanted to cheer when those automatic doors opened and I was standing in the check-in area with tons of other kids returning to college. They had parents hanging around them, handing them gum and Life Savers, asking them if they'd packed everything. I was anonymous. Not one person there was related to me, and my heart soared.

At school, I threw myself into final exams. My last was in a course called Great American Plays. We'd had to read a play a night. My friend Zoe had obtained a copy of the previous year's final, and it had questions like "Pork chops?" You had to know what play pork chops figured in.

Zoe and I, fueled by No-Doz, stayed up all night shouting clues at each other. "Water?" *The Miracle Worker.* "Dog?" *Come Back, Little Sheba.*

When the hall phone rang, it was four in the morning.

"It's my dad, who else?" I picked up the receiver. "Hi, Dad." I didn't even wait to hear his voice, and was punch-drunk enough to be nice. There was no response. "A prank," I told Zoe.

"*Sorry, Wrong Number,*" said Zoe.

I was hanging up when I heard, "Pills." Thickly. Like he had mud in his mouth.

"Pills?" I put the phone back to my ear.

"*Long Day's Journey into Night.* No, *After the Fall,*" shrieked Zoe.

I waved her to stop. "Dad, what is it?"

"I took No-Doz." Really thickly now. Tongue-too-fat-for-mouth thick.

"Well, that's no big deal. Believe me, I know."

He hung up. I hung up. "What happened?" asked Zoe.

"Nothing. We're taking No-Doz here and he's taking it there. That's weird."

We returned to my room. I sat on the bed and pulled my textbook, *100 American Plays*, onto my lap. It was the heaviest book in all my classes—ten pounds. I knew this because Zoe and I had weighed it. In protest we only dragged or slid it. "He doesn't have finals. Why would anyone take No-Doz who didn't have— Oh my God. He didn't say, 'No-Doz,' he said, 'Overdose.' "

I shoved the book off my lap and started hunting under clothes, papers, books. "What are you looking for?" asked Zoe. There it was, my address book, under a bag of potato chips. I raced to the phone.

I couldn't get the booth open. I yanked and yanked at the door. "Help." Zoe had followed me. She reached over and pushed. The door folded in.

"I need change," I shouted as I thumbed through the book for Maddy's number.

"Shut up," I heard someone yell groggily.

"Eve's father took an overdose," said Zoe, running to her room.

"You're kidding?"

"Eve's father took an overdose." I heard it repeated over and over, punctuated by yawns, as Zoe tore back, holding out a jar filled with nickels, dimes, and quarters.

I fumbled with the coins as I stuffed them in, misdialed, and tried too quickly to start over. I banged on the receiver to get a dial tone.

"Let me dial." Zoe pressed down on the receiver, held it

awhile, then released it and inserted several quarters. "What's the number?"

The entire floor was out of bed and gathered around the booth. I noticed that Joanne, the engaged person, was now sleeping with toilet paper around her head. While Zoe dialed for me, I wondered whether Joanne would sleep that way after she got married.

Zoe handed me the receiver. I heard ringing. An angry male voice answered: "What is it?"

"I'm sorry to wake you—" I stopped. I could barely speak. "This is Maddy's sister, Madeline Mozell's sister Eve. Get her, hurry up, please, it's an emergency."

While I waited what seemed like five minutes, but was probably only two, several girls got bored and went back to bed.

Finally Maddy picked up. "What's wrong?"

"Dad took an overdose of something, I don't know what. You'll have to call the police and get over to the house."

"Me?"

"You're the only one out there, for God's sake."

"But suppose he's dead. Suppose I find him plopped on the carpet. Or like, he could be in the bathtub." She started gasping, hyperventilating.

"Maddy, you have to."

"I won't go." She screamed this really loud, and kept on screaming. Probably everyone in the hall could hear.

"What's going on? Is that her father?" asked Joanne.

I yelled into the receiver, "Isaac, Isaac, are you there?"

" 'Lo."

"Isaac?"

"This isn't Isaac, it's Presto. If Maddy wanted to be with Isaac, she could, but she doesn't want to. She wants to be with me."

"Presto, please slap my sister, she's hysterical." I heard a slap. "Thank you. Would you please put her back on?"

She was crying tamely now, making sad little hiccuping sounds, as if she'd scraped her knee in the playground and the teacher had finally quieted her.

"Madeline, you have to do this."

"Why? It's not my fault."

"It's not mine either." Now I was crying too, heading her off at the pass. "Maddy, someone has to take care of this, so just do it, okay?"

"Okay."

"Thanks." We were sniffling in unison. I hung up.

"Are you all right?" Zoe asked.

"Yes." I wiped my nose on my sleeve. "I don't think I can study anymore," I said as Zoe trailed me to my room. "I think I have to"—I made a face at her, trying to smile—"go to bed." I closed my door.

☎

That was my father's first hospitalization, and my sisters and I were a great team. After I got the crazy call, Maddy checked him in, and Georgia did the follow-up. "Not enough to kill him. Big surprise," she reported.

"I didn't get a wink of sleep. I probably flunked my final," I told Georgia, knowing I hadn't. I was too much of a trouper to flunk. I was one of the supercompetent Mozell sisters. I could abort my father's suicide and pass a final exam the next day. "Look at you. You're fine," my mother had pointed out. Was she right, or was I proving her right, living up to her expectations even now, especially now, when I could never get her seal of approval?

Four

At six a.m., the phone rings. "He's dead," I say to Joe, and grab the receiver. "Hello."

"Is this the beautiful, wonderful daughter of Lou Mozell?"

"Hi, Dad. Are you all right?"

"Why'd you lock me in the pen? 'Cause of Jesse?"

"What? What are you talking about?"

"Go to hell." He hangs up.

I feel dizzy from the jolt—first to the body, then to the brain. Joe puts out his arm for me to snuggle into. I shake my head.

"He's been in that geriatric/psychiatric ward a week and he's definitely not better. I wish they would slap some handcuffs on him. At least then he couldn't phone."

"How about a straitjacket?" suggests Joe.

"Right." I throw off the covers and get up. I jerk open the closet and look for my robe.

"He doesn't know what he's doing." Joe pats the bedside table, hunting around for his glasses. He puts them on and watches me from the bed.

I go into the bathroom. Why am I in here? "What am I looking for?" I yell to Joe.

"Your bathrobe."

"Right." I take it off the hook and go back into the bedroom. "I hope this memory thing my father has isn't catching."

The phone rings again. Joe reaches for it, but I get there first. "It's *my* father," I say nobly.

He removes the receiver from my hand. "Hello." There's a long pause. I try to read Joe's eyes, which seem faintly amused. "He's calling collect now," he tells me, covering the receiver. "Yes, I'll accept the charges. Hello, Lou." Another pause. "No, of course Jesse isn't mad at you." He hangs up.

"Thanks."

"No problem. He's not my father." Joe turns over to sleep some more. The phone rings again. He groans and picks it up. "Yes. I'll accept. . . . You're not in jail and Jesse isn't mad at you." Blunt this time. He hangs up. "Shit. What a way to get up in the morning."

This is something Alexander Graham Bell never anticipated. I believe I read somewhere that he grew to hate his
own invention, but I don't think it was because he had a
senile parent phoning him ten times a day. I'm sure he didn't
know that people who couldn't recognize their own pants
would remember their children's phone numbers—could actually recall a seven-digit number plus an area code. I hate
Alexander Graham Bell. Of course, right now I hate everyone.

"I think we should buy telephone stock," I say later, at
breakfast, while I am pacing back and forth, eating granola.
"Not now, but when we baby boomers hit eighty."

Joe doesn't look up. He's reading his newspapers from all
over the country—the San Jose *Mercury News,* the Waco
Tribune, the Boulder *Daily Camera*—to find stories for his
radio show.

"Jesse, when I'm eighty, be sure to buy telephone stock."

Jesse doesn't look up either. He's reading the back of the
milk carton.

"Do I have to visit him today?" I wonder aloud.

Joe does not ask who "him" is. "No," he says.

"But I haven't seen him since I checked him in. Jesse,
you'll be happy to know that this morning your grandfather
remembered your name. It was a miracle."

"That could not be considered a miracle, Mom. That is
simply a scientific inevitability." Jesse's mouth develops a
little sneer. "When the brain deteriorates—and your dad is
like wacko—the frontal lobe damage causes a person to remember things they forgot and forget things they know."

I don't respond, and I deem this an extraordinary feat.
"That reminds me, I have to phone that man you had the car
accident with. I've already tried him twice, and he hasn't
called back."

"So forget about it."

"You should probably do this yourself. You know, I really am busy."

"If you think you're busy, you should try high school." Jesse continues to eat as he carries his cereal bowl to the sink. "I'll be back late. Ifer and I are going to a séance. You know, Mom, all doors are entrances. Think about it." He puts his bowl in the sink. "Bye."

I pour another cup of coffee, even though after two cups my whole body rattles from the caffeine. I allow myself to sit. For a moment it's completely quiet. Not even a breeze; nothing to ruffle anything. Stop, right now. Stop, with this feeling in this room: Joe at the table reading his papers, the smell of coffee, the warm cup in my hands, two sips before the jitters.

"Joe, when are you leaving?"

"Tomorrow. I'll be home in about a week."

"I wish you weren't going."

Joe pays no attention to this, which I resent and admire. "Aren't you late?" he asks pointedly.

I start my general pre-departure routine. Finding my purse, going through my briefcase, checking for pens, Filofax, a legal pad. "Have you seen my sunglasses?" I run upstairs. Search the night table, the bureau, the bathroom, stop at the mirror. Oh God, is that my face?

This is not the first time this has happened. Not the first time, since I turned forty, that I have passed a mirror and stopped short, startled by my own reflection.

These sideways unexpected encounters are the most jarring, these candid glimpses when I have not taken time to prepare my face to be seen and my brain to see it. All I notice are the lines around my eyes. Are these new? The creases running south from the edge of my nose. Definitely deeper. My mouth, of which I am extremely fond, have been ever since a girl in my bunkhouse at Camp Tocaloma told me it was rosebud-shaped, my mouth is starting to turn down. I need a vacation. No. This is just me. Me at forty-four.

I look the way I always have, but the face of the future is threatening to take over. I have two faces in one, a nonreturnable bargain.

One day, when Joe and I passed an old couple walking arm in arm, I warned him, "Soon we'll be them." "I hope so," he replied. He was admiring their coziness, but that's not what I meant.

The first time I "got" death, I was eight years old and standing in my elementary school playground, waiting in line for my turn at handball. "When you're dead, you don't know it." The kid in front turned to me, announced this, and then rubbed his fist around in his eye. "When you're dead, you don't know it." Every time I went to sleep I would count frantically, lie in my bed going from one to a hundred as fast as I could, so I wouldn't think about it, and eventually I succeeded. I didn't think about it for years. But when I started being surprised by my reflection, the thought came back, and lately every morning I wake up with that little boy's face staring into mine: "When you're dead, you don't know it." Also, for the past year I have changed my hairstyle every two months. Somehow this seems connected.

Why am I here? "Joe," I yell, "do you know why I came upstairs?"

"No," he shouts back.

"Oh, I remember. My sunglasses." I find them on my desk, next to Dr. Omar Kunundar's phone number. Good grief, I almost left without taking care of this. I sit down at my desk and dial. I hear the voice of a very businesslike woman.

"Hello, this is the office of Dr. Kunundar. If you are having an emergency, please press one and leave a message. If this is a nonemergency medical call, press two and leave a message. For other business, press three. Thank you."

I press three. "Hello, this is Eve Mozell again. A week ago, my son Jesse opened his car door into Dr. Kunundar's car. I would like to discuss the accident as soon as possible and would really appreciate it if the doctor could give me a call at 555-4603."

These words don't convey how charming I am on an answering machine. I am sincere and warm, polite but inviting. It's all in my voice, and it's one reason I'm good at my job: I do special events. People hire me to throw fund-raisers or convention parties. I am a great planner, great at anticipating what might go wrong so it doesn't. No Surprises is the name of my company. I do most of the planning on the phone, so I end up leaving many messages for people, like about whether we want a pasta station or a roast beef station, or about this adorable mariachi band I have located. I have "phone talent." I easily become buddies with people over the phone.

So why haven't I heard from the doctor after I've left several messages, even if he's out of town? I assume it's because he hasn't heard my voice. Because this nasty nurse, obviously she's nasty, has been screening his calls.

I phone my assistant.

"Hi, Kim, I'm running a little late. Any messages?"

She gives me the number for Madge Turner, who is on the board of several medical associations in southern California and who hires me frequently to do their special events. I am planning one for her now. "Hello, Madge, this is Eve Mozell."

"Hello, Eve, how are you?"

I consider answering truthfully, spilling out my general state of anxiety. "Fine, I'm fine, thank you. How was the cruise?"

"It was very relaxing."

I like talking to Madge because she always says the most obvious thing. If she were on *Family Feud*—"One hundred people surveyed, top five answers on the board"—Madge's answer would always be the top one. (Why do people take cruises? Number-one response: To relax.)

"That's nice, I'm glad to hear it."

"The food was delicious. They had canapés with salmon and caviar every evening before dinner. Do you think we could have salmon and caviar?"

"I think so. I'll price it out."

"I ate way too much." (What do people regret about cruises? Number-one response: Ate too much.)

"I was talking to the people at the Biltmore—"

"Eve." She cuts me off. I hear nervousness.

"Yes."

"Could we change the location? Wait, don't say no. I know the invitations have gone out."

"The party is only a month away."

"I know, I know, but if you send me the RSVP list, I'll take care of mailing the location change. I'll organize a little group to make follow-up calls, I promise you. And I'll get us out of our obligation to the Biltmore. You know, the Biltmore's downtown and I hate downtown. Besides, I had the most brilliant idea and I had it right in the middle of the Pacific Ocean."

"Well, great, what is it?"

"We should have our party at the Nixon Library."

I don't say, You're kidding. I don't say, In all the time we've worked together, I've never known you were a Republican. Part of my job is restraint, being careful where I put my foot. I try to be chummy, never frank. "They do parties there?" is all I say, mildly.

"Oh yes, it's quite wonderful. It's not really a library, it's a museum. There are fountains and a reflecting pond. And they have the place he was born right on the premises in case people get bored and want to take a little walk. I have the name of a woman there."

I write it down, get off with Madge, then phone Kim and ask her to set up an appointment for me with the woman at the library and to send the RSVP list to Madge immediately. I come banging down the stairs. "I'm going," I call out. But I can't leave without complaining. I detour into the breakfast room. "You know this party for four hundred fifty ear, nose, and throat doctors? Well, Madge Turner is changing the location to the Nixon Library."

After a long beat, Joe looks up from his paper. "Who goes to that place? Probably the most white-bread group in the country."

"I suppose you think it would be interesting to talk to them."

He laughs. " 'What Nixon means to me.' I bet you'll have a great time."

"I don't think so. I'll see you later."

☎

At five o'clock, I visit my father. I call Joe and tell him he does not have to come too. "I should hope not," he says.

There's one thing I like about doing something the second time, even when it's unpleasant: I like knowing the ropes. The elevator is to the left, past the admissions office. Seventh floor, I don't have to check the listing. After I ring the doorbell, I have to state my name in the intercom, my business (visiting my father), and the door will be unlocked from the inside. I will store this knowledge. It will comfort me. Maybe I can pass it on to someone. Maybe my friend Adrienne will have to commit her mother.

Also, the sights and sounds that I closed out the first time, that even scared me, become curiosities. Then familiar, even familial. I like this process.

The first thing I see is a woman sitting in a wheelchair facing the phone booth. She has the receiver in her hand. She has pulled it as far out of the booth as it will reach so she can talk. And she is screaming, "Come and get me."

Her hair is white, there isn't much of it, and it's pulled back by a child's barrette. She is little and her chin is pointed. I wonder who is on the other end of the phone. I wonder whose number she doesn't forget.

I go past her to the cage. "I'm looking for my father, Lou Mozell."

"Just in time," says the nurse.

"For what?"

She leans forward so her mouth is almost against the grate, and whispers. "They get difficult now. We call it sundowning."

I nod in understanding. She points to the left. "His room is the third. Doris will show you."

Doris, who has frizzy hair the color of straw and two very fat cheeks that scarcely leave room for her mouth, which runs like a straight road between them, comes out of the cage. I follow her down the hall. "So he's being difficult?"

"He wants to leave."

"Well, that's understandable." I state this loyally, in a tone that says, For God's sake, what would you expect? Then I hear him.

"Goddamnit, you bitches, get in here." He is shouting loud enough to be heard over the crowd at the Los Angeles Coliseum.

He sits in his wheelchair in the middle of the room, stranded—a passenger in a car that broke down on its way to nowhere. His pants aren't fastened at the top, and there's a rope around his waist holding them up. "Could you buy him some suspenders?" Doris asks.

"What's wrong with his belt?"

"It doesn't seem to work on all his pants." She bends until her face is level with his. "Your daughter's here."

"I'm not blind," says my father.

I sit down on the bed. "So how are you?"

"I'm hungry." His face wrinkles up tight, as if someone took a screwdriver, put it in the center, and twisted it.

"I think you're having dinner soon."

"Order room service."

I say as patiently as possible, "Dad, this isn't a hotel."

There is a pause. "Well, what is it?"

"It's a hospital. They're going to fix your medications."

He thinks about this for a bit. "They don't take Georgia's magazine here," he says petulantly.

"I'm not surprised."

"What kind of a hotel doesn't get *Georgia*?"

"Hotels don't subscribe to *Georgia*. Anyway, this is a hospital and hospitals never subscribe to *Georgia*." I am very bad at being patient.

"You put me here because of Jesse, didn't you?"

"No. Listen, do you want some company? Do you want

to go sit with the other—" I am about to say inmates, I realize, so I stop the sentence there.

"Sure, kiddo, let's go for a walk."

My father stands up and pitches forward, crashing onto the floor. It's sort of beautiful—he's straight all the way, as if he's tracing the quadrant of a circle. The sound when he hits is a gigantic squish, air being punched out of a cushion.

"Help, help!" I shout. Is this it? Is he dead?

I am flat against the wall staring down when Doris runs in. My father lies there like a permanent fixture.

"Jocko!" Doris's voice is so commanding she could be summoning troops. "Fortunately your father's fat," she says to me. "They fall better if they're fat."

I nod as though I agree or understand or know something. Then Jocko appears. He is as big as a Bekins van. His head is shaved except for some hair on top that sprouts like a plant. The sight of him probably has sent many old people who are mentally on the edge right over.

He wraps his arms around and under my dad, and pulls him up stomach first. "We really need a crane for these situations," Doris confides as Jocko pushes my father onto his knees. Then he lifts him from behind and puts him back in his chair. My father is conscious but silent. He looks quite puzzled.

☎

"He fell over," I tell Dr. Kelly. We are in an empty patient room a day later, having our official end-of-first-week consultation. Dr. Kelly is wearing high-top sneakers with her medical whites. "Why can't he stand up anymore?"

"It's part of his dementia." She opens his file and spreads the pages on the bed. "All your father's tests are normal. His EEG, his EKG, blood work. We did a CAT scan this morning." She mentions a few more workups. I lose track, and I know I should take notes, because Georgia is going to quiz me later.

"Look, my father's been nuts before. He's been mixed up about who he is and where he is. If you adjust his lithium and whatever else he's on, he'll come right back."

She shakes her head.

"Is there someone else I can talk to?" I say this bravely. It makes me nervous to confront any doctor, even this soda-pop version. I don't say, "I want to speak to someone over you—the doctor in charge," but I try to imagine I am Georgia, who inspires fear. Who can make salesgirls scurry in all directions.

Dr. Kelly stiffens. "I know your father's case."

"Fine." I cave in that quickly. And now her voice is sterner. Meaner. I owe this to you, Georgia. "Look," I say, smiling, trying to win her back. "My sister's concerned that we know everything, that's all, that no stone is left unturned."

"Your father has the dwindles."

"The dwindles?"

She nods.

"You mean he's dwindling?"

"Exactly." She acts proud of me—I have caught on to an extremely difficult concept.

"Are you sure it isn't Alzheimer's?"

"Well, we can't be sure of that until after he's dead and we do an autopsy, but this severe dementia and loss of motor skills came on fairly rapidly. I think"—she says "I think" as if she were drawing on years of experience—"it's just the dwindles."

"How long do you live with the dwindles?" It sounds as if I'm asking, How long will he live? But maybe I am really asking, How long will I have to live with his dwindles?

"A year or two."

"Why does he keep bringing up my son? He says I put him here because of Jesse."

"Could he be referring to something in the past, some event?"

I don't have to think about this. "Yes."

"He's perseverating."

Perseverating? I insult her and she pays me back by using an SAT word. Who knows what this means? I don't bother to ask. She shuffles the pages together and slides them back in the file.

"Oh, Dr. Kelly?"

"Yes?"

"The other day, I couldn't remember why I went upstairs. Is that normal?"

"How old are you?"

"Forty-four."

"Yes."

I go to my father's room. He's leaning over trying to reach his shoe, which is untied. He doesn't have the dexterity to tie his shoe even if he could reach it, and he can't walk anymore, so it doesn't matter whether his shoes are tied. He is no longer able to trip on his laces.

I stand in the doorway, watching coolly, like a plant manager assessing some employee's capability. You're not going to live two more years. Not one more year. I don't believe it. He looks up.

"Dad, come on, let's do something. Let's go find company."

I push him out the door and down the hall. The last time I pushed someone along like this it was Jesse in a stroller.

A man walks toward us in a lively way, on the balls of his feet. He has a healthy head of white hair and a trim body. He resembles an aging, weathered camp counselor, someone who might lead us all in jumping jacks. "I bet you don't recognize me," he says to my father.

"Sure I do." My father puts out his hand.

The bouncy man grasps it. "Great to see you again. I've been traveling."

"Me too," says my father.

"The Orient, Baghdad, Taiwan. But you know, I was thinking"—the man turns his head to one side, then the other, like a bird on a branch deciding which way to fly— "it's great to see you."

"Me too." My father is smiling and so is the man, as their conversation goes 'round and 'round, a horse on a racetrack with no finish line.

"Would you like to get by?" I pull the wheelchair to the side.

"I'm going in there." The man points to the dining room door. "Would you open it?"

I try. It's locked, so I knock. Doris peeks out. "Excuse me," I say.

She opens it further, spots the bouncy man behind me, and slams it closed. "Wait here," I say to my dad, as if he could go somewhere.

I run to the cage. "That man"—I point—"wants to go into the dining room, but Doris slammed the door in his face."

The nurse leans close to the grate and whispers. "He gets into everything."

"Oh," I say, as if it makes perfect sense. Who would want that? "Well, we'll see you later," I tell the bouncy man, who may have lost his mind but who does not have the dwindles. His family will expire from exasperation long before he dies.

"I have no idea who he was," says my father. Was. That's the correct tense. He was someone else once. My dad was too, I guess. I'm not sure.

I wheel him into the TV room. Old people sit and stare at a television, which is showing a weather report of conditions at nearby beaches.

"I hope you aren't jealous of your sister," he says suddenly, very loudly.

"Of course I'm not," I reply, noticing that several old people have turned to look. People who are otherwise not interested in anything. I smile at them to show that this conversation is harmless.

"She's a big success." He booms it.

I don't answer. Maybe this train of thought will go away.

"Georgie Porgie, pudding and pie." He's chanting and happy. He's ten and on the jungle gym, hanging upside down and swinging. "She's Georgia, the magazine," he chants. "We named her and then they named a magazine after her. Who ever thought when we gave her that name it would end up a magazine? Wasn't that brilliant? I'd like some applause."

Several demented people clap.

"This is her sister." He has swung to the top of the jungle gym and is shouting to the entire playground. I smile, nodding at everyone. My father turns his head toward me sharply. "What's your name?"

☎

"He's always been like that," says Joe, who is packing.

"True."

"But now he's senile. If you could see his brain, I'm sure it would look like Swiss cheese." He smiles, pleased at the notion of my father's brain with gigantic holes in it. "Of course, it's the holes that make Swiss cheese interesting. Although Swiss cheese can never really be interesting. Like your father."

Joe does three half-hour shows a week for National Public Radio. What that means to me, married to him, is that at any moment some idea takes hold, like this mini-essay on Swiss cheese, and then he's no longer talking to me but experimenting with an idea that, in some form or another, may end up on the air. His show, *USA from Here,* features oddballs. Joe spins their lives into tales.

He loves it. He was spinning tales before he was on the radio. He grew up in New Hampshire, in a small town, a place where it was safe to be curious. His parents still live there contentedly, in an 1846 white clapboard house with vines of roses encircling the windows and a weathervane standing at the peak of its shingled roof. Joe could always tell which way the wind was blowing.

With the confidence of the truly secure, Joe does not pay tremendous attention to how or what he packs—except for his tape recorder, which is always carefully snapped into its leather case and stashed in the small zippered pouch on his hanging bag. Clothes are selected almost at random: the first shirt his hand touches in the drawer, the pair of pants nearest

the closet door. Our bathroom is full of duplicates and tripli-
cates of things Joe forgot and had to buy on the road.

"My father's interesting," I protest.

"You're praising your father? He's not dead yet."

"What are you talking about?"

"You know, when Nixon died, they turned him into a
hero. Revisionist history. But your father's not dead."

"He's dying."

"He's not dying and he's not interesting." Joe talks to me
as if he were correcting my wrong answer to a test question.
"Mainly he's trouble."

"You pack like a complete slob." I say this with a smile
that I tack on after I hear myself speak. It doesn't fool Joe.

"What is this about?"

"You always get there and don't have what you need,
that's all."

"So I buy it. Or don't."

"Right. Forget it." I go look in the mirror. Is this new
haircut weird, or is it my imagination? My hair is short
around my ears, then takes a two-inch drop in the back. It
looks like upstairs, downstairs. "If my father is senile, why
does he know how to upset me? Do people always get senile
in character?"

"Ask Jesse. That sounds like something he'd have an
opinion on." Joe zips his bag, folds it in two, and starts buckling the sides.

"Why? Because you don't want to talk to me?"

He stops buckling and stands up straight. He pushes his
glasses back on his nose. It's a remarkably aggressive gesture
for being so simple. Casual, affable Joe is deceptive this way.
He uses his index finger and pushes the glasses back firmly,
and it is now immensely clear that he's looking at me pierc-

ingly, and not just with two eyes but with four. "That is not what I mean, Eve. The reason you should ask Jesse is, he has an opinion on everything. What's wrong with you? Where's your sense of humor?"

"That is so unfair." I am dimly aware that I sound exactly like Jesse at some age. Some earlier age that I miss right now. The phone rings. I hope this is Dr. Omar Kunundar, car accident victim. "Hello?"

"Well, so . . ." says Georgia.

"I hate my hair. And this is my third new hairstyle in six months."

"You don't hate your hair. You hate your face."

"I do?"

"Yes. But you cannot do anything about your forty-some-year-old face, so you change your hair, thinking that will make your face look young, the way it used to."

"Oh God, you're right."

"Of course I'm right," says Georgia, closing the subject. "What's the verdict from the doctors?"

I ask Joe to hang up the bedroom phone after I take the call in another room, my study, where I have clocked thousands of hours of phone calls with Georgia, leaning back in my swivel chair, as I do now—lean back and get comfortable before I tell her. "He has the dwindles." I wait for the gasp of amazement. I get it.

"What? That's the diagnosis?"

"I swear to God."

"That's not a diagnosis. It has only two syllables. Did you speak to the head guy? Oh, good grief, hold on. Can you believe I'm still at the office? I have to check this caption."

When she comes back on the line, I skip over the head-guy question, hoping she won't notice. "They say his brain is going and it's not coming back. They're going to try to adjust his medications so he doesn't shout and get abusive, but they can't guarantee it." I get no response. It's possible Georgia is doing work again and has forgotten I'm on the phone. "Hello, are you there?"

"I was just thinking. This is really sad."

"I know. Oh, wait a minute. Jesse," I call, "is that you?" He opens the door and lounges against the jamb. "Your dad's leaving soon. Don't forget to say good-bye."

"Duh," says Jesse.

"You know, Jesse, it's really not necessary for you to talk to me like that."

"Sor-ry." Two syllables, not a diagnosis, and definitely not an apology.

"Are you doing something tonight?"

"Nah, I don't think so. Ifer's grounded. She called her mom a PMS ho."

"Well, no wonder she's grounded."

"Her mom is a PMS ho, it's the truth."

"Well, fine, I'm on long-distance with your aunt Georgia, I'll be off in a minute."

"You mean an hour." He closes the door.

"Sorry, Georgia. Anyway, I was feeling sorry for Dad, wheeling him down the hall, and he was being kind of charming. You know how Dad has charm."

"Crazy-man charm, which is not to be confused with real charm," says Georgia dryly.

"Right. So we got into the TV room and he announced, 'Guess what, everyone?'—I swear to God, Georgia, he managed to get the attention of people who have no attention span—'Guess what? My daughter is Georgia the magazine.'"

Georgia hoots in delight, which fuels me. "'Wasn't I brilliant to name her Georgia?' He actually said that, as if the magazine wouldn't be called whatever he named you."

"Should I send a complimentary subscription?"

"To UCLA Geriatric/Psychiatric?"

"Why not?"

"You mean so Doris, the nurse, can read about the perfect vacation on Majorca?"

"We don't run irrelevant articles like that, and you know it," says Georgia. "So he can brag."

"He does anyway. He's fixated on you. He asked if I was jealous." I do another imitation. " 'Are you jealous of your sister?' " I blast it the way he did.

"No!" Georgia is incredulous. This is satisfying. I feel as if I am landing the world's biggest fish.

"Then he said, 'This is her sister . . . what's your name?' I'm not kidding, he said that."

I know Georgia is practically <u>rolling</u> on the floor. "That is hysterical. Don't you think that's hysterical? You know, Eve . . ." Her voice drops three octaves. Well, that's a slight exaggeration, but Georgia has two voices: her low authoritative voice, which is her Georgia-the-magazine voice, and her normally pitched Georgia-the-human-being voice. Now she switches to her Georgia-the-magazine voice. "There is some evidence that withholding parents get more devotion from their children than giving parents do. We're running an article about it. I hadn't thought about this, but perhaps withholding children get more than giving ones. I've got to go. Putting out this tenth-anniversary edition is a complete nightmare—I can't possibly convey what I'm going through."

I go back into the bedroom and throw myself on the bed. Joe is finishing up, putting some magazines and papers in his briefcase. "So what's the cake lady like?" I ask.

I'm going to pull myself together. I'm going to settle in

and listen to Joe tell me a story. I'm going to watch him smile my favorite smile, the one that starts slowly, sneaking up, and then bursts out big and wide. "She stands on a stepladder and ices the cakes with a Ping-Pong paddle. 'I buy 'em by the gross at Mel's Sporting Goods 'cause when I ice 'em lime green, I just can't wash it out.'" Joe imitates her gravelly, froggy voice. "'I wear my rain slicker—'"

I start thinking about my father. His glee when everyone in the TV room was looking at him. That center-of-attention-in-second-grade look on an eighty-one-year-old man. His front teeth turning yellow, the tufts of hair coming out of his ears. He's metamorphosing into some beast, something that walks on all fours and grins for no reason. But in a ludicrous tribute to the strength of his personality, the second-grader in him still dominates.

"You're not listening to me," says Joe agreeably.

"I'm sorry. I don't want you to go."

"Eve, I'll be back soon. You sound like a child."

Me and my dad. I roll over and off the bed. "I'm going to start dinner. Jesse must be starved."

I start banging around the kitchen. Taking out olive oil, garlic, filling a pasta pot with water, turning on a burner. *Don't go, don't go, don't go.* I'm beginning to sound like that little blonde actress in all those fifties movies. The one with the short pageboy. Not Deborah Kerr, shorter. Who was she? She never actually said, "Don't go," she was too docile. Her husbands went wherever they were going and you knew the plane would crash and it did, but there's always the scene when she doesn't know it. She's innocently playing with her children. Or is it that she's all dolled up and lighting candles on the dining room table for his welcome-home dinner? Anyway, then the phone rings. Surprise.

"Bye," says Joe. He gives me a kiss.

"Who's that fifties blonde actress, kind of bland?"

"Kim Novak?"

"No, not sexy. Square."

"I don't know. I have to go. I love you."

"I love you too." I wonder if withholding wives get more devotion than giving ones. I hear Joe pick up his bag. I think I hear him swing it over his shoulder, but maybe I just know that comes next. Then the front door opens and quietly shuts.

As I reach over to get a potholder off the wall hook, my arm touches the edge of the pot, which is hot. I yelp.

There's no one around to ask what happened.

I put my arm under cold water and wrap a dish towel around it. Holding it carefully, as if my arm is fragile, I go into the living room. I wander around, then I do what I always do, sit in my favorite armchair, which, if I curl up, fits me snugly. I sit there doing nothing. Trying to feel all right. Wishing Jesse were young again so I could have someone to cuddle.

☎

The next morning, at seven-thirty, the phone rings. "He's dead," I say. Then I realize Joe isn't there to hear me. "Hello?"

"May I speak please to Mrs. Mozell?"

"Ms. Mozell," I say, irritated. This man has just made me married to my father. "Is this a political call?"

"Excuse me?"

"Nicaragua. El Salvador. Look, I don't give money on the phone. And it's the crack of dawn. Don't you guys usually call at dinnertime?"

"This is Dr. Omar Kunundar."

"Oh, Dr. Kunundar, I'm sorry, I'm so glad you called, thank you." I'm falling all over myself, totally obsequious. I quickly swing my legs out of the bed. Wake up, get a grip. I have just assumed a man from the Middle East is from Latin America. In my nicest, chummiest voice, I say, "Please forgive me. I believe that my son, Jesse, opened his car door into your car."

"Yes, I am on my way to the hospital."

"Right now?"

"No, when your son opens his door. Like a wall, I hit it. I am very sorry too."

"It's his fault."

"Yes, I know."

"Well, my husband and I were wondering. . . . You know how insurance companies are these days?"

"No, I have not heard."

"Well, they're very hard on teenagers. They charge a lot of money to insure a sixteen-year-old. And if Jesse gets another accident on his record, his coverage will skyrocket, you know, go up." Oh God, is that condescending? "So we were wondering, did you already notify your insurance company?"

"No. I am too busy yet."

"Well, good. We would really appreciate it if you would not tell the company and we could pay you directly."

"My lights are falling off," says Dr. Kunundar.

"I'm sure they are. We'll be happy to take care of it. If you just get some estimates—"

"I do not know if this is all right."

"It's fine, honestly, it's fine, but of course, if you don't feel comfortable . . ."

"I'm sitting down, thank you. I have three ears and a nose this morning, but I will call you back when I speak with your mother."

"My mother? Why do you need my mother? I haven't seen her in over twenty years. My sister Madeline talks to her. I haven't a clue what my mother's up to." There is a long pause, unfortunately, and during this time I cannot believe I have said what I have said.

"This is very sad to hear. It is sad to be without a mother. But it is my accident."

"Well, it was my son's fault."

"What I mean is . . ." He speaks very slowly, as if I were dense. "I mean that I have to speak to *my* mother. She is in Burbank. If this is illegal, I will have to call the authorities. She will tell me. Good-bye thank you." No comma, all together.

"Good-bye." I stare at the receiver. I actually do this before hanging up. Joe's always pointing out when actors do this in movies: they get upsetting phone calls and take a beat to stare at the receiver before hanging up. This is completely fake, says Joe. No one confuses the person on the other end of the phone with the phone itself. But I just did.

The phone rings again. Two calls before eight. "Hello." I say this politely. On my best behavior. Perhaps it's Dr. Kunundar again.

"Nine-one-one, nine-one-one."

"Dad?"

"They're stealing my money." And he howls. Like some animal being clubbed to death, whose sounds wake the jungle. It goes on and on and on.

"Dad, stop, please. Nurse! Nurse!" Now I am shouting.

"Yes?"

I recognize Doris's voice. "I think my father needs a sedative."

"He's had enough for a horse," says Doris.

"Ask Dr. Kelly to call me, please."

"I surely will."

"Thank you."

I drop back on the bed and pull the covers up to my nose. "Mom?"

"What? Honey?" I say this muffled through the sheets.

Jesse sticks his head in. His hair is wet from his shower and he looks so fresh. "I'm out of here."

"Did you eat? You should always eat something in the morning."

"Everyone says that, but it's not true."

"Fine, I believe you, forget I said it, have a really nice day, Jesse."

"I'm taking Dad's car."

"Fine. We'll take your car to the . . . not the mechanic. What do you call those places where they rebuild cars?"

"Body shops?"

"Right. We'll go after school."

"Cool." He closes the door.

I don't move while I listen to him go down the stairs and out.

The phone rings again. I should let it ring, but I can't. I probably need a twelve-step program to break the phone-answering habit. I pick up the receiver and listen, but there's no more of that air-in-a-tunnel. A person can't anticipate long-distance anymore; besides, we're in the same city. "Hello?"

"This is not your father."

"Oh, Adrienne, hi." What a relief. "Adrienne, who's that short actress with a pageboy in all those old movies?"

"Teresa Wright?"

"No."

"What about that other one? Whose last name's a guy's name, but what is it? She's funny."

"This one wasn't funny."

"Oh."

There is going to be a quiz show for Adrienne and me where all the contestants are over forty. It'll be called "Name That Person You Already Know."

Thirty minutes later, we are still on the phone. I am in my bed, and I suspect that Adrienne is, well, not in bed, since she is calling from New York, where the time is three hours later, but on it. Until she married Paul nine years ago, she shared her king-sized bed with her belongings: her sketch pad, her dental floss, several books and magazines, Kleenex, the TV remote, her telephone, her Rolodex, a bag of cinnamon cookies from Leroy's Bakery. Now these things are piled on her night table, a little mountain of necessities, leaving room for her husband. But during the day, while Paul covers sports for the *Daily News*, she is still parked on the bed, where she gets most of her ideas just lying there. As she sketches her cartoons, her beloved TV, which sits on an old pine blanket box, is never off. Adrienne loves the television as much as I love the phone.

"I think my father is dying." I have said this out loud twice now. I am placing myself inside the circle. Everyone's parents die. Everyone dies, even Y-O-U. There ought to be a way out. Once I went skiing with Joe, and I fell on purpose so I wouldn't fall by accident, but that approach wouldn't work here, would it?

"Did Dr. Kelly say he's dying?" asks Adrienne.

"No."

"You sound upset."

"I'm not. Why should I be? I don't love him. Are you scared of death?"

Adrienne doesn't even think it over. "No."

I should have expected this. Adrienne's hair turned gray and she didn't dye it. "Why? Why not?" This isn't a question, it's a plea. Save me from this. Save me from the boy with the fist in his eye.

"I suppose because I saw my father die." I can hear Adrienne munching a cinnamon cookie. "He was lying there, and he was in so much pain he shuddered."

"You mean like a death rattle?" That's a term I've heard forever. What is it, and will I recognize it when I hear it?

"No. Just every few seconds, his body would tense up and shake. God, it was creepy. Then he died. And you know how in yoga they say relax your feet, then your ankles, and they work their way up until your whole body is limp? That's what happened to him."

"Are you saying that death is the ultimate in relaxation?"

"I guess so."

"I never relax. If you relax, that's when it happens."

"What?"

"Whatever."

"Eve, I don't think your father's dying. But I think the thought of it is producing anxiety."

"I'm not anxious about my father. Jesse had a car accident —he's fine—but now I have this terrible mess with the insurance."

"Your agitation is all about insurance?" She says this evenly, to underscore her disbelief, and that makes me counter aggressively.

"Do you know how much it costs to insure teenagers?"

"Eve, I can hear you."

I lower my voice. "Adrienne, if I can't persuade this doctor Jesse hit to let us pay him directly for the accident, the cost of our coverage will be astronomical. We could lose it altogether. And you haven't talked to this guy. He's a nose doctor who's a total headache. But basically, everything's un-der control. I'm sure if I can get him back on the phone, I can handle him."

"And that's all you're worried about?" asks Adrienne.

"Yes."

Five

I graduated from college in 1973 but left before the ceremonies to avoid having my father there. My mother's presence wasn't an issue. I'd refused to see or speak to her ever since my trip to Big Bear. When Maddy tried to report some hike they'd all taken or relay an invitation to visit, I wouldn't listen.

My father was still drinking, but aside from his overdose

while I was studying for my Great American Plays final, he hadn't tried anything drastic. I kept to a policy of going home only for an odd week now and then. I decided to move to New York City; this put me near Georgia and a safe three thousand miles away from him.

I met Adrienne through a classified ad she had placed in *The Village Voice,* requesting "one female roommate who is sane and has never attended est." We shared the top floor of a five-flight walk-up. The two bedrooms were each the size of a shoe box. Our living room couch was a single bed with pillows piled against the wall on the long side. We had one asparagus plant. It sat on the air conditioner, its lacy stems vibrating because the air conditioner was always on; we ran it year-round to block out the roar from Sixth Avenue. I had a coffee table, of which I was proud. It had once been a display case for, I fear, nothing too attractive. Still, it was glass on all sides with pretty pine trim, and the back had sliding doors. We put Adrienne's salt and pepper shaker collection inside.

Thanks to Georgia's husband, who knew the deputy parks commissioner, I went to work at the New York City Parks Department, planning special events: concerts, Bicycle Day, the opening of the new seal pond in Central Park. Adrienne sat in the apartment all summer, watching the Senate Watergate hearings until her money ran out. Then I helped her get a job at Parks too, in the Graphic Design Department, where she designed our posters.

At first Adrienne and I shared a phone number. But after a few weeks she began saying, "It's probably your dad," whenever the phone rang. Soon after that, she got a number of her own.

"Hey, kid, I'm thinking of moving to New York." My father called right in the middle of Nixon's 1974 State of the

Union address, just as he was saying, "One year of Watergate is enough."

"Dad, that's a terrible idea."

"This town is dead."

"Well, maybe, but you wouldn't like New York anymore. It's so dangerous, I mean there are"—I racked my brain for something scary—"Chinese street gangs. Muggers galore, I am not kidding."

With that, Adrienne turned off the TV and made no pretense of not listening to my conversation.

"Let's face it, kid, those network bastards don't want what I do. They're into reality now. Mary Martin Moore."

"You mean Mary Tyler Moore?"

"Yeah. Who cares, I don't care. I shoot the breeze. I shot it yesterday. I guess I'll shoot it tomorrow."

I quickly dialed Georgia. "This is such a nightmare. You won't believe what a nightmare this is. Dad wants to move here."

"Well, I'm sure he won't."

"Georgia, there's nothing keeping him in Los Angeles. He's divorced, his series is canceled."

"You take everything he says much too seriously. Did you ever consider that you enjoy getting upset?"

"I don't enjoy getting upset."

"Have it your way," Georgia said, in a tone that indicated she was humoring me.

"Georgia, I don't enjoy getting upset." I looked at Adrienne, who was nodding indignantly in agreement.

"Fine. Are we meeting for lunch next Monday?"

"Sure."

"You pick the restaurant."

"No, you pick it."

"Eve, I don't care."

"Okay, The Hare and the Tortoise."

"Is that a serious place? Does it have tablecloths? I hope it doesn't have spider plants drooping over the tables."

"I don't remember. Yes, it has tablecloths. Look, if you don't like it, you pick the place."

"No, that's fine, where is it?"

"Fifty-fourth between Park and Lex. What time is good, Georgia?"

"It's up to you."

"Twelve-thirty."

"Let's make it one."

I hung up. I didn't say anything to Adrienne. She turned the TV back on, we both watched Nixon in silence, then abruptly Adrienne hit the power button, turning the TV off. "I hope you don't mind my saying—"

"What?"

"Every time you're upset and you call your sister, you feel worse."

"No I don't."

Adrienne took off her shoe and slammed it on the floor. "Goddamn these roaches." She went to get a paper towel to pick up the dead roach. "Where'd it go?" she asked.

"Isn't it there?"

She looked around the floor, then under the couch. "No."

"My father's like a roach. Just when you think you've gotten rid of him . . . Oh God, suppose he moves here?"

"You'll hardly see him, it's a big city. And when you have to, I'll go with you, I promise."

"Thanks. You know, Georgia told me last week that a person's ears and nose keep growing forever. I mean the rest of you completely stops and your nose and ears go on and on and on."

"Why did she say that?"

"Because it's interesting. She's always learning things like that."

Adrienne smacked at another roach. "I missed." She slipped her shoe back on, crossed her legs demurely, and fluffed her hair as if she were now a lady again. "I don't mean to criticize Georgia, but you think she dresses so amazingly—"

"I think she's chic."

"She looks like someone's mother, someone's very chic mother. I bet she has her hair done every week."

"No, she doesn't."

"I can't tell whether she's twenty or forty."

"She's twenty-six."

"Well, she doesn't look young. She looks youthful."

☎

The next day, while I was writing a press release about higher entrance fees to the Central Park ice-skating rink, Madeline called from Los Angeles.

"I have to talk fast because I'm broke."

"Do you want me to call you?"

"No, I charged this to a fake number, but you usually only get caught if you talk a long time."

"Maddy, that's illegal."

"Oh, Evie, don't be so uptight. What's new?"

"Dad may be moving to New York."

"This is my lucky day," sang Maddy. "Ruby Tuesday,

this neat store in Venice, took thirteen sets of my bead ear-rings on consignment. Presto's friends with the manager, but he really liked them. He would have taken them anyway. I had to call the minute I left the store."

"That's great, Maddy."

"And now Dad's moving to you. Ha, ha-ha, ha-ha."

"It's not for sure. Besides, it's not as if you ever see him."

"But I know he's in L.A., and that's practically the same thing. Who put him in the hospital when he took all those pills?"

"That was two years ago. And you didn't put him in, you just called an ambulance." This last remark is good-natured only on the surface. I change the subject. "So, are you going to college?"

"God, do you and Georgia make plots?"

"Excuse me?"

"That's all she asks about too. She never asks about Presto or my earrings. Eve, would you do me a favor?"

"What?"

"Would you ask Georgia if she'll put my earrings in the magazine? If she'll use them in a fashion spread?"

Georgia was now the associate fashion editor of *Harper's Bazaar*. When she had landed the job, she had called. "Do you realize that I'm only twenty-six? This is big."

Then my father had phoned me. "Your sister's going to be president."

"Of what?"

"Hearst. The country. Who knows?"

I answered Madeline. "Why don't you ask Georgia your-self? Why should I have to ask her?"

"My phone's disconnected, okay? Anyway, she never takes my calls. Sometimes she doesn't call me back for a whole day. I don't ask you for things. I hardly ask you for anything. I never ask anyone for anything."

"Fine, I'll do it."

Maddy brightened immediately. "Thanks, Eve. This really means a lot to me. I'd better get off, before I end up in San Quentin."

☎

I sat in The Hare and the Tortoise pretending to make notes in my Women's Liberation Appointment Calendar, which Adrienne had given me for Christmas, and glancing up every few seconds to check for Georgia.

Finally she appeared, bestowing on the hostess her half-smile, the one in which her lips stayed together but the corners of her mouth turned up. She was dressed in a very long sweater—it was a turtleneck that continued past her hips to become a dress, and it was cinched with a wide leather belt, reminding me that she had a better waist than I did.

I was always making these calculations: How do we compare? Being a sister, especially a middle sister, I could understand myself only in comparison with someone, and usually that meant with Georgia.

I suppose I fixated on her because she came first, was there when I arrived. We both shared our parents' dark hair and dark eyes, so the obvious physical distinctions between us were few. And Georgia was so definite, not just now but always, in what she thought, in all her choices. Faced with her certainty, I had trouble fathoming where she stopped and I began.

If Georgia proclaimed an affection for anything—say,

macadamia nuts—I couldn't prefer cashews without feeling I'd betrayed her. I never admired her straight and narrow aristocratic nose without remembering that mine turned up slightly, giving me the eager look of a kid while she had the serious appearance of a woman. Today I saw that her waist was not just ideally small and round, but smaller and rounder than mine, which was an oval leading not to broad, but to broader, hips. Madeline was so much another person—five years behind me, much taller, willowy even—a kind of free, not freer, spirit, who swung her arms loosely when she walked. Georgia acted as if she owned the street, Maddy strode along oblivious to it. I tended to watch where I stepped, trying to make my way without causing anyone else too much discomfort.

As I observed Georgia weaving her way over, quickly sizing up the food on tables she passed, I noticed that, around her shoulders, on top of this sweater dress, she had tied another sweater, a matching sweater. I had never seen anyone who was not on a playground walk around with her sweater tied around her, but seeing this style on Georgia made me want to tie everything I owned around my shoulders.

Which reminded me of my father's call several weeks before. "They pay your sister to wear clothes," he had said. This particular call had come when I was doing that humiliating thing known as "waiting for the phone to ring."

I'd met an architect while handing out press releases at the opening of an adventure playground in Central Park. Philip hadn't designed the playground, his boss had. Philip had done the specifications for the jungle gym. He'd asked for my number.

The phone had been sitting next to me on the couch while Adrienne and I watched the evening news, all about Rose Mary Woods and how she had accidentally erased eighteen and a half minutes of a White House tape. I waited two rings, not to appear eager, then answered.

"They pay your sister to wear clothes. Bet you never heard of that before."

"Big deal."

"You said it." He hung up. The phone rang again. Again I waited two rings. "Hello."

"Get a load of this. They pay Georgia to wear clothes."

"Dad, you just called me."

"I thought I dialed Maddy. Don't be mad."

"I'm not," I lied, barely disguising it.

"You know your old man. He gets carried away." He hung up again.

Georgia sat down and blew a kiss across the table. "Hello, darling." Adrienne was right, it was hard to tell what age Georgia was. This kissing bit she had done for a year now, but the "darling" was new. Even though it was an affectation, she knew it was, you could tell by how she said it. "Darling." I liked the sound of it. It was comforting. I leaned closer across the table, a tree leaning to the sun.

"Have a menu." I handed mine over. I saw her eyes whip down it; then she laid it neatly next to her napkin. "I snacked all morning at the office. You eat. I'll just have a tomato juice. Could you have the waiter bring a tomato juice with a slice of lime on the side?" she asked the hostess.

"Dad says they pay you to wear those clothes."

"They don't pay me. They just give me free clothes." She cupped her hand coyly along the side of her mouth, as if someone might overhear. "They normally do this only with the fashion editor. This is the first time they've done it with the associate fashion editor." She returned her hand to her lap. "This dress is Halston."

"Is that a material, like cashmere?"

Georgia smiled. "God, the things you don't know. Halston is a very famous designer. You know, Eve"—this was the first time I'd heard her voice drop a level and sound vaguely as if she'd been brought up in Europe—"if you don't know something, it's usually a good idea to wait awhile and see how the conversation goes, because sometimes you can figure it out for yourself." Then she added, in her normal tone, "That was a really good piece of advice."

"I know all about Halston," I bluffed. "I was just kidding around." I changed the subject. "You know Madeline's earrings?"

"You mean the reason she's not going to college. Because she's becoming an earring factory."

"I know it's completely dumb." We both started laughing. "Does she actually think she can live off this?"

"Who knows?" Georgia squeezed lime into her tomato juice.

"She asked me to ask you if you would put them in the magazine. In a fashion spread. Actually, she practically started crying, she begged me to ask you, but don't tell her I said that."

Georgia seasoned the tomato juice with pepper. "She should go to college."

"She doesn't want to."

"Here, taste this. Isn't it delicious?"

I took a sip. "Yeah."

"She'll never meet men if she doesn't go to college."

"That's not too liberated, Georgia."

"Is that one of Adrienne's opinions? Adrienne probably doesn't shave under her arms. I'm as liberated as she is. I'm simply being practical."

"Well, you don't have to worry about Madeline and men. She meets guys just waiting for a green light."

"Sure, those kind of guys." Georgia raised her eyes to acknowledge the waiter. "I'm only having tomato juice."

"I'll have the chef's salad."

"Does her chef's salad come in a big wooden bowl?" Georgia asked.

"I'll check." He disappeared.

"He doesn't even know how the chef's salad comes? What kind of a restaurant is this?"

"The food's good. Philip and I eat here. It's near his office."

The waiter returned. "Yes, it does."

"Then you don't want it," said Georgia. "It's too much. You'll get tired just looking at it. Have the crab bisque. I saw one go by."

"Crab bisque, please. So will you use Maddy's earrings?"

"I'll look at them, but they're probably not avenue enough."

I didn't ask what that meant. I figured it would become clear, but it didn't.

"Tell her to send them to me," Georgia said.

"If Dad moves here, will we have to spend Thanksgiving with him?"

Georgia assumed a pose. She put her elbow on the table. Her arm and hand were straight up and her chin was balanced on the tips of her fingers. She narrowed her eyes and thought. "Yes."

☎

Six months later, Adrienne, Philip, and I were going uptown in a taxi to meet my father. He had been living at the Algonquin hotel for a month and now had found an apartment. I had to drag Adrienne away from the TV. Nixon had resigned the presidency that day and she was watching his speech over and over on the news. "Parallel lives," said Adrienne. "Your father moves in, Nixon moves out."

It was a muggy August night. We stuck to everything—our clothes, the cab seat, one another. The taxi had to dodge geysers from several fire hydrants that had been turned on by kids and were sending torrents of water into the street. We were all three soaked with water and sweat when we reached my father's apartment at Seventy-first and Third.

It was a tall white brick semi-luxury building, the type that promises cookie-cutter apartments with low ceilings and wallboard instead of plaster. "I can't enter this place," said Philip.

"Is this a political position?" Adrienne blew upward in a futile attempt to cool herself off.

Philip did not need to consider this. "Yes."

"Nouvelles political positions," said Adrienne. "Refuses to enter ugly buildings. I could do a cartoon based on this, would you mind?"

"That would depend on where you sold it," said Philip.

"I'll try *The New Yorker* first," said Adrienne.

"Fine." He walked over to the bus stop.

"Philip, my father is renting an apartment here."

"So?"

"He's all alone. You could at least be kind enough to go up and look at it. You could even say something nice."

"I'll say congratulations. That's as far as I'll go."

We entered the building, got on the elevator, and rode up in silence. The door to 6A was wide open. "Dad?" I called.

"Eve? Hey, it's my Evie. Hi, kid." He started crying.

"He always cries," I explained. "He says hello, he cries."

"It's a family tradition," said my father, taking out his

handkerchief. "Eve, this is . . . what did you say your name was?" He looked at the woman who was with him. She was short, and not plump but solid like a sausage, packed into a flowered pantsuit. She wore large square glasses and looked like a woman in those "Don'ts" features Georgia had run in *Mademoiselle*.

"Virginia Hazen. Call me Ginny." She offered her hand. "I'm your father's realtor."

"Nice to meet you." I introduced Adrienne and Philip.

My father threw his arms out. "This place is a hit, don't you think?" We looked at the room, which, if it had not been L-shaped, could have been the interior of a plain white gift box.

"The couch can go here," said Ginny, standing against the long wall. "And the dining room table here." She moved over to the alcove.

"It's great, Dad."

"Fantastic," said Adrienne.

"Congratulations," said Philip.

"Too bad there's not much of a view." My father walked over to the window and looked across Third Avenue to an apartment house remarkably similar to this one. "Big deal, I'll put up venetians."

"I can arrange that for you," said Ginny.

At that moment, I noticed that my father's shirt was misbuttoned. One side of the collar poked up two inches above the other. It was like wearing a "Needs a Wife" sign around his neck.

He clapped his hands, signaling that his attention span had expired. "Who can stand an empty apartment? Let's go eat. Ginny, you like spareribs?" He didn't wait for an answer. "We used to get the best spareribs, didn't we, Evie?"

"We sure did."

"Where was that?" asked Adrienne.

"Ah Fong's on Glendon, right?"

"Right, Dad."

He led the way back down the hall. "Georgia's coming. Did you hear, Eve, Georgia's coming?"

"Yeah, of course, I know. We're meeting her at the restaurant."

Ginny locked the apartment and gave my father the key. We all crowded into the elevator. "God, it's great to be together, isn't it, Evie?"

Sorry, no answer, no way. I watched the floor numbers flash—five, four, three . . .

The elevator doors opened. Thank God, more air. Breathing room. I was the first one out, through the lobby and onto the sidewalk.

The streets were not empty exactly, but lonely. In August most Upper East Side residents split for their vacation homes, and those who remained looked droopy, as if they belonged on the sale rack. The humidity had the effect of leg weights, causing people to move slowly, sloggingly. The only reason Georgia and Richard were in town (they shared a rental with friends in Bridgehampton) was that she had to cover for her boss, who wasn't.

Adrienne, my father, and I started down Third Avenue. Philip trailed behind with Ginny. I could hear him haranguing her about how these apartment buildings were faceless monsters.

"How do you like Ginny?" my father asked.

"She's very nice."

"I'm thinking of marrying her."

"What? How long have you known her?"

But my father was on to something else. "Hey," he boomed. "Hey, there's Georgia." He waved his hand back and forth like a windshield wiper at Georgia and Richard a block away. Georgia wore a rain cape of a flamboyant flimsy material, and when she waved back, it unfurled like a flag.

"How much do they pay you to wear that?" my father asked.

"It's parachute silk, don't you like it?" Georgia twirled.

"Hello, Lou." Richard shook Dad's hand. Even in this heat, he was dressed properly—blue blazer, striped rep tie, white shirt—although he kept wiping his forehead with a handkerchief. Richard had probably been his high school's student body president and most likely to succeed; and still, in his early thirties, he looked arrogant and innocent, as I imagined he appeared in his yearbook picture. He was fine-looking, not handsome, but parent-pleasing. He had a per-fectly apportioned amount of black hair, parted neatly with every hair in place. Georgia had good hair too. Thick, short, also black and straight, it had spun out when she twirled, then dropped right back in place. Adrienne had speculated that they probably first fell in love not with each other but with the way their hair matched. "Adrienne, darling, nice to see you again. Philip." Georgia kissed everyone's air and Richard shook hands, three shakes each. "Who stuffed him?" my dad whispered.

My father's future wife was standing off to the side. "Oh, Georgia, Richard," I said. "This is Virginia Hazen."

I could see Georgia scan Ginny, taking in every flowered inch, before she smiled and was gracious.

Georgia swept into the restaurant with us in her wake. "Mozell reservation for six, but we're going to be seven this evening." She followed the maître d' to the table; we followed her, then stood stranded while she negotiated a table she pre-ferred, a round one with a lazy Susan in the center.

"Isn't this better?" she proclaimed as we all sat down.

"Round tables are better for conversation than square. We almost bought an apartment but didn't because the dining room was long and narrow."

"What year was the building?" asked Philip.

"Prewar," said Georgia.

"What you like drink?" asked the waiter, who had a somewhat incomplete knowledge of English. My father ordered a scotch and water. Richard ordered vermouth. After asking what kind of white wine they had, Georgia requested Chinese beer, and so did the rest of us.

"You order food now?" asked the waiter.

"We want the good stuff," said my dad. "You take care of it, Georgia."

She did: spareribs, egg rolls, shrimp fried rice, lobster Cantonese, chicken chow mein with extra almonds.

"Childhood Chinese," said Adrienne.

"We'd all like chopsticks, except my father. Ginny, would you?" asked Georgia.

"Heavens no," said Ginny.

"Five, then."

My father put up his hand to stop the waiter from leaving. "Do you know who you're talking to?"

The waiter looked around, confused, but nodded politely.

"Who?" asked my father.

"No problem with chopsticks," said the waiter, bowing slightly. The smile was still glued to his face, but clearly he was feeling he'd gotten caught in oncoming traffic.

"You're talking to the fashion editor of *Vogue*."

"Associate fashion editor." These were the first words Richard had contributed to the conversation.

"And it's *Harper's Bazaar*, thank you very much," said Georgia. She smiled at the waiter, dismissing him, and launched into a story, without taking a breath, about this eccentric famous fashion designer who took a stuffed animal everywhere, a teddy bear named Fred who even had his own seat at the Philharmonic. Georgia was one of the great ball carriers. Richard had married her probably to absolve himself of all social responsibility. Georgia absolved everyone. While she regaled us with how she had sent Fred flowers when he was in a doll hospital, I could hear Philip start in again on Ginny. "There are five renowned living architects," he said to her. "I suppose you know who they are?"

"Lay off already." I practically spit the words at him.

He clamped his mouth shut in a manner that indicated he had no intention of opening it ever again. Georgia hesitated a flick, just long enough for me and only me, her sister, to know she had noticed the interchange, before she continued to describe Fred's itty-bitty smoking jacket.

"You done with this story yet?" my father inquired querulously.

"Why not?" Georgia agreeably answered.

"Good, let me tell you about the revolver."

"What revolver?" I asked.

"Ever heard of *Luck Runs Out*?" he said to Adrienne.

"I know you wrote it. I've wanted to see it, but—"

"Great movie." My dad cut her off. "Could have been as big as *Casablanca* if it had had a love story. Tell her how you met him, Eve."

"Who?" asked Ginny.

"John Wayne, who else? So he's a Republican, so what?"

"I was five years old and I remember nothing."

"He patted her on the head and told her her old man could write. Gave me a revolver when we finished shooting. Said he'd carried the damn thing in every movie he'd ever made."

"I thought he gave you a bullet."

"Who was there, were you there?" My father's voice was suddenly loud. He waved his sparerib menacingly, and mustard sauce fell on his shirt. "I'll be right back." He got up, knocking his chair into the woman seated at the table behind. Richard quickly jumped up and righted the chair as my father lurched his way through the diners. I didn't turn but followed his course in a wall mirror. After he left the room, he stopped in the bar, ordered two more drinks, and downed them.

Did anyone else see? I caught Georgia's eye.

She unsnapped her purse, fished around, and took out a small pillbox.

"Only Georgia would have a pillbox," Adrienne pointed out later.

"She was rescuing me," I declared.

"Did you hear what Richard said?"

"What?"

"He pointed out that Georgia was *associate* fashion editor. That was hostile."

"No, it wasn't, Adrienne. He's an uptight lawyer. They're always trying to be technically correct."

"I don't think so," said Adrienne.

Anyway, Georgia took out a Valium. Carefully, even ceremoniously, she placed the tranquilizer on the edge of the lazy Susan, gave it a spin, then stopped it when the Valium was in front of me. As I picked up the pill, she pinched one out for herself and raised her teacup in a silent toast.

☎

"Dad said he was going to marry her. I think he'd met her that week. And Philip was unbelievably obnoxious. We would have had a huge fight on the way downtown, but

Georgia had given me a Valium and I fell asleep practically before I walked in the door. In fact, Adrienne had wanted me to watch *Citizen Kane* so I could see her favorite moment, but I barely made it to the bed."

"What's her favorite moment?"

"Have you seen the movie, Maddy?"

"No."

"Then it wouldn't mean anything to you."

"I know I didn't go to college, but I'm eighteen years old and capable of understanding something in a movie even if I haven't seen it."

"I don't even know what the moment is. I shouldn't have said that. Anyway, Dad didn't pick up the check, Richard had to. Do you know Richard didn't say one thing throughout the meal except for pointing out that Georgia was not fashion editor but *associate* fashion editor. Is that hostile or what? He hardly talks. Maybe he doesn't have a tongue."

"He has a tongue. He stuck it down my throat."

"Madeline, are you serious?"

"Remember when he was out here? And he took me to dinner? Georgia ordered him to, I guess. I borrowed these Greek sandals with straps going all the way up my legs because I thought it would really freak him out. Also, I picked a Mexican restaurant. When he walked me to my car, he kissed me on the mouth and stuck his tongue down my throat."

"What'd you do?"

"Nothing. I said, 'Thanks for dinner,' and slammed the door."

"Oh God, should we tell Georgia?"

"I'm not telling Georgia."

"But wouldn't you want to know if you were married to someone who French-kissed your sister?"

The operator cut in. "I have an emergency call for Eve Mozell."

"Oh my God! Okay, operator, I'm getting off."

"Let me know what it's about, okay?"

"Okay. Bye, Maddy." I hung up. "It's an emergency call," I yelled to Adrienne as the phone rang. "Hello?"

"Eve."

"What's wrong, Georgia, is it you and Richard?"

"Why would it be me and Richard?"

"I don't know, I just didn't know why you were making an emergency call."

"Our father bought three houses, a car, and a bicycle."

"Since we had dinner with him? Since last week?"

"Actually, he bought them all in one day."

"Can you do that?"

"Of course you can do that. Ginny took him to Westchester. Why would you think this call was about me and Richard?"

"I don't know. It just flew into my head. Dad can't afford three houses."

"We know that, Eve. Thank God Richard's a lawyer. He'll get Dad out of it. He can get anyone out of anything. Thank God."

"Thank God."

"I talked to my therapist. He says we should put Dad in Bloomingdale's."

I did not ask if he was being sent to a department store. It did not seem likely. "Bloomingdale's will take care of it?" I said cautiously, a very slight question at the end. Maybe, on some floor I've never been to, there is therapeutic shopping. My father is given money, set loose, and he has to not spend it. He learns to control himself at Bloomingdale's and then is no longer tempted to buy three houses, a car, and a bicycle. I shook my head at Adrienne, who was standing in the door-way, trying to make sense of all this.

"He's drinking like a fish and taking God knows what else. They'll dry him out and then determine what's wrong with him. They're absolutely brilliant at drugs. I'm sure psychotherapy is a waste of time. My shrink says the best thing to do is ambush him tonight."

"Right now? Can't we wait until tomorrow morning?"

"Now," said Georgia.

When my taxi pulled up, she was waiting in front of Dad's building. Even in crisis, she looked pulled together: her hair brushed and shiny, probably a hint of blush, definitely lipstick. She stood her usual ramrod straight and had actually taken the trouble to accessorize her suit with a silver dangling pendant in the shape of a lima bean. Well, it's important to look nice when you're going to a department store, otherwise how can you tell what anything will look like on you? Georgia had told me this once when I met her to go shopping dressed in a T-shirt and jeans, which was what I was wearing now.

Georgia smiled down the doorman. "We're going to visit my father, don't bother to ring." We sped by and into the elevator. "I'm dreading this," I said. She stood there silently, swinging the lima bean back and forth. We got out at six and she pressed the buzzer.

No answer. She tried the door. It was unlocked. An unlocked New York apartment? What did this mean? Had he been beaten and robbed? Georgia turned the knob slowly and pushed the door in an inch. A blast of music. "Everything's Coming Up Roses."

"Not dead," said Georgia. "Definitely not dead. Dad!" she called.

"In here."

He and Ginny were sitting at a card table in the living room. A bicycle-built-for-two was parked nearby, and the only other piece of furniture was a couch upholstered in a flowered print very similar to the sort Ginny favored in her pantsuits. The couch still had plastic on it.

"Hi, girls," said Ginny.

"Gin." My father laid down his cards, grabbed the bills in the center of the table, and stuffed them in his pocket.

"I lost again," Ginny said good-naturedly. "Heavens, I can't beat the man."

"Would you mind leaving?" Georgia was her most imperious. "We'd like to talk to our father."

"I'll be out of here in a jiff." Ginny swallowed the rest of her red wine and picked up her shoulder bag. "I hope we're going to be good friends." She stood on tiptoe to peck me on the cheek, then went for Georgia, who took a step backward. "Well, I'll be toddling off."

"Hey, guess what your old man did. I bought three houses today."

"We know," said Georgia.

"Was it on the AP?"

"No, you called and told me."

"Three houses." He shook his head happily. "It's the trifecta."

"Dad, sit down," Georgia ordered.

"Georgia, were you ever young?" asked my dad.

Georgia ignored him. "Sit down, Dad."

"Who made you king? That's what I want to know."

"Goddamnit, shut up," I shouted. My dad stared at me.

"We're taking you to the hospital," said Georgia. "You're out of control."

"Go to hell." My father started wheeling the bicycle to the door.

"Where are you going?" Georgia demanded.

"Out. Perchance to ride. Perchance to live."

Perchance? What drama was he in? Who was he playing?

Georgia barred the door. Stood in front like a sentry. "You're drunk and you're crazy."

"But I'm not married to Richard," said my father.

"Shut up," I screamed. "Put down that stupid bicycle." Tears were running down my cheeks. I'm doing this only for effect, I told myself. If I flip out, he'll shape up. This will scare him.

"Dry up, you're faking," said my dad.

How did he know? How could he tell? "I'm not faking, don't tell me I'm faking," I screamed louder.

"Calm down," said Georgia quietly. "Dad, if you do not get in the car with us and check into the hospital, you are never going to see Eve or me again."

My father thought about this. His tongue moved over to one side of his mouth and poked out his cheek.

"Go to hell," he said again, but without conviction. He tried to turn the bicycle around, but it was too big for the entryway.

"I'll take it," said Georgia. "Eve, pack some of Dad's clothes, would you?"

I went into his room and opened his closet. In the corner was a wilted nylon suitcase. I placed it on the bed, which was unmade, and opened a bureau drawer. His clothes were all rumpled in a heap. I didn't want to touch them. It felt danger-ous. There could be a surprise hidden in this mess.

I squinted a little so I couldn't really see what I was picking up, as I packed socks, underwear, and with luck pajamas. Fortunately, in the next drawer I found clean shirts with cardboard in them. Safe shirts. I was working really fast. I zipped the suitcase and took a suit out of the closet. I layered an extra sports jacket over it, and carried everything to the living room.

My dad was on the couch, refusing to look at Georgia or me. She was at the card table, shuffling the deck over and over.

"I guess I've packed enough."

"Where are we going?" my father asked.

"Bloomingdale's."

He did a slow take. "Is it open now?"

"That's what they call New York Hospital's psychiatric facility in Westchester," said Georgia. "It's on Bloomingdale Road. They're going to dry you out and find out why you're acting strange."

"I'm not strange," my father shouted.

"You are strange," I shouted back.

"Come on, Dad," said Georgia. It was not a request.

My father got up. Georgia grasped his arm, but he pulled away. He took a beat to stand tall, to right his shoulders. Now I knew the part he was playing. He was Alec Guinness in some English prisoner-of-war movie. He was about to be marched into solitary in *The Bridge on the River Kwai.* You can lock me up, beat me, starve me, but you'll never destroy my dignity. Playing this part and loving every minute of it, he walked steadily, though shakily, to the door.

We said nothing, through the door, into the elevator, out of the elevator, and into the limousine, which Richard had hired. We said nothing all the way up the Hutchinson River Parkway to White Plains and Bloomingdale Road.

"It looks like Sarah Lawrence College," Georgia observed when we turned into the hospital complex of ivy-covered brick buildings. That was the only comment anyone made, except for my father's final "Go to hell" when he signed himself in and was led away.

It was close to three in the morning when Georgia and I left.

I sat in the limousine rubbing my eyes. "Don't." Georgia pulled my hands down. "Don't ever tug at your face."

"I was mushing, I wasn't tugging."

"Just don't. Your face is falling anyway. It starts falling the day you're born." She searched inside her purse. "Aha." Triumphantly she held up a black square of paper. "After Eights."

"What's that?"

"It's a chocolate-covered mint inside a little envelope all its own. It may be the greatest thing the English ever invented." She handed it over, then located one for herself.

We nibbled our mints. "Was it ever nice at home? I don't remember if it was ever nice."

"Oh, it was," said Georgia. "Remember how Dad used to take us shopping for dresses?"

"Because Mom didn't want to."

"True. But he loved to so much. 'My daughters need clothes.' Georgia puffed up her chest, imitating him. "He would announce it so everyone noticed us."

"What else?"

"We played games at dinner, charades or twenty questions. Sometimes Maddy sang 'The Twelve Days of Christmas,' and we would all sit with our napkins clamped over our mouths so we wouldn't laugh."

"I remember. She was totally tone-deaf. Why did she ever imagine she could become a rock star?" I thought about

Maddy at age five, in her red Dr. Denton's, pouring her heart into "Five go-old rings" as she stood on her stage, my parents' coffee table. "Georgia?"

"What?"

"Remember earlier tonight when I was screaming?"

"Yes." She said this in a very kind way.

"I was pretending. How did he know that?"

"You weren't pretending. You flipped out. Don't you ever read The Magazine?" She always called *Harper's Bazaar* The Magazine, as if there were only one published in the world.

"I look at the pictures."

"Eve, last month they reviewed a book called *Outside Inside.* By this psychologist. It was fascinating. The thesis is—"

Thesis. My brain was too tired for that word.

"When a person freaks out, sometimes they step outside themselves and watch. Outside, inside, get it? It's a kind of self-protection. Do you still have last month's issue?"

"I don't know."

She patted my hand. "I'll send you a copy."

I was getting drowsy, drifting into a half-sleep where everything seemed quite pleasant. If only I could have stayed in this big solid car, being carried along in some direction safe from fathers and telephones. I lay back, with my head resting on the top of the seat, and stretched my legs. I could just see the tops of the trees go by, and then the tops of buildings when we got into the city. We dropped Georgia off. Then the driver took me home.

☎

To cope with my father's first hospitalization for his over-dose, we sisters had assigned each other roles: I did this, so you have to do that. Now, with his second, we had a routine. If Georgia and I had committed him, Madeline knew without being told that she would do the follow-up.

Patients didn't have phones at Bloomingdale's. My father couldn't call me. And with Maddy keeping tabs on how he was faring, I was in paradise. That fall, when my phone rang I grabbed it. I never hesitated before speaking. I said hello enthusiastically. Unfortunately, I'd broken off with Philip and no one new had turned up, which meant that now that I looked forward to answering the phone, there was never anyone exciting on the other end. Mostly, in the evenings, I hung out with Adrienne and her boyfriend, Sandy.

Adrienne became enamored of Indian food. "It goes with me," she announced, pulling jars of garam masala and chutney from the kitchen cupboards.

Adrienne was earthy. A wild frizz of brown hair, solid shoulders, big breasts. She was unconsciously sexy in the way that a very welcoming person can be sexy because she's so warm. She turned curries into experiments, throwing in tomatoes one day, potatoes and chickpeas the next, the way she enhanced herself every day with clanking silver jewelry in any number of combinations. The result was never a hodgepodge —neither her appearance nor her cooking—but always some inspired exotic combination.

In October, we celebrated her first sale of a cartoon: "Nouvelles Political Positions." To *The New Yorker,* no less. Adrienne, Sandy, and I toasted the absent Philip for being so inspiringly obnoxious. We sat on the floor, as if we were in the Indian desert, surrounded by a host of condiments—peanuts, chutney, coconut—as well as pappadums, these toasty things Adrienne was very excited about. The curry simmered on the stove, and the TV was on, showing *Citizen Kane.*

"Here it comes." Adrienne held up her hands for quiet during her favorite part. "Merry Christmas," said Charles Foster Kane's guardian, holding out a brand-new sled. The guardian was a miserly-looking but hale middle-aged man. "Cut to kid," Adrienne narrated as the camera showed young Charles making a nasty face. "Cut back," she shouted as the camera cut to the guardian again. "And a Happy New Year," said the guardian. He was now white-haired and stooped.

"Isn't that an amazing way to show time passing? Merry Christmas, he's your basic average-aged adult. Happy New Year, he's ancient. Unreal." Adrienne dug ravenously into her curry. Viewing this had refreshed her appetite.

"That's really your favorite part?" Sandy asked doubtfully.

"This is life," said Adrienne. She snapped her fingers.

My phone rang.

"I'll take it in the other room so you can watch." I carried the phone into the bedroom and kicked the door closed. "Hello?"

"Eve?"

"Hi, Georgia."

"Eve, would you mind if Richard and I go away for Thanksgiving? We've been offered this apartment in London. You know, I'm having trouble getting pregnant, and I thought if we were in London . . ."

"Why are you asking me?"

"Because of Dad. Don't think you have to spend Thanksgiving with him. He doesn't deserve it. Madeline says he's perfectly happy in that loony bin. He's even popular in group."

"Don't worry. There's no way I'm going."

"Good. I'll call when I get back."

"Have fun. Good luck with the baby."

☎

At noon on Thanksgiving Day, I was staring into the refrigerator. Leftover lamb curry, eggs, one onion.

"Are you sure you don't want to come to Thanksgiving?" asked Adrienne. "Sandy's parents would love to have you."

"Thanks anyway. I'm going to get takeout."

Adrienne was putting away her inks on the drafting table that was now in our living room. She'd just finished another cartoon, called "Reasons They Broke Up." She did it in a white heat right after she'd seen the inside of Sandy's closet, where he hung his clothes in cleaner's plastic, then placed them in larger plastic bags, and where his shoes were kept in baggies tied with twists. Reason number one was "Likes plastic too much."

"Did you show Sandy the cartoon?" I asked.

"No, I'll wait until we break up, after the holidays. You sure you'll be all right?"

"I'm fine."

I bundled up and went out on Sixth Avenue. It was freezing, the kind of cold that bites your flesh. I tucked my chin down, trying to bury as much of my face as possible under my thick wool scarf. Everyone was walking fast, with hunched shoulders.

New York City is a hospitable place if you're alone on a holiday. Everything is open—food stores, flower shops, the newspaper stand. I patted my mittened hands against my cold ears as I scooted into Hugo's, a twenty-four-hour deli.

I wandered up and down the aisles, thawing. What did I want? An ice cream sandwich maybe, cole slaw, rice pudding. Nothing needed to go together, and everything could be dessert. There was a cooked turkey in the deli tray with one leg and half a breast sliced off. The skin was wrinkling. Georgia would undoubtedly be able to give it some advice.

But nothing appealed to me. I braced myself and went back outside. A man came toward me gesticulating, having an elaborate argument with no one. His dirty jeans drooped. The hood of his grungy sweatshirt was stretched over his head, and inside, barely visible, were bloodshot eyes so sunken they might have been in retreat. He stopped at a pay phone, picked up the receiver, and started talking—that is, his lips formed words, but no sound came out.

"I'm not going to be moved by this person under any circumstances," I told myself. "This is not a message or a sign or anything." I suddenly realized what I wanted to eat— blintzes. I went back into the deli.

"Blintzes, please. Two, no, four cheese blintzes."

I could see the man through the store window. He slammed the phone down. His conversation with himself had not gone well, and he walked off, continuing to gesticulate.

"Anything else?"

"That turkey. Will you sell me the whole thing?"

I got in a cab with everything except the blintzes, which I gave back. I had turkey, potato salad, cranberry relish made specially by Hugo's for Thanksgiving, an Entenmann's pumpkin pie, paper plates, and plastic knives and forks. "I want to go to the New York Hospital on Bloomingdale Road in White Plains. It takes about forty minutes to get there, I'll show you the way. Would you take a check?"

"Not a chance," said the driver.

"Then please take me to an Avis place. Do you know where an Avis place is?"

Half an hour later, I was driving up the parkway feeling excited, as if I had somewhere to go and it wasn't an insane asylum. It was very beautiful at Bloomingdale's. Towering oaks, elegantly bare; the ivy had turned gold and burnt orange.

No one was in the reception area. There was a note saying to pick up the phone and dial 321. "Hello, this is Eve Mozell. I want to see my father, Lou Mozell."

"Sure, honey. Someone'll be right down."

I sat with my shopping bags. There were decorations on the wall, children's cutouts of Pilgrims and turkeys with a sign above that said "Mrs. Weber's Third Grade Class, White Plains Elementary." I wondered if the parents came here to see the exhibit.

The elevator opened and a man in a janitor's outfit waved me in. He turned the key in the elevator locks, and pushed eight.

When the doors opened, I stepped into a room the size of a phone booth, with another door straight ahead of me. The man unlocked that one too, a large metal door, and swung it open to reveal my father standing with his arms open. I went right into them.

"Evie, baby."

"Hi, Daddy." I started crying.

"What's wrong?"

I shook my head. I didn't know. Maybe it was the lock. Maybe it was seeing the janitor turn that key and seeing my father, his arms open, waiting, behind a locked door.

"Hey, I'm the one who cries." He handed me his handkerchief.

"You always have a handkerchief. Even in here, you have a handkerchief." I sniffed and started laughing, but then I started crying all over again. "You look great," I said finally. He did. His shirt, for instance, was pressed and buttoned correctly. For the first time in years, he didn't look as if he'd dressed in the dark.

The janitor had taken my bags out of the elevator and set them down next to us. "I brought you Thanksgiving," I explained.

"Ha. What a winner. When I had you, I had a winner."

He picked up the bags. He actually picked them up. Had he ever before carried anything for me? We walked down the brown hall past small identical rooms. It was like a dorm. A man came toward us reading *Time* magazine. He looked up. Big smile. "Hi, Lou." The second he passed, my father whispered. "Used to be head of Xerox."

We passed a woman. "Hi, Gloria."

"Hi, Lou."

"Her husband should be here, not her."

We passed several others. Everyone greeted my father happily. One person was in pajamas. "Don't ask," my father said, squeezing my shoulder.

The furniture in his room was the equivalent of government issue: iron bed, plain gray blanket, one pillow, metal cabinet for clothes, two wooden chairs, one with arms. A couple of the latest issues of *Variety* lay on the floor. He pointed to the armchair. "You sit here," he said grandly. He picked up his pillow, socked it twice, put it on the long side of the bed, against the wall, and sat back against it. My father actually plumped a pillow. That was so competent. "How are you?" he said.

He was really asking. He wanted to know.

"Oh, I'm okay. I broke up with Philip."

My father nodded. "I don't remember him too well. What was he like?"

I reminded him that Philip was an architect. I told him about the projects he worked on, and how he was fanatical about the appearance of everything he purchased, even his shaving brush. That he knew the history of every old building in New York City. My father paid close attention, laughing at the bit about the shaving brush, raising his eyebrows approvingly at Philip's love for Manhattan.

"Did you like him?"

"I thought I was going to marry him. I thought I loved him."

"Love." My father shrugged. "In marriage, you can exist without love, but never without like."

"I didn't like him, you're right. How did you know? Why was I with someone I didn't like?"

"Company." My father grinned. "I'm an expert on that."

"Did you like Mom?"

"Your mom was everything. The sun, the moon, the whole enchilada. But she didn't like me." He wasn't mopey, just matter-of-fact.

"Well, I don't like her." I got up and started unwrapping the bird. "Let's celebrate."

I gave Dad some containers to open, expecting the tops to flip off and the food to fly out, but he carefully peeled the tops back and stacked them. "This was a terrific idea," he said.

"Have I ever done anything you didn't think was terrific?"

"Nope."

"Maddy likes Mom," I said.

"Well, you and Maddy had different mothers."

No wisdom at all, nothing for years, then a deluge. Or maybe it just seemed that way compared with the emptiness before.

I'd had Hugo's slice the turkey. I didn't think there'd be carving knives available. My father forked some slices onto a plate, then, in neat little piles, put potato salad, cranberry relish, cole slaw. He presented the plate to me and pointed to the armchair so I would sit down again.

"You know, Evie, you were always—"

"What?"

"The most sympathetic."

That was the only shadow on the whole day, that compliment for something I vaguely understood was my undoing. But I brushed it off and out of my head. We were having a sort of picnic and I liked it. Our first family picnic: Thanksgiving 1974 in a loony bin in Westchester. "Aren't you going to eat?"

He was staring out the window at an oak tree with three beautiful leaves hanging on for dear life. "It looks nice out there when you're in here. Of course, when I'm out there, I never notice."

That was true, of course. He never noticed anything. The sun rose and set without so much as a nod of acknowledgment from my father. Had he figured that out in group?

"I'm being 'paroled' soon. I was hoping you'd come to the wedding."

"Dad, you're not getting married. Every time I see you, you say you're getting married. You're a manic depressive. That's why they put you on lithium. That's why you bought three houses, that's why you always decide to get married after saying hello."

"No, I'm getting married next summer. To a real nice nurse."

"Are you sure?"

My dad laughed. Even his laugh sounded healthy. "She's got a daughter too. What the hell's her name?" He thought.

Aha, the old dad is there. Can't be bothered to remember the name of his future stepchild.

"Lola. She's twenty. Wants to be a model. I told her Georgia would shake the trees for her." He went to the door and called, "Hey, baby, come here."

I sat there with a paper plate on my knees as a woman walked by the door, stopped as if someone might be watching, then whisked in. Her skin was brown, her hair orange, her lipstick red. She was very colorful. That was mainly my first impression. I couldn't stand it that I couldn't race home and call Georgia or Madeline. Georgia had neglected to give me her London phone number, and Maddy's phone was disconnected again.

"Claire, meet Eve. I just told her we're getting married."

"It's the God's honest truth. We hope you'll come to the wedding."

"Well, sure. Would you like some Thanksgiving dinner?"

"No, thanks, honey, I'm not much for food."

☎

"She's not much for food," I told Georgia a week later, the second she got back. "What does that mean?"

"Is she thin?"

"Yes, very thin and very tall. Taller than he is."

"How old is she?"

"Georgia, she's black."

"What do you mean, black? A black person?"

It was thrilling. Probably my most thrilling moment on the phone. It was a direction no one expected him to take. It meant absolutely nothing and it was thrilling. Having it happen and getting to tell them.

"That's cool. That's the coolest thing he's ever done," said Madeline.

"I don't think he's marrying Claire because she's black. I don't think he's making a statement about race relations."

"Maybe not, but we're an interracial family now," said Maddy. "I already march, and you should too now."

"March where?" Georgia asked when I told her Maddy's response. "There aren't too many civil rights marches these days."

"I think she means for peace. Maddy's really into peace. Peace and whales."

"Fine, darling, she's into peace. But hasn't she noticed, the war is over? Someone should break the news. By the way, how old is our new stepmother?"

"She's forty-three. Dad's sixty, that's not so bad. I think this will really be good for him, get him out of himself, more involved. She has a twenty-year-old daughter who wants to be a model. Her name is Lola. He wants you to help her get work."

"Blacks age better than whites."

"They do?"

"There's no comparison. Have you ever seen pictures of Marian Anderson? I wanted to run something about this, but the editor wouldn't go near it with a ten-foot pole."

"I can't believe he's marrying a nurse. How did we get so lucky?"

Six

After shutting the front door, I do what I always do: go into Joe's study to check the answering machine. Five calls. Probably all from my father. Probably all screaming, Where are you?

He's been locked up in UCLA Geriatric/Psychiatric for two weeks, but I haven't heard from him in five days. I should go this evening.

I dump my briefcase on the floor in the front hall, next to Ifer's backpack, and approach the machine warily, preparing to hear my father's threats, complaints, whines, weeping. I press Playback.

"Hi, Eve, I'm back from Montana. Something wonderful has happened. Call me."

"Hello, dear, it's Madge. I thought the meeting went splendidly. Wasn't his birthplace adorable? Just think—those four Nixon boys lived in one little attic in two little beds. I guess they had to get along, and they darn well did. Should we have name tags?"

"Hi, Eve, it's Adrienne. I'm working late and Paul's out covering the Mets, so when you get in, no matter how late, call me."

"Is this ABC Window Dressing, yes? I am Ogmed Kunundar. I have here the measures. Thank you. Two-one-three—"

This must be the doctor's mother, possibly as demented as he is. I copy her number while I hear Joe's voice, stiff, hating the machine: "Finished with the cake lady. Off to Chicago tonight to interview Max, the bagel man. I'll call from there."

I sit down at his desk, a soothing place to be. Sometimes I wear his sweaters when he's away, and often I read in his study. His disorder, which upsets me when he's home, provides a comfort zone. I dial Adrienne.

"Good news, my father hasn't phoned from UCLA in five days. I actually have peace and quiet. What's up?"

"I was watching *Rebecca*, with Joan Fontaine—" Although she has never smoked, Adrienne has a cigarette voice, deep and throaty. She can make the most innocuous statements reek of drama.

"Yes?" I say, hoping some thrill is coming.

"Was that the actress you were trying to think of?"

Her voice also leads to frequent letdown. "No. Joan Fontaine is thin. This one I'm thinking of is sort of wide."

"Wide? Joan Crawford?"

"No, not big like Joan Crawford. Oh God, I can see her, what is her name? She's sweet, short, and boring. I think her name starts with an *l*. Is that why you called?"

"Basically."

"Maybe he's waiting for me to get in the bathtub."

"Who?"

"My father. He's waiting for me to be luxuriating in a bubble bath. I'll have to jump out, drip water all over the floor to answer the phone, and then discover it's him. Oh God, I should go see him. But I'm exhausted. I was at the Nixon Library all day trying to decide whether roast beef should be served in front of an exhibit of Tricia Nixon's wedding dress. At least my father hasn't phoned. Thank goodness he hasn't phoned."

There is a long pause.

"Hello?" I say. "Are you still there?"

"You seem wired," says Adrienne.

"And you sound like a broken record," I reply, not unpleasantly. "I'm not wired, I'm tired. I'm getting off. I'll talk to you soon."

I hang up, feeling restless. It's five o'clock, the hour when I'm normally here in Joe's study regaling him with my day. I would be describing the trio of dummies in the Nixon Library: Pat, Tricia, and Julie—the girls dressed for their weddings, Pat as the mother of the bride. Of which bride, I wonder. Did they dress her in what she wore to her older daughter's wedding or her younger daughter's? I would have moved Joe's tapes onto the floor and parked myself in his wicker armchair with my feet propped up on his wastebasket.

Joe would be leaning back, bending his desk chair as far as it could go, his hands clasped behind his head. He would be devouring my words. But I am used to Joe's travels. I reward myself by doing things I never do when he's here. Like consume an entire dinner of guacamole dip.

I go into the kitchen. Why am I here? That settles it, I'm definitely not going to see my father today. I don't even know why I'm in the kitchen. Oh yes, guacamole. I stick the Post-it with Ogmed Kunundar's number on the wall and take a few avocados from the fruit bowl. I dial her on the kitchen phone, then, with the receiver clamped between my chin and my shoulder, cut open the avocados.

"Hello, is this Mrs. Kunundar?"

"Yes, who is calling?" She has a piano voice, but all treble clef and every word a different note.

"This is Eve Mozell." I am talking the same way, words all over the scale, as if I have joined her in some extraordinary level of politeness. "I believe you phoned me by accident because you thought I was a window-dressing place, but you probably meant to call me about your son, Dr. Kunundar."

"They are all doctors. You mean which?"

Which one? Oh God, I can't remember. What was his first name? "I'm not sure, but he and my son had a car accident. I asked him if I could settle this without going through the insurance company and he said he would ask you. Does this sound familiar, Mrs. Kunundar?"

There is silence.

"Hello?"

"It was Omar. Omar is genius."

"I'm sure he is." I slice a lemon.

"Have you heard of lasers?"

"Yes."

"Omar can fix your nose with a laser."

"That's amazing." As I squeeze lemon juice onto the avocados, the phone squeezes out from under my chin and the receiver shoots across the room.

"I'm sorry. I dropped the phone."

"You are a family of accidents, then?"

"Well, no, I hope not. I was cooking and talking, that's all. Mrs. Kunundar, I know the car accident was my son's fault. I will be happy to pay your son directly for the repairs."

"Omar says you do not see your mother."

"Yes, that's true."

Silence again. It's like silence from a therapist. There's no way to know what it means.

"Look, Mrs. Kunundar, what I'm suggesting isn't illegal. It's simple and easy for both of us, but if it's a problem, please forget it."

"And your father?" Is she interrogating or curious?

"My father. What about him?"

"Do you see him?"

"He's in the geriatric hospital at UCLA. I see him all the time. I'm going right after we get off the phone."

Big lie. I just used my father's illness to gain sympathy. That is so tacky. So utterly shallow. What's worse, now I will have to go to the hospital to prove I'm not a liar.

"I hope he is not very sick," Omar's mother says with an intonation that approximates the C-major scale. "Is it something with his nose or his ear? Perhaps you should discuss with Omar. Also I have a foot son and a heart son."

"It's actually my father's brain. He's forgetting things, not my phone number of course, unfortunately, I wish, but—" I stop dead. Why did I say this?

"You have a lot of trouble. I will tell Omar."

"Thank you."

She hangs up.

Is it good that I have a lot of trouble, or bad? Have I passed or failed? Did she understand what I meant, that I wished my father would forget my number, or was what I said so callous and undaughterly that she couldn't comprehend it? The phone rings. It's my father. Now when I'm totally discombobulated, it's definitely him.

"Hello?"

"Is this ABC Window Dressing?"

"Mrs. Kunundar, this is Eve Mozell again." I restrain a desire to scream.

"Why?"

"You called me. You have my number mixed up with ABC Window Dressing. Maybe you should dial information."

"I am very sorry." She hangs up.

Now, for sure, I am too wiped out to go to the hospital. I mash the avocados up and put in a lot of salt. I deserve a lot of salt today.

I call Jesse in his room on his number.

"Hey," says Jesse.

"Hi, sweetie. Do you and Ifer want some guacamole?"

I hear them stampede down the stairs. Ifer arrives first. She is wearing ripped jeans, which reveal all sorts of glimpses of her bare skin, and a scoop-necked sweater that ends right under her breasts. "Hiya," she says, pulling her sweater up at the top and then down at the bottom. She plops into a chair at the kitchen table. "You look weird."

"I do?"

"Are you all right?"

"Actually, I may be a little upset."

"I knew it," she exclaims.

"You are definitely psychic," says Jesse, taking the chips

and guacamole off the counter, and swinging his leg over a chair to sit.

"Do you mind if I have some too?"

"Sure, Mom, you don't have to get cranky." He puts the guacamole in the center of the table and scoops a mountain of it onto a chip. "What's wrong, anyway?"

"I don't know. At least my father hasn't phoned." I look around for some wood to rap on. The table, of course. I knock it twice. "Thank God, he hasn't phoned. He's in the hospital," I explain to Ifer.

"He's not sick, he's cracked," says Jesse.

"Jesse, for God's sake."

"Oh, that is so sad," says Ifer.

"He's been there two weeks. Why do I suddenly feel anxious today?"

"May I put my hand on your forehead?" asks Ifer.

"What for?"

"Mom, it's just to get your vibrations."

"Oh, in that case, sure."

Ifer presses her fingers against my head. "Excuse my nails, they're China-wrapped." She closes her eyes.

"Don't move," says Jesse.

"You're upset," she says finally.

"I know, that's what I told you. The question is, Why?"

"I can't tell you why," Ifer says solemnly. She eats a chip and licks guacamole off her fingers. "That's something only you can tell yourself."

"My father hasn't phoned."

"God, Mom, you said that already."

"That's why I'm upset." It's as if the apple just fell on my head. "Why hasn't my father phoned?"

I leave Jesse and Ifer to demolish the guacamole, and go upstairs to phone Madeline in private. I don't ask what her big news is. I don't ask about her trip. I unload my anxiety without preliminaries, as if her vacation to Montana took place in the middle of a phone call I am now resuming.

"I'm terrified to go back to that hospital."

"Why?"

"Dad hasn't telephoned in five days. It's like he's dead."

"Don't they tell you when someone dies?" asks Maddy.

"Of course. I just mean he may be alive, but if he's stopped calling, he's dead."

"Can we pull the plug?"

"You can't pull the plug unless he's plugged in to begin with."

"Hold it, Eve, I'll be right back, that's my call waiting. . . . Listen, I've got to take this, I'll go with you to see him. I'll meet you there tomorrow, I promise. In front at one."

"But what's your big news?" I say this to a dial tone.

☎

The next day Madeline is waiting for me, sitting on a bench in the courtyard in front of our father's present residence, the UCLA Mental Health building. The courtyard has two jacaranda trees, which, since it is the end of May, are blooming. These are perfect trees to inhabit the front yard of a loony bin, because they bloom lavender—the entire foliage turns purple. What an astounding sight. It's impossible to look at a lavender tree and not wonder whether, in spite of how beautiful it is, something is haywire. Madeline waves. We exchange light kisses on the cheek.

This is the way it is with us sisters. Hours clocked on the phone, lives intertwined, but when we're actually face to face we hold back. My father may cry easily. He's soppy with feeling. But we take our cues from our mother. We are not a huggy group.

"How do I look?" she demands. "Do I look different?"

"You look relaxed."

She also appears to have spent a lot of money in a western shop. She is wearing cowboy boots, a blue workshirt, a fancy tooled belt with a silver buckle, and a red kerchief around her neck. If Joe were here, he'd be humming "Home on the Range." He says Madeline never takes a trip without coming back dressed as the place, and he likes to provide musical accompaniments to her outfits. He whistled "La Cucaracha" when she dressed in ruffled peasant blouses and a concha belt after a trip to Cancún. She turned up in lederhosen after skiing in the Alps and he yodeled.

Madeline peers into my face. "I look relaxed, that's all?"

"Did you have your eyes done or something?"

"God, Eve, I'm not your age."

"Then what?"

"Never mind." Very coy. She pushes all her hair from one side of her head to the other. She does this frequently to her flowing, rather glamorous hair, which she has taken to describing as chestnut-colored on her résumé.

She follows me into the building. "Howdy," she says to a man who is wheeling himself out. She smiles at him.

Since Maddy became the receptionist on *Living Dangerously*, she smiles at passersby and holds it, giving them time to recognize her.

"It's creepy here, I'm warning you," I say as we get into the elevator. "What's your big news?"

"I'll tell you later." She holds up a brown paper bag. "I brought a schnecken for Dad. If he acts strange, we'll give it to him. He loves schneckens."

"He has the dwindles. He's in and he's out. They say he's

not coming back. I mean permanently." We get out on the seventh floor and go down the hall to Geriatric/Psychiatric. I push the buzzer for someone to let us in.

"Did you talk to them about herbal medicine?"

"No, but you're welcome to."

Doris opens the door. Maddy gives her a big smile too. Doris does not return it. Her mouth, that road between her cheeks, is narrower than ever. A one-lane blacktop. "Hello, Doris. This is my sister, Madeline." Doris nods like a humorless German maid who is paid to open the door but will not be polite about it. Adrienne would know what movie she was from, definitely some murder mystery in which she ends up in court as a hostile witness. "Where's my father?"

Doris tips her head toward the sitting room. I put my arm through Maddy's. "Come on."

I pull her along. I'm on home turf, moving comfortably. Maddy stares at the cage, at the nurses inside, whose images are crisscrossed by bars. There's a scream coming from somewhere. It rolls right off me, while Maddy stiffens—she has entered enemy territory.

We turn left into the sitting room, where the TV is on as usual and the wheelchairs and seats are organized in rows. My father is in the back. It's as if someone forgot him at a drive-in movie. Parked him in the last row and split, but he couldn't care less. He stares at the ground. His body slumps forward. His shoulders seem narrower, weaker, his middle larger than ever.

I realize that Madeline doesn't pick him out until I say, "Hi, Dad."

"Oh," she gasps, then swallows it—the actress in her goes to work covering the shock and dismay. "Hi, Daddy," she says in a forced upbeat tone.

I touch his arm. It's white, bloodless, like a specimen

from a glass cabinet. As I rest my hand, I notice him eyeing it. He looks up at me confused, then back at my hand. What's strange about this? My hand, the touch? "Hi, Dad," I say loudly, even gaily. "How are you?"

"What time is it?" he asks, bewildered.

I check my watch. "One-fifteen."

I turn two chairs around to face him, forming an arbitrary conversation zone in the middle of these orderly rows of seats. We stare at each other. "I couldn't think of anything to say" achieves a new level of meaning. "I just got back from Montana," Maddy announces finally. "Do you like my hat?"

"What time is it?" asks my father.

"One-sixteen."

The bouncy man sticks his head in the room. He winks, disappears, then sticks his head back in. No one pays attention but us. "Peekaboo, I know you."

"Me?" asks Maddy. She smiles radiantly. At last, a fan. "You've probably seen me on television."

"You've probably seen me on television," he says, trotting over.

She is momentarily puzzled. "Oh, are you on too?"

He pumps her hand and doesn't stop. "Great to see you."

"Same here." She wrests her hand away but speaks politely to balance it out. "What's your name?"

"No hard questions," says my father.

Maddy and I burst out laughing. My father is surprised. He laughs too. "Hey, Dad, Madeline's hat is like the one John Wayne wore in your movie."

No reaction. No reaction to *Luck Runs Out* the one time in my life I have brought it up.

"I'm on my way," declares the bouncy man for all to hear. "Would you open that?" He points across the hall at the dining room door. Madeline gets up.

He's not supposed to go in there, should I stop her? "Maddy, wait," I blurt, as Doris, seemingly from out of nowhere, throws herself in front of the door. She blocks it spread-eagled as if protecting her log cabin from Indians.

Maddy freezes, her hand extended. About to seize the doorknob, she is instead eyeball to eyeball with Doris.

My father doesn't seem to notice any of this. He continues to gaze about grumpily as Maddy returns, taking baby steps, eyes fixed on the floor. She puts her hand on her chair seat, checking out its stability before sitting.

"What time is it?" my father growls.

"It's one-twenty now."

He looks at my shoes. "What is it, Dad?"

His eyes travel up my legs. "You know I've always liked you." He has a sly smile.

"I like you too," I say lightly.

"You were always very attractive." He draws out the last two words as his eyes climb higher.

I jump up, out of my seat. "Well, thanks."

His eyes are now fastened on my breasts, and in some weird way, they pin me in place. "We never got it on like I did with your mom, but I want you, Lola."

"Lola? I'm Eve. I'm your daughter." Observe the rules, I am begging, please.

"I don't have daughters, I have sons." He's a drooling wolf, about to pounce.

I grasp Maddy's arm. "Come on, we're going. Good-bye, Dad."

"Wait a sec." Madeline fumbles with her purse, trying to stuff the bag with the schnecken in.

"What time is it?" asks my father.

"One twenty-three." I grab Maddy's purse myself and

yank her. We start walking fast, holding on to a shred of normal demeanor by not doing what we want, which is to scream and run. Out of the sitting room, down the hall, our legs move fast and faster. "Let us out," I shout, an inch from panic, as we dead-end at the locked front door. Someone in the cage hits the buzzer, releasing us.

Out we fly. "Stop him!" someone yells. I whirl around, expecting my dad. Expecting this man who can't work his own wheelchair to be in hot pursuit. But it's the bouncy man —he has followed us outside the locked ward and is trotting happily toward freedom, the red exit sign at the stairs. Doris flies into the air and tackles him. She lies on the floor, her arms wrapped around his legs, holding him in place.

I tear to the elevator and push Down. I smash the button twenty times. The doors open. Maddy and I get in. As they close, Doris is still lying on the floor, gripping his ankles. She has just captured a bird, a Dr. Seuss bird that was about to flap its wings and fly away, its long legs dangling.

☎

"Don't tell me he doesn't know what he's saying, he knows what he's saying. He's horrible, disgusting, and revolting."

Madeline and I have careened into the nearest coffee shop. I have ranted all the way here. Maddy keeps looking this way and that, telling me under her breath to take it easy.

"Take it easy? Why?" I demand in a loud voice.

"Someone might recognize me." She uses a stage whisper and offers tentative smiles to other customers as we are led to a table. It is immediately comforting—this lumpy brown leather booth, the many signs in script with exclamation points, like "Soup de Jour for sure!" This coffee shop has been here awhile. It's not as old as my father, so it isn't falling apart, but it has some history. "I really do hate him," I say.

Maddy's elbows thud onto the table and her head drops into her hands. "No wonder Mom left him."

"Look at this, my hands are shaking." I rub them against the table, then back and forth against my neck.

"Eve, stop it, you look crazy."

I put my hands in my lap. "Why *did* she leave him?"

"At first it was just sex," says Maddy.

"With Tom Winston. What a thought."

Maddy suddenly straightens up, no doubt remembering her public—she can't be seen with her chin lolling on a coffee shop table. "I think he's pretty hot. At least he sure gets worked up over eagles. He practically saved the American bald eagle single-handedly. But then remember when Mom drank heavily?"

"When she faked suicide?"

"Right. I bet during that time she wasn't seeing him, and that's when she realized she was in love."

"Did Mom tell you that?" I have this vision of them—girlfriends flopped across a single bed, exchanging secrets while they clutch stuffed animals and giggle.

"Of course not. Mom—talk about something personal?"

"I thought she talked intimately to you."

Maddy shook her head. "I've just thought a lot about it. Sometimes I do think about things, Eve."

I let that pass. "What's Tom like?"

"Oh, finally you want to know. Well, he can go on for hours about John Muir or how to estimate the age of a ponderosa pine, but basically he's nice. Normal."

"Maybe that's what Mom couldn't resist." I thought of my father. How his emotional controls were never quite locked in place. Today . . . God, today . . .

"You should have told me Dad would be so weird," Madeline says, her lips quivering. Uh-oh, the trembles—that's what Georgia and I used to call it when Maddy was little and working her way up to a big cry. "Watch out, she's got the trembles," I would shout meanly, which would make her quiver more. "You shouldn't have just taken me there," she says.

"I didn't know what he'd be like. Do you think I was expecting that? Besides, you haven't exactly been here."

"I was on vacation. My only vacation all year."

"I only said you haven't been here."

"I know what you were saying."

"May I take your order?"

We both look at the waitress blankly. "You ladies need more time?"

"Do you have buffalo steak?" Maddy asks.

"No."

"Be serious, Madeline, this is Los Angeles." I laugh so she will think I'm kidding around.

She ignores me. "What's the soup?"

"Beef with barley."

"Barley?" She considers, I assume, the Montana of it. "I'll have that."

"Scrambled eggs. No, that's too risky," I say.

Madeline yawns pointedly.

"It is, Maddy, you never know what they can do to scrambled eggs—put water in them, or milk, cook them to death. BLT on rye toast, and an iced tea."

"I'll have a Coke with lemon," says Madeline. "He looks terrible too. He needs sun."

"Maybe you could get him a day pass and take him to the beach." I say this mildly, to cover my hostility.

"Maybe I will."

There is silence. Neither of us can think of how to get out of where we are. Finally Maddy says, "I hope that never happens to my body."

"What?"

"A pumped-up middle and everything else deflated. Everything except his big fat jowls. When did he get those jowls? If I ever look like that, shoot me."

"I think he looks like Richard Nixon—the way Nixon did before he died. Except that Nixon had all his marbles. Imagine Dad discussing détente on the *Today* show. Nixon had slumpy little shoulders just like Dad. I always feel that if Dad had had an audience or a bunch of cameras recording his release from all those loony bins, he would have raised both hands in the V-for-victory sign. Also, Dad always ended up in a pit again, like Nixon, and had to dig himself out. Of course, Julie and Tricia loved their father, which is different from us." I notice that Maddy has gone glassy-eyed, looking at me as if I'd lost my mind. "I'm planning a party at the Nixon Library," I explain, "and when I was there yesterday, they were showing his *Today* show interview, when he was eighty, over and over on videotape."

"Why are you hosting that party? Where are your values?"

"It's business. I'm throwing an event there for a slew of ear, nose, and throat doctors."

"Things like that show up on you," says Maddy. "Like Dorian Gray." She smiles at someone she doesn't know in the next booth: Yes, you recognize me from television, remember? "You know, Eve, there's this great doctor in Santa Monica, Dr. Mao, and I swear, if Dad would drink his herbal tea, he'd be fine. This is like all those times he went cuckoo from being manic."

"It isn't." I pick up my sandwich to eat but lose my appetite before I get it to my mouth.

"He should have been on tea all these years, instead of lithium." Maddy is wolfing down her soup and slices of buttered bread as if she's breaking a fast.

"I think the problem's beyond tea."

She admonishes me with her soup spoon. "Chinese medicine's been around for a million years."

"Everyone always says that. Just being around doesn't mean anything. Dad's been around for eighty years, and look at him. If you think herbal tea is the solution, you deal with it. Go talk to the doctors. Take over the whole thing, it's fine with me. You weren't here."

"Take it easy. We're just discussing this."

We hit silence again. She can break it, not me, no way. I occupy myself by taking my sandwich apart and putting it back together. Maddy shoves the lemon down into her Coke and starts stabbing it with her straw. "So how are you?" she asks.

"Okay, considering I have to deal with this. Look, I would really appreciate it, when they release him, if you would take him back to the Home. Talk to Angie, make the arrangements, it's your turn."

Madeline nods.

"Thank you."

The waitress stops at our table, staring down at my uneaten sandwich. "How is everything?"

"Fine, thank you."

Maddy waits until she's out of earshot. "So don't you want to hear my surprise?"

"What?"

She flips her hair to the other side of her head and holds a pose. "I'm pregnant."

"You're pregnant?"

"Yup." She delivers this like a cowboy on a Montana ranch.

"Who's the father?"

"Eve, I'm not sixteen years old and you are not my mother. Aren't you going to say congratulations?"

"Congratulations. That's fantastic. When are you due?"

"January."

"Did you tell the show?"

"Not yet. They won't mind. They'll write a pregnancy into my character."

"Oh."

Maddy takes the paper bag out of her purse and extracts the schnecken.

"So who's the father?"

"How's Jesse?" she flashes back with a wicked smile.

Why not? It's safe territory. I go for it. I tell her about the Kasmian religion, about Ifer, about the car accident. "Joe's away, so naturally I have to deal with it, and the doctor Jesse hit may be a semi-lunatic. I even had to speak to his mother."

"I get the picture, Eve."

"What?"

"You're stressed and you want me to take Dad back to the Home." Maddy uses a bored-out-of-her-wits monotone. "Fine, it's my turn. I'll do it."

As soon as I get to my office, I call Georgia and inform her she's going to be an aunt again.

"Madeline says they'll write the pregnancy into her character."

"Wait a minute. Refresh my memory. She's a receptionist on this soap, right?"

"Correct. Her name is, I forget. Her name is something and she has an unrequited crush on her boss but mainly she says, 'May I get you coffee?' "

"Oh my God, this is crazy," says Georgia. "Did you suggest an abortion?"

"No, I did not. Juliana, that's her name."

"No wonder you didn't remember it. It's a soap name, it doesn't exist in the real world. And she doesn't know who the father is?"

"She knows. She wouldn't tell me."

These are the times we live for—these amazing family developments that no one but a sister can truly appreciate. In the contemplation of Maddy's pregnancy, Georgia and I experience bliss: a moment of intense and perfect intimacy.

"You realize they're going to fire her, don't you?" says Georgia.

"They are?"

"Of course they are."

"But why? If her character hardly has a story, why do they care if she's pregnant or not?"

"You'll see."

"She thought Dad needed sun."

"What?"

"She said he looked terrible and he needed sun. Isn't there some joke about this? A man's in the hospital with no brain, and the doctor says, 'You look terrible, you need sun.' She also said he should drink herbal tea. I told her to call the doctors. She can tell them herself. She could at least take care of something."

This is what I do, rail to Georgia about Madeline for the thing I'm actually mad at Georgia about: abandoning me. There's an instant when I panic that Georgia will notice. I never express my anger with her, Adrienne says, because she's the closest thing I have to a mother. I've already lost one mother and I won't risk losing another. Instead I take my anger out on Maddy, hoping/not hoping that Georgia will notice, and then am incredibly irritated when she doesn't, when she just rattles on: "You know that thing you did where you looked in the mirror and you couldn't believe your face? We're doing a piece about that for the tenth-anniversary edition."

"I reacted like that because I was so harassed and upset from putting Dad in the UCLA loony bin," I say, now reminding her pointedly of my hardship.

"I doubt it. I'm calling the article 'The New Adolescence.'"

"Huh?"

Georgia sighs. It's a sigh that laments my dimness. "You know how you think you'll never accept your body or your looks when you're a teenager, and then you get to accept them?"

"Like, 'I hate my legs.'"

"Right, but then you learn to like your legs if you're you or learn to live with your legs if you're your friend Adrienne. Well, it turns out this is only temporary. In the middle of your forties, you start to hate your legs or your face all over again, or spend hours contemplating your sad sagging behind because it's aging."

"I don't contemplate my sad sagging behind."

"I don't mean you, specifically. I'm speaking of American women in general. You recall how Hillary Clinton kept changing her hair right after the election?"

"Not really."

"Well, she did. 'The New Adolescence'—it's a great title. You know what else we're doing? The D word."

I have no idea what she is talking about. I assume it will become clear. Assume—Georgia taught me that.

After I hang up, I ask my assistant, "What do you think the D word is?"

" 'Divorce,' " says Kim. "You didn't tell her about my divorce, did you?"

"Of course not."

My office is a large, airy room Kim and I share ten minutes from my home. The building is very Los Angeles, which is to say that it looks like something out of New Orleans. Much of Los Angeles appears to have been transplanted from somewhere else. The native look is Spanish style, beige stucco with tile floors, but it is common to drive down a residential street past a white manor house with columns (shades of Atlanta), a Tudor house, even a clapboard colonial. People have put up whatever makes them happy, and so our office, which goes with nothing else on the block of plain brick medical buildings, looks as if it originated in the French Quarter. All the offices on the second floor open onto a circular balcony with fancy wrought-iron railings. Kim and I look down at a cobblestone courtyard with bougainvillea, geraniums in clay pots, and two cast-iron frogs with gaping mouths at the gate.

When I am on the phone, Kim hears everything I say, although she has good manners and pretends not to. During my call to Georgia, she proofread a speech I wrote—Madge Turner's welcoming remarks for the party. She hands it to me and I hand her back the program, which I reviewed while I talked to Georgia. She runs down my list of calls. "Madge still wants to know about the name tags. The Citrus Singers have confirmed. They want to clog dance as well as sing."

"Sure, why not."

The phone rings. Kim answers, "No Surprises." She holds out the phone. "It's Dr. Kelly."

"Hello, Dr. Kelly."

"Hello, Eve."

This is the height of pathetic: to call this person Doctor while she calls me Eve.

"How's my father?"

"After you and your sister left today, he had a terrible screaming fit."

"Oh? About what?"

"He was just angry. Using very bad words, you know."

Very bad words? I don't know and I don't ask.

"We put him on the elephant tranquilizer." She laughs.

"It's for elephants?"

"No, I was making a joke. It should kick in soon, and he'll be stabilized. We're estimating his departure for a week from tomorrow."

"My sister Madeline is going to pick him up. Please let her know the exact time." I give Dr. Kelly the phone number.

"Eve?"

"Yes."

"We have a group here, a support group for adult children of dwindling parents: ACDP. Perhaps you and your sister would like to attend?"

"I don't think so, but thank you. And thank you so much for taking such good care of him." Now I have made myself practically sick: I feel as though I'm always fawning over people who don't deserve it. In fact, it's knowing that they don't deserve it that makes me fawn. I feel sorry for them.

"We aim to please," says Dr. Kelly. "Bye."

"Maybe the D word is 'dwindling'?" I say to Kim.

"Maybe 'depressed,'" says Kim. "Did you tell Georgia I've been depressed since my divorce?"

☎

Late that night, I am naked in the bathroom, contemplating my behind in the full-length mirror. Why have I never noticed this sagging event? Woman faints from sight of own tushy. It's a cartoon for Adrienne to draw: a naked woman passed out on her bath mat, eyes wide with horror. What vision has she seen? What caused her to get out of her bathtub and keel? Has Joe noticed this forty-four-year-old backside of mine?

"Mom!" Jesse yells. "Mom, you've got to get down here."

"I'm busy," I shout.

"Mo-om."

I throw on a robe, a robe I now plan to wear *while* I bathe so I never again risk seeing my own behind. I stick my head over the banister. "What?"

Ifer is at the front door, droopy, a refugee. Dirty bare feet. Hair hanging in her face. She is pasty under the best of circumstances. Her hair technically is blond, but actually has an absence of color; her face too, more white than flesh-toned. Tonight, in her sorry state and lit by the harsh hanging fixture in our entryway, she has acquired a sickly greenish tinge. In her arms she clutches a cat, a mangy thing whose tail hangs out of the ratty towel it is wrapped in. Jesse has his arm around Ifer protectively.

I come down the stairs not too quickly. "Mom, can Ifer move in?"

Ifer sniffs a gigantic sniff.

"I swear her mom's a bitch." Jesse fixes his big brown eyes on me. My eyes. My father's eyes. "Mom, you've got to let her, she'll die if you don't."

"I don't think that's a good idea." I walk into the living room. They trail in after.

"I swear, I'll do anything," Ifer says to me. "I'll wash the dishes."

I sit on the couch, across the room, far from them. "I have my hands full right now with Jesse's grandfather. I don't see where—"

Jesse clasps his hands together, begging. "Please."

"No."

A moan escapes from Ifer. "Sit down, you'll feel better," Jesse tells her. She perches on the very edge of the chair like someone who doesn't want to impose. "Listen, Mom, your dad's on the way out."

"How can you say something that callous? I can't believe I've raised a son who would say that. You should consider what you say."

"Me?" Jesse points to himself. "I don't have a problem. But did you ever think there's something wrong with *your* attitude? What *is* your attitude toward death?"

"My attitude?" I realize I'm trapped. I don't have the energy to escape. Try as I might to have absolutely no meaningful conversations with Jesse, sometimes he gets me in a weak or ornery mood. "What I think about death is . . . when it's over, it's over."

Jesse shakes his head in dismay. "That's not very evolved, Mom."

"It isn't?"

"No." Ifer is up and eagerly on her way to my side. "Kasmians believe that everyone has at least two lives on this planet." She speaks intensely, perhaps even spiritually.

"By then your soul has soaked up everything it has to learn and moves on to another planet," says Jesse.

"Suppose you learn nothing being alive? Suppose being alive is like some course in high school that you flunk and have to take over?"

Jesse and Ifer are now standing over me, delivering the lecture of their dreams. "Maybe then you get three lives on each planet, I'm not sure," says Jesse.

"But then you basically move around the universe," Ifer adds. Jesse nods wildly in agreement.

So I think my father's dying, but really he's departing for Mars. Then why am I scared to die? I could be going to Jupiter or Venus. "As far as I'm concerned, my father is already on Mars. He's given me nothing my whole life and I'm never going back to see him."

"Cool." Jesse smiles.

"That is so great, Mrs. Marks," says Ifer. "Your mom is so great, Jesse. Mine is totally fake. Do they have any more room in that loony bin your grandpa's in? Because my mom should be in there too."

Grandpa? That makes my father sound like someone out of *The Waltons.*

"Can she stay?" asks Jesse. Ifer lowers her chin and makes it tremble, just as Maddy used to.

"Let me call your mother, Ifer, and tell her where you are. You can stay here a few days if it's okay with her."

Jesse and Ifer slap palms. He puts his palm out for me to slap. I do it but feel ridiculous. "Could I talk to you a second? Excuse us, Ifer."

Jesse and I go out to the hall. "What is it?" he asks.

"I don't want the cat."

"Mom, Buddha is not a cat."

"Don't take that tone with me, Jesse. I don't want to hear

how Buddha has the six-thousand-year-old soul of an Indian guru. Buddha is a cat and I hate cats. I'm a dog person."

"You don't have a dog."

"I don't want that cat in here, do you understand? I have enough to deal with. Borrow my car, drive the cat back to Ifer's, leave it, and come back."

"That sucks, Mom."

"Do you want Ifer to go too?" I see him debating a response, some nasty retort he doesn't make. He goes back to the living room.

I have taken a stand. No cats. I feel a whole lot better.

☎

At two a.m. the phone rings.

I sit up in bed. He's dead, he's definitely dead. "Hello."

"Mom?"

"Jesse?"

"I need help."

"Where are you?"

"In my room."

"Are you nuts? Why did you call? Why didn't you just come in here? Are you trying to scare me to death?"

"You always call me on the phone."

"But I'm asleep."

"You call me when I'm asleep. You know, I say, 'Wake me in an hour' or in the morning or something, and you call and wake me. God, Mom."

"Forget it. What is it?"

"Buddha's dying."

"The cat? I told you to take the cat back to Ifer's."

"I know, please don't get mad, but we didn't."

"Jesse, I'm hanging up. If you want to talk, come in here."

☎

Half an hour later we arrive at the emergency room of the La Cienega Animal Hospital. Ifer is sitting in the backseat, clutching her cat and sobbing. She and Jesse bolt out of the car the second I stop.

When I walk in, Jesse is elbowing his way to the front of the line—there actually is a line at two-thirty in the morning. "Excuse me, excuse me, we have an emergency," he says, as if everyone here at this hour didn't have an emergency.

"My dog was just hit by a car. Get out of here." A man elbows Jesse back.

"Sor-ry." Jesse says it high, then low, like a musical door-bell. He makes a face at the guy as he and Ifer take their places behind him.

The waiting room looks very much like the sitting room at UCLA Geriatric/Psychiatric. Everything linoleum and vinyl, easy to wash off, hard to destroy. There is a woman sitting with three bulldogs, two on her lap and one on the floor. She's fat. Her chins rest on her chest and her bare pudgy feet are wedged into men's . . . not Hush Puppies, but something like that. What are those men's shoes that are associated with daddies? Anyway, is she my age? Do I look older than she does, or younger?

"Mom? . . . Yoo-hoo."

"Look at that lady," I whisper. "She's covered in dog hairs."

"Gross," says Jesse.

I feel bad to have said this—to have pointed out that the

woman is a shag carpet. I didn't want to say that I am obsessed with aging and am standing in line wondering whether I look older than a woman with three bulldogs.

The biggest bulldog is gasping for air, making loud, frantic, deafening wheezes as if it has a drastic case of asthma. Ifer looks up from where her head is buried in Buddha's scroungy fur. "Could you imagine living with that?" she asks. She buries her head again.

"May I help you?" We move quickly to the window.

The nurse or whatever this person is called at an animal hospital definitely looks younger than I do. She looks about three years older than Ifer. A shiny, bright-faced college student who undoubtedly washes her hair every single day, and holds it back with an elastic headband when she soaps her face. She is spanking neat and healthy, as opposed to Ifer, who looks just this side of trash.

"You've got to save Buddha," begs Ifer. "She's throwing up all over the place, and when she's not, she just lies there."

"She threw up?" I say to Jesse. "Where?"

He doesn't answer.

"I hope not on the rug."

"Buddha," the nurse writes. "What's her last name?"

"Marks," says Ifer, sobbing. "I'm putting her in your family," she says to me, before going off again into fullfledged hysterics.

"Female?"

"Yes."

"Spayed?"

"No, I would never do that." Ifer wipes her nose by drawing her entire forearm across it. Jesse pats Buddha's head.

"It will cost fifty dollars for Dr. Robertson to see Buddha," says the nurse. "Credit card, cash, or check?"

I suddenly realize why I'm here. I was so startled to be awakened, so carried away by the drama, I didn't realize I'm the one with the money. "Credit card," I tell her.

"This night's a real bummer for animals," says the nurse.

"It is?" Jesse lights up. "Weird. Weird-o."

A guy dressed in blue scrubs comes out of the back. He looks like the guy who wheeled my father into the loony bin. He takes Buddha, and Ifer bursts into another round of tears. I find myself with my arms around her. "She'll be fine. I'm sure she'll be fine."

"Can I live with you forever?" Ifer asks.

"No." I hug her tighter. "Not under any circumstances."

We sit and wait. If only Joe were here instead of me. He would be happy. The nurse would have confided how she gets her hair so bright and shiny. The woman with three bulldogs would have poured out the saga of her dog's sinus problems. Joe would go home with stories. I will go home in a bad mood, worried I will be too tired to do my work tomorrow.

Fifteen minutes go by. I'm beginning to get that spaced-out feeling you get at airports. "Your Aunt Madeline and I used to hang out at airports when our parents were fighting."

"What did they fight about?" asks Ifer.

"My mother fell in love with someone else."

"I don't blame her," says Jesse.

The enormous asthmatic bulldog is transported into the back by two men in blue. The fat lady comforts her other dogs: "Sweet munchkins, don't be sad."

"Hey, Buddha's parents," the nurse calls. "The doctor will see you now."

We all go into the examining room, which is very small and has a metal-topped table in the middle. In a second the doctor shows up. He's slim, tall, and handsome, with glasses for wisdom. He looks, in short, perfect: old enough to be a doctor you trust but not so old he doesn't know the latest medical developments; handsome enough to make you swoon, but not so handsome he looks brainless. Why does Buddha have someone who looks like a doctor, while my father has someone who looks like she's going to jump in the air and do splits?

The doctor is carrying Buddha in his arms, and while he talks to Ifer, he strokes the cat and scratches her behind the ears. He uses her name, something I marvel at. I can't imagine calling Buddha Buddha.

"Buddha is a very, very sick cat," he says. "She has a serious ear infection. I suspect it's entered her blood-stream. . . ."

Dr. Robertson, do you take care of old people too, I am wondering. Animals and old people. The way doctors have handles like OB-GYN, could you become an A-OP?

"Mom will do that."

"Excuse me, what?"

Dr. Robertson goes blithely on. "Good. It will save Buddha's life." He bestows on me an irresistible smile.

I can't say, I have no idea what you've been talking about, I was in a walkabout, fantasizing your new medical specialty.

"She'll need two pills every four hours for fifteen days," says Dr. Robertson.

It starts to dawn. "Hey, wait a minute."

"Two pills. Just drop them down her throat."

"But I'm—"

"You don't want to do it?" interrupts Jesse. "You want us to do it. Cool, we'll stay home from school."

"Yeah, we'll miss finals," says Ifer.

"I'm sure your mom doesn't mind." Dr. Robertson

hands me Buddha. I pass her on to Ifer, who kisses her on the mouth.

Dr. Robertson shakes all our hands. "Good-bye, Mrs. Marks," he says. He doesn't call me Eve.

Jesse and Ifer go out to the car, while I pay the bill and get the pills.

As we drive home, Ifer croons, "Poor little Buddha, poor little Buddha."

"You know, I really do have a lot on my hands right now." I can't not say it. I just can't. "With your grandfather and all."

"But Buddha's got a lot of life in her," says Ifer.

"Yeah. Your father's finished."

I stop the car in the middle of the street. It's a very dramatic, foolhardy act, except that it's so late there's not another car about. I look Jesse in the eye. I penetrate deeply, as I did when he was five and he threw his apple juice can out the window: "A cat is not the same as a person."

"You can love a cat as much as a person," says Jesse.

"More," says Ifer.

"Doesn't that make them the same, Mom?"

"Jesse, for God's sake, don't you have any sympathy for your grandfather? He's lost his mind."

"He doesn't feel anything for me."

"I'm sure he does . . . did."

"Right."

"You keep referring to him as my father."

"That's what he is, Mom, technically. That's like the first relationship, right?"

I start driving again. Ifer resumes crooning, "Poor little Buddha, poor little Buddha."

"Do you think Dr. Robertson is older than I am?"

"No way," says Jesse.

☎

Ifer is lining the wicker laundry basket with two bath towels, making a bed for Buddha. It's four in the morning, and I'm trying to think how I can get through the day. I will surely be exhausted. I can put off my meeting with Madge Turner—the party, now two and a half weeks away, is on track. I won't see my father because there's no point anyway, he's out of his mind. Tomorrow Joe returns. I really need Joe.

"Why don't you like your mother, Ifer?"

"She's trying to control me. She's a total, complete control freak. What I wear, what I think, where I go. She calls me Jennifer. My name is Ifer. I don't correct her anymore, I just don't answer."

"A parent's got to respect your integrity," says Jesse, who has the refrigerator open and is staring into it. "She was supposed to die. I don't know what happened."

"What are you talking about?"

He examines some American cheese, peeling back the plastic wrap, then rejects it. "We asked the Ouija board when she would die."

"You what?"

"Don't have a cow. We didn't tell it to kill her, we only asked, and it said—" Ifer and Jesse now chant together, "T-O-M-O-R-R-O-W."

"That's today," says Jesse. He resumes his search through the refrigerator. "Well, really yesterday because it's four in the morning so now it's really tomorrow."

"Oh," Ifer shrieks. "I didn't tell you, I didn't tell you." Her hands are on her head and she looks as if she's about to pull out her hair in ecstasy. "My mom got sideswiped!"

"No!" says Jesse.

"Yes!" says Ifer.

They stare at each other with their mouths hanging open, spooked by the wisdom of the Ouija board.

I slam the refrigerator shut to get their attention. "Ifer, the cat sleeps with you in the den, is that clear? You're lucky your mother loves you. I don't want to hear one more word about sideswiping. Do you get it?" I am bellowing an inch from their faces. They nod docilely.

"Good. I'm going to bed."

I am almost up the stairs when I hear, "God, Mom." The last word. I'm never going to have it.

☎

On a screen, a dot is flashing next to Joe's flight number, indicating that his plane is landing. I have been sitting in the lounge next to his arrival gate, reading in *People* magazine about a woman who gave one of her kidneys to a waitress in a coffee shop where she ate breakfast. I would not give one of my kidneys to a waitress, even if I went to the coffee shop every single day and chatted with her about her divorce, her kids, and how there is too much useless mail coming into your home so that you don't open half of it and who knows what to do about it. If she listened for hours about how I almost burst into tears this afternoon when I looked at the mail, I still wouldn't give her a kidney. But would I give one to Georgia or Madeline?

Suppose their kidneys failed simultaneously? With my backbone of rubber, my inability even to tell the veterinarian that I don't want to be saddled with Buddha, I would probably end up giving both my kidneys away. At least I don't have to worry about donating to my father. He is too old and too sick for a kidney transplant. I hope.

A crowd gathers at the window as the plane can be seen rolling toward the gate. Joe is back. I am relieved. Elated. I'm going to feel safe again. Standing away from the crowd, so I have a view over it, I see him or rather the top of his head, the mini-haystack of hair that he's forever pushing out of his eyes. "Joe!" I wave with both hands like a crazed referee.

He comes toward me in his loping, cheerful gait. "Hi, darling." He drops his bag and puts his arms around me. As if I had been away and he were welcoming me home. "I've missed you."

"Me too." I tilt my head up for a kiss.

"You didn't have to come to the airport."

"I know."

As we walk to the escalators, he puts his arm around my shoulders and laps it over my arm, which he holds on to tightly. I feel all tucked in.

"How were the bagel man and the cake lady?"

"She was the sweetest," says Joe. "A doll, which happens to be her favorite word. 'You're a doll,' she kept saying." He takes a moment to watch a man whose two daughters, in cheerleading outfits, have greeted him waving pompoms.

"That would never have happened in my family," I say. "What do her cakes taste like?"

"Not bad, except for the one she calls a ginger ale cake, which is made with ginger ale and grapes. 'Gold and purple, doll, my high school colors.' She's plump and round, like a peach, and she wears pink stretch pants, and stuck in her belt, like a six-shooter, are a Ping-Pong paddle and—" He stops. His arm falls off my shoulder. He stands there puzzled, not paying attention as other passengers say "Excuse me" and bump around us. "What is that thing you put plaster on with?

She uses it to sculpt scenes in the frosting. It was in my broadcast, did you hear it?"

"No, I missed it. Did you bring the tape?"

"Yeah, sure." He stands there stumped.

"Put your arm back, okay, sweetheart?"

Joe wraps me up again and we start walking, step matching step. "What is that thing called?" says Joe. "It's not a spatula, but doesn't it start with an *s*? When we get in the car, we'll put on the tape."

"Adrienne and I are still trying to remember that short wide actress from the fifties."

"Doris Day?"

"Short and wide, Joe."

"What about the one who was married to Reagan?"

"Oh, I know who you mean, the one with bangs, but it isn't her. This one has bangs too. She has totally dumb hairdos. Blond. God, it's roasting."

We have just hit the outdoors, where the Santa Ana winds are blowing. Normally, on a southern California spring day, the sky is overcast in the morning, then the clouds burn off into a clear afternoon, temperature in the seventies. But every so often the Santa Anas kick up, the temperature soars into the nineties, and hot air swirls around you. It feels as though we have stepped inside a vacuum cleaner.

In anticipation of stickiness, I separate from Joe. We move quickly across the street to the parking lot and the car so we can be rescued by air-conditioning. "What's this?" Joe is looking in the half-open window at Buddha curled up on the backseat.

"It's Ifer's. She's moved in. Temporarily."

"Who? The cat or Ifer?"

"Both. She and her mom are fighting, so I said it would be okay if she lived with us for a while as long as it was okay with her mother. Unfortunately, it was okay with her mother. She asked how long we wanted her."

Joe puts his hand out for the car keys. "But why is the cat with us, right now, in the airport parking lot?"

"I took her to the office today. I have to give her pills every four hours or she'll die."

Joe slams the trunk closed and we get in the car. He doesn't say anything until we're at the parking lot exit. "You don't have enough to do?"

"What?" This is a game I play called False Innocence. I know exactly what he's talking about and I know he's right, but if I admit it, I'll have to do something about it.

"Eve, you shouldn't be taking care of the cat."

I know how to get him off my case. "Her name is Buddha."

He smiles. "She's probably sacred, right?"

"Probably. In the Kasmian religion."

"Was there a founder of this religion? Mr. Casmo? Or is it from 'cosmos'?"

"It's with a *k*. I saw it written on Ifer's jeans when I put them in the washing machine."

"You're washing her clothes?"

"I do Jesse's, and they just go in with his."

Joe nods.

"Actually, Jesse is driving me crazy. He keeps saying things about my father, like, 'His brain is fried,' or 'He's bought the farm,' as if my father's not even a human being."

"You've talked about him like that for years."

"Not really."

"Oh, no?"

"Not in the same way. That's not fair."

Joe makes a little wave with his hand—Have it your way

—and turns on NPR. I stew. "I want you to come with me to UCLA to visit him. Tomorrow morning."

"Fine, Eve, of course I'll come."

"And I wish you would talk to Jesse. He has no intention of seeing my father and he doesn't care about him."

"Shush," says Joe. "They're supposed to be running my promo now, what happened to my promo?"

I switch the radio off. "You are so self-centered."

Joe pulls over to the side of the road and stops. "Do you remember what your father did? Because I do." He is talking to me the way I talked to Jesse, as if *I* had thrown *my* apple juice can out the window.

"I remember."

"I don't forgive him for it."

"He feels guilty. Even in this demented state he feels guilty about Jesse."

"He did it to you, Eve. So I don't know what all this sympathy's about or why you expect Jesse to care about a grandfather who's ignored him."

I look at Joe but don't see him. I focus on this little pulse on the side of his head. "Because it's kind. Because he's dying."

Joe throws his hands up. "How do you know? How do you know, when no one else knows?"

"Well, for one thing—"

"What?"

"He's stopped phoning."

"Thank God." Joe pulls back into traffic. My father's stopped phoning, Joe can get on with his life. "You're building this whole thing up," he says. "He's never been normal, now he's less so, that's all."

"I don't want you to go with me."

"Where?"

"To visit my father, Goddamnit."

I look out the side window—it's the closest I can come to turning my back on Joe in the car. "Having you here is worse than having you away."

He doesn't respond. My remark hangs there, all alone, unencumbered, giving it extra kick. I'm not giving you a kidney, Joe, no way, so don't ask me.

☎

We don't speak the rest of the way home, except when I ask if Joe wants the radio back on and he says no. It's just a stab at pretending that we're not angry with each other, and I have no idea why I do it, since he should be apologizing to me. I wait in the car while he deals with his luggage and gets inside the house. I don't even want to share the front door with him.

When I go in, the wind slams the door shut behind me and the force of it opens the door to Joe's study. He is sorting through the mail that is piled on his desk, organized by me, with newspapers on one side, personal mail in the middle, and then a disgusting bundle of things with the words "car-rt sort" on them, whatever that means. I hope it takes him a week to go through all the charity appeals, magazine appeals, and campaign appeals. I hope he has received his fifteenth offer of life insurance from MasterCard. I hope someone wants him to plant a tree in Israel, and that he has at least six requests for a subscription to *The Nutrition Action Newsletter.*

I stomp up the stairs and then realize that the reason

I have a scratch from my wrist to my elbow is still in the car.

I bang open Jesse's door without knocking. He jerks up from where he's flopped across his bed, listening to music. Ifer is lying on her back on the floor. She barely blinks. "Are you all right?" she asks me.

"Your father is here, Jesse, and I left Buddha in the car. You'd better go get her." I leave the room.

"God, you could knock," I hear on my way out.

"What, Jesse?" I stick my head back in. Ifer looks nervously back and forth between us.

"Noth-ing."

The phone is ringing. "Oh God." I go into my bedroom and dump my purse on the bed. "Hello."

"May I speak please to Mrs. Mozell?"

"It's Ms. Mozell or Mrs. Marks, take your pick," I snap. "Listen, Dr. Kunundar, I spoke to your mother—"

"She is worried about you."

"What?"

"She says you have a problem very serious with your father and you should not be worrying about cars at a time like this."

"Oh." I sit down on the bed. I sit as if someone had bopped me on the head and I had no alternative. "You mean you will let me pay for the repair?"

"Of course, that is no problem, but you know I am a doctor."

"Of course."

"So I may ask, How is your father?"

"I don't know. According to his physician, he's become senile, but he could live a long time."

"That is sad."

"How kind of you to say."

"May I ask also, is any fixing possible?"

"We've already taken our car to the repair shop. I was worried about yours."

"I am meaning your father."

"Oh no, he can't be fixed."

"That is very, very sad. When did this start? Was it sudden?"

"Well, he was difficult when I was growing up. He was an alcoholic and a manic depressive, and now that he's senile, it's like he's the same, only worse."

"Hmmmm." He makes a cozy, mulling sound. "You are kind to take care of your father. You are good."

"No, I'm not. I went to see him two days ago and he freaked me out. Before that, I hadn't been for a week." This must be what it's like to be Catholic. All alone in a room, confessing to a voice.

"I think you should go again. It will be okay."

"You are like a Ouija board."

"Like a what, please? I do not know this."

"A Ouija board tells the future."

"You must throw this out right now."

"Excuse me?"

"You must not be superstitious." He is emphatic. What would he make of Ifer? He would probably want me to throw her out too.

"Do you like cats, Dr. Kunundar?"

"I do not wear hats. It scares the patients."

"I said 'cats.' "

"Oh, that is my accident. I work too hard for a pet. I am in operations too much. Maybe someday, but not a cat. Fish is better for me." He laughs.

"I think it's better for me too."

"Mrs. Marks—"

"You can call me Eve."

"Oh, you are the first woman. Eve." He says my name in a velvety way. "Sometimes when they are like your father, they are in and they are out. You knock on the door, you say hello, no one is there, or someone else is there. If someone else is there, it is best to say 'Excuse me' and call again. Then you go back later and see if he has come home."

"If he were home, he would telephone me."

"Maybe not. But you must go to your father because it is necessary for your heart. And I will go to the mechanic because it is necessary for my car."

"Just get one price, Dr. Kunundar. You don't need to get several, what is that thing called? Estimates! God, I couldn't even think of the word 'estimate.' Is it normal to start to lose your memory? I'm"—I balk at telling my age—"in my early forties."

I don't want to consider why, when I have never concealed my age, I suddenly will not tell a doctor I'm forty-four. Do I want to seem desirable? Am I flirting? If I am, it's Joe's fault, I'm so angry with him. I feel a hit of guilt. I push it away, tamp it down, but dimly I know that what has just happened is not quite betrayal, but it's something.

"A little forgetting is nothing," says Dr. Kunundar.

"Good. Well, this is really sweet of you. Just tell me the estimate and I'll mail you a check."

"Right before."

"Excuse me? Oh, you mean 'right away.' "

"Yes good-bye."

Joe walks in and throws his hanging bag on the bed. I get up. "I'm going to see my father. Would you mind getting dinner for Jesse and Ifer?" This is not a question. I leave.

When I get to UCLA, the Santa Ana winds are blowing

more fiercely. They whir through the jacarandas, tearing off blossoms, and whip litter up off the street. I have to shield my face while crossing from the parking lot to the tall brick Mental Health building, but the minute the heavy entrance door clicks shut behind me, it's tomb silent. It might even be peaceful.

Maybe he's in and maybe he's out. If he's out, I'll call again. As I go up in the elevator, I prepare myself with Dr. Kunundar's wisdom.

I buzz, and a nurse I have never seen unlocks the door. "I'm here to see Lou Mozell."

"He's in his room," she says, and continues on past me. "I'm out of here, yes!" I hear her say as she smacks her palm on the elevator button.

My father's door is closed. I knock. "Dad?"

"Evie?"

I look in.

He's lying on the bed, curled up on his side, still dressed. His body has a soft, malleable quality, like bread dough. It has almost no definition. His eyes are open. Big and watery.

"Hi, Dad."

He tries to push himself up, but either his arms are too weak or he can't tell them what to do.

"Here, let me help." I try to lift him by his shoulders. I pull; he slides right out of my hands. I pull again but stop because it feels as if I could pull his shoulders off, just disconnect them from the rest of him. There is too much dead weight. To get a better grip, maybe even leverage, I have to move closer. I have to hug him. I stand rooted to the floor. "It's okay, Dad. You don't need to sit up."

"I want to." His voice is there, the safe one. I check his face less fearfully. Yes, he's in now.

"I don't think I'm strong enough to help you. Would you like me to get a nurse?"

"What time is it?" he asks.

"Seven thirty-two."

When I was an antsy kid, wanting to go somewhere or waiting for something like my birthday party to start, I would ask over and over, "What time is it?" "You're watching the clock," my mother would exclaim, exasperated. That's what my father is doing now—watching the clock. With his attention span blown, along with his ability to concentrate, there's nothing else for him. He's in time hell: it's too late for everything and life stretches out interminably. "What time is it?" It's the saddest question. Do you know what you're waiting for, Dad, or is it the only question left?

I look around his room. There's no life here, really. No magazines on the bedside table. No pens, or scribbled notes, or photos of people he might intermittently recognize. His clothes are scattered on the floor. I pick up his shirts, his shorts. A pair of pants. They are shiny brown with a silver glint like the fake fabric of a carpet. The waist is huge.

"God, Dad, you're so fat."

"I know," he says with a sort of wonderment. A genuine "How did it happen?"

And for one second it feels like a real conversation. Like he's normal and the only "How did it happen?" about him is not his entire crazy life and not this final frying of his brain, but just "How did he get fat?"

I measure the waist of his pants, using the width of my hand open wide as a ruler. One, two, three, four, five. Not quite six. What's that? About forty-six inches. "I think you need some new clothes."

I glance over. He's trying to push himself up again. He

huffs, he puffs, and there is the slightest little lift; then he thuds down permanently. It's the opposite of a baby, who tries and tries and finally succeeds. He tries and tries and finally fails. I collapse into a chair, the pants a heap in my lap.

"We had something special, didn't we, Evie?"

You won't let me go without an answer, will you? You won't go without hearing what you want to hear. "Yes, Dad." It's so much easier to say than not.

"What time is it?"

"Seven thirty-five."

"I want to go to sleep."

"Okay."

I walk over to the cage. "My father needs some help getting undressed. He wants to sleep."

Two nurses come back with me to the room. They stand at his bed and stare down at him. "You want to go to sleep, Mr. Mozell? It's very early," one of them says.

"Aw, what the hell," says my father.

I kiss him on the check. "Bye, Dad. Bye, Daddy."

"What time is it?" I hear him ask as I close the door.

The Santa Anas are now blowing fitfully, as if they can't decide whether to go or to stay. I hit a calm spot as I walk back into the house. I pass Joe's study. The door is closed, but I know he's still there—we always hang out in our respective studies when we're angry. I hear music coming from upstairs. Undoubtedly Jesse and Ifer's. I start up, toward bed. I'm not going to speak to Joe. I have no desire to. I turn on the stairs and head back to his study.

"The thing that really bothered me—" I have opened his door but am not looking at him. I am speaking to his space. "The thing that really bothered me is that when I went to pick you up at the airport, you didn't ask how my father was."

"I know how your father is." Joe leans back in a particularly self-satisfied way and puts his feet up on his desk.

"Really." I give the word Georgia punch.

"I spoke to Doris."

"Doris the nurse?"

"Did you know she plays the harmonica with a group called the Harmonettes? They went to Agoura Hills High School together—two nurses, a nun, and a flight attendant. Two months ago, they went on *Star Search*. Doris, on *Star Search*!" Joe's normally bright eyes are on high beam. "They're entertaining at the National Bowling Championships in Dubuque."

"I suppose you may do an interview with them?"

"Right."

"The point isn't how my father is, it's how I am." The Santa Anas rear up and clap two windows shut for emphasis. "It's completely beside the point that Doris is a harmonica-playing geriatric nurse."

I rage up the stairs. Joe is out of his chair after me. "You're as crazy as your father," he shouts. I slam into the bathroom and lock the door.

"Eve?"

I don't answer.

"Eve, for God's sake, knock it off."

I will not knock it off. I'm going to stay here in this bathroom. I will not talk to you and I will not be charmed. I am going to contemplate my sad sagging behind and my chin, which is threatening to double, and the unwanted lines around my eyes. I'm going to stare at them until I feel really bad, and I know, I absolutely know in my gut, that this overwhelming need to feel awful (or is it angry?) is my father's fault.

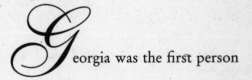eorgia was the first person

I knew to buy an answering machine. The summer of 1975, a

few days before my father's wedding. She recorded her maga-

zine voice on it, the one that was an octave lower than her

normal voice.

"Hello, this is Georgia Mozell. Yes, it's true . . .

I've taken my last name back. Please leave a message, preferably short, after the beep."

"Yes, it's true . . ." There was a long pause after this. Georgia always knew how to create dramatic effect.

I spoke to the machine. "Hi, it's me. I was wondering what you're wearing to this event. I guess you've already left."

"Don't hang up, I'm here. I'm screening calls. This machine is wonderful. It's like having my secretary at home. Go right out and buy yourself one."

"To record whose calls? I haven't had a date since Philip. Let's see, we broke up last October, now it's July, that's—"

"Nine months," said Georgia. "Eve, you must be optimistic." I knew she wasn't talking just about me. "You cannot be single and not have an answering machine."

There it was. No sooner did Georgia have this invention than she had a rule about it. "It's the single woman's security blanket." A rule and a cover line.

"What are you wearing to the wedding?"

"Basic black. I think I shall wear it for the rest of my life."

"In honor of your divorce?"

"No, silly. Because I've decided it's best to find one look and stick to it."

A look was something I could never manage. It required more than bottoms and tops. It required scarves, pins, a variety of shoes. In other words, accessories. I owned one purse. Even at the age of twenty-four, I knew I would always own one purse. At this time it was a large brown leather thing with a flap, and I knew I would wear it to my father's wedding even though it did not go with . . . what? While talking to Georgia, I'd been standing in front of my closet unable to decide what to wear.

"Georgia, I've got to get dressed. I'll see you later."

"Eve?"

"What?"

"Did Richard ever kiss you?" She said it so fast I almost didn't understand it.

"What? No. Why?"

"Oh, I don't know. I saw this idiotic cartoon by your roommate Adrienne, 'Reasons They Broke Up,' and reason four was 'French-kissed your sister.' "

"I was never French-kissed by Richard."

"I didn't think so."

There was an uncharacteristic quiet here. Georgia was always in a hurry.

"Are you okay?"

"I'm fine, dar-ling." She mocked herself, putting extra zip on the last word. "Bye."

"Bye."

The phone rang.

"Hello."

"I'm a Yankee Doodle dandy . . ." He was singing, actually belting the song, maybe he was even using hand gestures.

"Hi, Dad."

"Yankee Doodle, do or die . . . Did you ever think you'd hear Lou Mozell so happy again?"

"I'm glad."

He hung up.

The phone rang again.

"Hello, this is Lola Carlton. Your father is marrying—"

"Sure, of course, hi." Do I say congratulations? Do I warn her about what her poor mother is getting herself into? Do I tell her not to give my father her phone number under any circumstances?

"I'm looking forward to meeting you. I've heard so much about you from your dad. He raves and raves."

"Really, that's nice. I'm looking forward to meeting you too."

"I wonder if you would mind if I brought my portfolio to the wedding?"

"Portfolio?"

"Of the work I've done. Modeling."

"Oh, you want my older sister, Georgia. She's the fashion editor."

"Isn't this Georgia?"

"No, it's Eve."

"I'm really sorry."

"It's okay."

"Your father gave me this number. I'm so embarrassed."

"He sometimes gets mixed up." I gave her Georgia's number.

"Bye." The phone rang again.

"Hello."

"Yankee Doodle, da-da, da-da, just to ride the ponies . . ." Now he was wrapping it up, shuffling off to Buffalo on the telephone.

"Dad, take it easy. Are you getting manic?"

"I'm fine. We're having Virgin Marys. There are more flowers here than you ever saw in your life. I bought fifty dollars' worth."

He hung up.

Madeline phoned next. She wasn't here for the wedding. She had moved to Seattle and was working for Greenpeace.

"Hi, Eve, did it happen yet?"

"No, it's one hour from now and I'm still not dressed. Georgia just asked if Richard French-kissed me."

"Why'd she think it was you?"

"Well, why not, it could have been me. Thanks, Maddy."

"I just mean, why doesn't she ever think anything's me? How'd she know about it, anyway?"

"Because Adrienne did this cartoon, don't ask, I can't even get into it. Anyway, I really have to get ready. I'll call after."

Adrienne came to the wedding too. Adrienne attended every family event with me for moral support. On our way out the door, while I was hunting at the bottom of my big brown bag for my keys, I told Adrienne that Georgia had said I should get an answering machine. "What's the point? It's not like I have any dates."

"What I don't understand," said Adrienne, "is why one minute Georgia was going to Paris to get pregnant, and the next she and Richard were through."

"She explained that to me. She said that sometimes couples try to have babies when they should be breaking up."

"Alternatives to divorce," said Adrienne. "Maybe there's a cartoon in that."

"Please don't," I said. "Please, please don't."

☎

My father's apartment door was wide open. Adrienne and I peeped in as if we were checking out someone's hotel room that happened to be having maid service when we walked by. I could see bunches of daisies in those generic green-glass flower-shop vases, one on a living room side table and another, identical one in the middle of the coffee table.

"Suppose he's manic? He was manic on the phone."

"First of all, he's been out of Bloomingdale's since January and he's fine. Second of all, Claire's a nurse. She'll make sure he takes his lithium. He couldn't have found a more ideal mate." She gave me a shove, the way they push parachutists out of planes on their first jump.

"Hello, Dad, Claire," I called.

Claire poked her head through the kitchen doorway and waved. "I'm here, come on in." Very hearty, as if we were all going on a hayride. "I could use six more hands."

"I'm afraid we have only four. You remember my friend Adrienne Singer."

Claire wiped her hands on a dish towel. "Sure do. Pleased to see you, Adrienne. Aren't I the blushing bride?" She let out a cackle.

The counter, the stove, the top of the refrigerator—every surface was covered with platters of hors d'oeuvres: deviled eggs, stuffed mushrooms, black olives surrounded by green olives surrounded by celery sticks surrounded by carrot sticks. There was a plate of spiraling slices of cheese, American lapped over Swiss lapped over Muenster. The sink was stacked with dirty dishes.

"My God, how many people are coming?"

"Let's see, there's you, me, Dad, Lola—that's my little peanut—Georgia. Have a rumaki." She picked one up by its toothpick and jabbed it at my mouth, which I opened just in time. I clamped down, she yanked the toothpick out, then did the same to Adrienne. "Water chestnuts and chicken livers, the specialty of the house. Take a platter, would you?" She reached into a bowl of parsley and tossed handfuls on the platters like confetti, slapped the parsley bowl back in the refrigerator, and pulled her apron over her head. She moved fast.

Adrienne and I each took a platter out to the living room. There were champagne glasses, about twenty-five of them, in neat little rows on the card table.

"She's nice," whispered Adrienne. "Thin, but nice."

"I told you she was thin. Did she call my dad Dad?"

"I think so."

"Dad's in the bedroom. Wait until you see what I bought him to wear," Claire chimed in right behind us. She held a platter in each hand. I could see her entire wedding outfit now: beige silk blouse with the tails out, and matching pants. The clothes hung on her like flags in dead calm. Around her neck was about a pound of seashells, which rattled against each other.

"I've been up all night getting this place spick-and-span. You don't get married for the second time every day. I had to charge out for champagne and more Bloody Mary mix for Dad's little Virgins." She cackled again. "Raymond would never let me put one foot outside the house on my wedding day, but then he was the most considerate man."

"Raymond?"

"Lola's dad, my first, dead of a heart attack four years ago, God rest his soul. Died right in the middle of a press job."

"I'm sorry."

"A what?" asked Adrienne.

"He was a dry cleaner. He dropped dead in the middle of pressing a pair of striped silk pants. Not mine, fortunately, or anyone else's in the family." We followed her back to the kitchen, where she opened the refrigerator and took out dips: two white, one green, one red. "I'm a real blender person. I love to throw them in and mix them up. Would you open these, honey?" she said to Adrienne, pointing to several varieties of chips in a shopping bag on the floor.

"Hello? Hello there?"

"Lola baby, we're in here."

We all looked up, way up. Lola was at least six feet tall.

She was also gorgeous. A delicate face, positively chiseled, on a long swan's neck. Her hair was slicked back. She was wearing an antique lace dress with a dropped waist—1920s, Georgia told me later—that made her look like a frothy white cloud.

I put out my hand. "I'm Eve. This is my friend Adrienne."

"Friend?" said Lola. "Is that 'friend' in a meaningful sense?"

"What?"

"Never mind." She gave a short wave of her hand, as if to say, Erase.

"Your mother's been cooking up a storm."

Lola looked around the kitchen, taking everything in. "As usual," she said dryly. "Where should I put this?" She gave a jerk to a large leather portfolio she was toting.

"In that closet, baby." Claire pointed toward the hall.

"I'm going to check on my father. I'll be right back."

I found him in the bedroom trying to tie his bow tie. He had two pieces of tissue stuck to his face where he'd nicked himself shaving, and he was wearing a red brocade jacket with black lapels. "I feel like I'm opening on Broadway. How do I look? Pretty dandy?"

"You look great."

"How you doing, kid?"

"Fine."

"I feel like a new man. I could dance the lindy. Want to dance the lindy at your old man's wedding?"

"Sure." Didn't he ever notice that the more excited he got, the cooler I got?

I started looking around his room. On the bureau was a framed photo of him and Claire under the marquee of *A Chorus Line*. He was holding his tickets up as if he'd won the lottery. They looked almost goofy with happiness. "Cost an arm and a leg," he said, seeing me pick up the picture. "Hey, do you think I should put the wedding in the newspaper? Announce it, the whole megillah?"

I snapped around. "No, absolutely not."

"Yeah, you're probably right."

"It's not exactly appropriate, is it?"

"What about Leonard Lyons? Georgia could give him a call."

"Leonard Lyons. He writes about celebrities."

"Well, Georgia's almost a celebrity. It could read, 'Her father, who wrote *Ghosttown*, got married . . .'"

"Georgia's not a celebrity. Besides, that's the *New York Post*. You want to be classy."

"You're right. You're a smart one, Eve. Georgia's successful, but you've got brains too." He gave up on the tie. "Can you do this?"

"No, but Georgia probably can."

"Aw, leave it. It's a style. She's nifty, isn't she?"

"Who?"

"Claire. Who else? You think I'm talking about Audrey Hepburn?"

"Did she pick out that jacket?"

"The socks too." He lifted his pants to reveal fire-engine-red socks. "Don't think your mom would go for 'em, but then I'm not marrying her, am I? Let's get this show on the road."

Georgia had just arrived, with the judge in tow. "We'd better move quickly," she said. "The judge is on his lunch hour."

It was a short ceremony. When the judge said, "For better or for worse," my father chirped up, "For better." Everyone laughed, so he butted in when it was Claire's turn and said it again. Then the whole thing was over and everyone was kissing everyone else. Lola popped the cork on the champagne, and we all clapped as if something extraordinary had happened.

She started pouring and handing out glasses. I gripped Georgia's arm. Dad can't drink, suppose he drinks? We stood there transfixed as she gave one to our father. "Don't you want a Virgin Mary?" I blurted.

"Sure. Why mix drinks?" he answered smoothly, pretending the question was innocuous, and returned his champagne.

"I'll make it for you."

"I'll help," said Adrienne.

I took the Bloody Mary mix out of the refrigerator, and turned to find that Lola had followed us to the kitchen. She emptied her champagne into the sink and filled the glass with water. As I made my dad's drink, she lounged against the counter and sipped slowly.

She made me nervous. Like a lizard on a stone, she might jump at any moment. "I'm glad your mom's a nurse, because my father takes lithium." I could feel Adrienne's amazed eyes; still I couldn't stop blathering. "I mean he's fine when he takes it, but it's really important he pop one every day and get checked regularly, otherwise he flips. Also he's an alcoholic, kind of, I guess," I added lamely.

Lola smiled. "My mom's great with pills."

"Good."

"You don't get that thin without help."

I nodded. Is she saying what I think she's saying?

"She made a lot of food," said Adrienne.

"Up all night, a whirling dervish. That's my precious mom." Lola slid her body slowly down the counter, wrapped it around the doorway, and was gone.

When we went back into the living room, she was sitting on the couch with Georgia, her portfolio open on the coffee table.

"Here, Dad," I handed him his drink.

"Thanks." He raised the glass. "Toast time."

Claire sat next to him on the arm of his chair. We all waited.

"Well, start already, Mister," said Claire.

"When I went into the hospit—" His voice cracked. His lips started twitching. "I was having a rough patch." He paused as if he had made a huge confession, even though there was no one present who didn't know this. "When my two wonderful, fantastic daughters checked me in, I thought my life was over." His eyes watered up. "But then I met Claire. She couldn't keep her hands off me. In the tub. Rub-a-dub-dub." From tears to obscenity in less than thirty seconds.

Claire winked. "I had to give him a sponge bath."

"I was tied down," my father said. Claire whooped and pounded her chair.

"They're made for each other," I whispered to Adrienne.

"Hot stuff," said my dad.

"We get the picture," said Georgia in her most magaziney voice, the one you did not refuse.

My father raised his Virgin Mary. "L'chaim." Everyone clinked glasses, reaching across the coffee table and couch, and over and under one another's arms.

"Okay, my turn." Claire stood. She mushed her hair around while she thought. "I've got to say I miss Raymond today," she said finally. "I figure he's up in heaven giving us his blessing, along with your own mother."

Georgia threw me a look. What disaster had our father invented to claim our mother's life this time?

"I'm sorry you can't meet him," Claire went on. "That

man could get stains out of anything. Tomato sauce on a silk shirt, red wine on a wedding dress. Once Louis Armstrong showed up with a tie. It was his favorite tie, white raw silk, and it had a stain the size of a silver dollar." She leaned forward and whispered as if sharing a big secret. "Soy sauce."

I looked over at Lola. She showed no expression whatsoever. How many times had she heard this? This was definitely Claire's John Wayne story. No doubt Lola could have moved her lips in synchronization, except, of course, the story had probably changed. The spot was originally the size of a dime.

"He said to Raymond, 'I hear you're magic man.' Not 'magic, man.' But 'magic-man.' " Claire chuckled some more. This part Lola obviously knew, word for word, line for line, intonation for intonation. "And Raymond said, 'I'll do my best, sir.' He was always modest, wasn't he, Lola?"

"Yes," said Lola.

"I'll drink to that," said my father. "L'chaim." Everyone clinked again.

Georgia stood up. "To new beginnings. To your marriage, to my divorce, and to my new job. I'm going to be the articles editor. Wait—" She held up her hand to stop everyone from going ape. "It's a lateral move, that's why I'm so happy about it. Nobody, but nobody, goes from fashion to articles. Soon I will know everything."

"About what?" asked Adrienne.

Georgia did not look her way. "Everything about the magazine, so I can be editor in chief." She lowered her hand, permitting everyone to clap.

"Georgia, that's amazing."

"Well, aren't you something," declared Claire.

Hugs and kisses, everyone squeezing around the coffee table to reach her. "Thank you, thank you." Georgia beamed.

"I want to say something. Hey, here's my two cents." My dad was shouting.

"Yes?" Georgia held her hand up again for everyone to quiet down.

"I always knew you were a whiz, because you got my genes." He wiped away some tears.

Lola was still sitting on the couch, her portfolio balanced on her knees. "Does that mean you won't be hiring models anymore?"

"Not directly. But I'll make sure you're seen." She said this graciously, queen to subject.

☎

My father and Claire stood in the doorway with their arms around each other and waved as the elevator doors closed. Georgia, Adrienne, Lola, and I rode down together, Lola's head sticking up above us like the top of a palm tree.

Georgia stooped to see her reflection in the brass plate around the elevator buttons and applied some lipstick. "At least someone in the family is married."

"What about your mom?" Adrienne poked me.

"Maddy says she and Tom don't believe in marriage."

"I thought your mother had passed away," said Lola.

"Hardly," I said.

"Wishful thinking on our father's part," Georgia added.

We walked out to the street. "I bet Claire takes good care of him. He used to be fun when he was normal. Wouldn't it be great—"

Georgia interrupted me. "It would."

"I think they'll be happy." I announced this because I hoped it was true, but I also wanted to see if Lola would agree. All she did was ask for Georgia's work number.

Adrienne took off to see *Jaws*. Unlike me, she adored scary movies. Georgia insisted that I had to buy an answering machine, and pointed me in the direction of an electronics store on Lexington Avenue.

An hour later, having made my purchase, I stopped at a coffee shop. It was an odd time, five o'clock, and the place was nearly empty. Between my saddlebag purse and the cardboard box, I barely fit into the shop, which had a narrow aisle with a counter on one side and four little booths on the other. I collapsed on a stool and stacked the box and the purse next to my napkin. The waitress was at the end of the counter talking to a guy, the only other customer. She had her wallet out and was showing him family pictures.

"Do you think he has a flat head?" she was saying. "All my husband's family have flat heads, right in the back, right here." She tapped the back of her head. "Boy, I hope my kid's head isn't flat."

The guy took off his glasses and examined the photo up close. "It's as round as a globe," he pronounced.

She smiled, gratified. "You think so? Oh, hold it, I'll be right back."

She scooted down my way. The guy smiled at me. He was tall and he slouched on the counter, his chin resting in his hand, his fingers tapping against his cheek. He seemed to have all the time in the world. Even his smile took a while to happen. One front tooth overlapped the other slightly, which made him look even more homespun. This guy didn't belong in New York. He should be passing the time of day in a general store. On the other hand . . . Adrienne had just finished reading *Looking for Mr. Goodbar*, which, like *Jaws*, was too scary for me, but she told me the plot. This guy was probably crazy, even though he looked nice; there was no way I was going to talk to a strange man. I studied my menu. I had a rule in New York City: If you read, no one bothers you.

"He's doing an interview with me. Mostly about my mother-in-law, who's hell on wheels, but I got off the track," said the waitress.

"Do you have a mother-in-law?" he inquired.

"No," I said curtly while I read "Grilled cheese sandwich. With tomato. With bacon."

"So what will you have?" the waitress asked.

"Tea and an English muffin."

"Hey, you bought one of those answering machines." She leaned over to study the picture on the box.

"I figure I can screen my father's calls. He phones nonstop."

"So does my mother-in-law." She called down to the man, "Hey, maybe you should interview her. She screens her dad's calls."

"Please, it's all right." I stuffed the menu back in the wire rack, and started going through my purse, even though there was nothing to find there.

"Being interviewed is fun, honey." She popped a tea bag in a cup and poured in hot water. "If he's interested in my mother-in-law, there must be something he can interview you about."

"No, there isn't," said the guy.

For some reason this smarted.

"But I'm glad you bought an answering machine," he added.

"Why?" I shot back hostilely. For this, I turned and looked him square in the face.

"So when I call you for a date, if you're not home, you'll get the message."

☎

"I can't believe Georgia forced you to buy that answering machine," said Adrienne. I got home shortly after she did. "Do you want some tea?" she asked. "Although I'm surprised I have the nerve to run water after seeing that movie."

"No, thanks. I just had four cups. Maybe I'll like the machine. Maybe someone will call."

"That's not the point. The point is, you didn't have any choice. Is that my phone ringing or yours?"

"It's mine." He couldn't be calling this soon, not this soon. "Hello?"

"This was one of the greatest days of my life."

"Listen, Dad, I'm really busy. I can't talk now."

"Sure." His voice was pensive, lonely.

"I'm glad you're happy, Dad, but I just got home and I have a lot to do."

"I'm scared, Evie."

"You are?"

"Yeah."

I sat down. A conversation may actually take place. He's married. Maybe he's different now.

"Suppose it doesn't work out?"

"I think it will, if you remember to be considerate, you know, interested in her, and not always talk about yourself. . . ."

No response.

"Dad? Dad, are you there?"

"Your sister could upstage the president, couldn't she?"

"That is so true. Do you believe she did that?" Now we were really having a conversation.

"You're the nice one, don't ever forget it."

I was led into a trap. Was I supposed to thank him for praising me at her expense? And furthermore, my compliment was an insult. I didn't want to be the family nice one.

"I'll talk to you soon." I slammed the phone down.

☎

"Our father isn't worried that his marriage won't work. He's worried that it will work," said Georgia late that night when we conducted our postmortem on the wedding.

"Huh?"

"It's called the 'opposite syndrome,' and it's practically the first article I assigned as articles editor. You say the opposite of what you mean because what you mean is too threatening. He's scared it will work out and he'll be happy. That terrifies him because he was so hurt by Mom. Also, he's very attached to being miserable."

"And to making us miserable."

"Mainly, obviously. Tell me something. Do you honestly believe that Louis Armstrong took his own clothes to the cleaner's? Also, didn't he live in Queens?"

"Did he?"

"I have a feeling I know that for some reason. And I believe Raymond worked in the Bronx. So what was Louis Armstrong doing taking his dirty clothes from Queens to the Bronx?"

"So she made it up?"

"Or something."

I dropped the bomb. "Claire could be a speed freak."

"What?"

"Lola hinted that she lives on diet pills."

"Really." I could hear Georgia chewing on this.

"I think Lola asked me if Adrienne and I, well, she used the word 'friends' in this strange way—"

"She's gay," said Georgia. "I met her a long time ago on a fashion shoot. One of the other models was her lover."

"God, she's gorgeous."

"Well, so, why not? Is there anything else?"

Anything else. I didn't tell her about the coffee shop. About meeting Joe. All I said was, "I'm glad you made me get that machine."

"You're welcome," said Georgia.

☎

I was in the apartment when Joe called the first time, which was one day later. But the next time, after our first date, I wasn't, and he left a message on the machine. "I'm crazy about you," he said. There was a beep, then his voice, then a click as he hung up. I played it a hundred times.

Finally, in December, I took him to meet my father and Claire. Joe had been offered his own radio show in Los Angeles. He was leaving in January and I was going to join him a month later. This was both a get-acquainted and a good-bye dinner.

"My father's sixty-one and he has absolutely no interests," I told Joe in the taxi on the way to the restaurant. "Once a week, he plays poker with some retired writers. Occasionally he says something about politics or tells show business stories. Mostly he's a nightmare."

"You told me that."

"Claire talks a lot, I think because she lives on diet pills, but she's kind of fun."

"You told me that too. I'm sure I'll love them." Joe put his arm around me.

"No, you won't." I sighed and leaned back against him. Joe was the most peaceful place I'd ever been. His arms were home, but nothing like the home I grew up in. We'd just gotten back from skiing near his parents' house in New Hampshire. That was when, as part of my increasing attempts to take the chance out of life, I fell on purpose the second I started down the mountain so I wouldn't fall by accident. Joe thought this was irresistible. As I rested against him in bumper-to-bumper holiday traffic, lulled by him and by the flickering Christmas lights reflected in the window, I wished that I did not have a father. No father, no mother. "I'm dreading this."

"It will be fine." Joe had no life experience to indicate it could ever be otherwise.

I saw them the minute we walked in, because my father stood up and yelled, "Over here." He was wearing his red jacket, and he had a bright green holiday handkerchief peeking out of his lapel pocket. Another gift from Claire, no doubt.

"Lou, Claire," said Joe, "it's a pleasure to meet you." I was still at the stage where I marveled even at how Joe shook hands. Very casual but firm. And that he used the word "pleasure." That really knocked me out.

Claire was drinking her usual, a white wine spritzer. My father was working on a Virgin Mary. Joe and I both ordered beers.

"I say we have lobsters," my dad said. "So it costs a little, so what? Joe's paying."

Everyone laughed. It was one of those nights when everyone was going to laugh no matter what was said, or practically.

"Four lobsters," my father told the waiter.

"And I'll have another one of these." Claire raised her glass, then gulped the last of her drink down. "Raymond hated lobsters. He hated them because his dry cleaner's was right near City Island and people were always bringing in shirts with butter stains on them."

"I thought everyone wore bibs when they ate lobsters," I said.

Claire shrugged. "He said butter stains were worse than tomato sauce, nobody knew it but it was true. Butter was worse than almost anything except—"

"What?" asked Joe.

"You'll never guess."

"Coffee?"

"Nope."

Joe squeezed my hand under the table. This was the sort of conversation he loved. "Ink?"

"Chicken broth."

"You've got to be kidding," said Joe. "I would never have guessed."

"Raymond said it was the fat. Have you ever noticed that if you leave a spot of chicken broth on a counter it can lift the finish?"

"Who cares?" said my father.

"I'd like another drink. Joe, would you get the waiter?" Claire fluttered her eyes. She was virtually a blinking yellow.

When the lobsters came, she broke open a claw and that was about it. The lobster lay like a dead body on the plate, bright red, as if it had expired on the beach with a terrible sunburn. My father ate like a pig. Big drops of melted butter dribbled down his chin.

Since nobody asked, I volunteered. "Joe does wonderful radio interviews, like with this man who saved string and has a ball in his living room the size of a piano. When we met, he was talking with all sorts of people about how they felt about their mothers-in-law. It was hysterical."

"I'm sorry Raymond isn't alive, you could interview him," said Claire.

"Did I ever tell you about John Wayne?" my father interjected.

I kicked Joe under the table, just to say, I warned you this would happen.

My father told the story again. And then there was silence. "I've got to give John a call," he said.

"Lou's some telephone talker." Claire pushed her plate into the center of the table. "When he was in Bloomingdale's, he was on the phone day and night."

My father smiled sheepishly. "I live half my life in the real world and half on the telephone."

The interviewer in Joe clicked in. He looked completely relaxed, his thin frame in a friendly slump against the back of the booth; only, his eyes got sharper. "Who do you like to phone?"

"My lampman," said my dad.

"What's a lampman?"

"The man who fixes my lamps."

"One of 'em was on the fritz," said Claire.

"He's good for a few minutes every day. Then there's Mary."

"Who's that?"

"Georgia's secretary. Never can reach Georgia. She's one of the ten busiest women in New York. I'm surprised they don't put her in *People* magazine."

Claire offered, "He called Japan yesterday."

"By accident," said my father. "I must have hit too many numbers."

"I'd like to do a story about you."

"Joe." I put my hand on his arm.

He ignored me. "About you and the telephone."

"Joe's show is going to be in Los Angeles, on KCRW."

"Never heard of it. When do you want to do it? Tomorrow?"

"That would be fine."

"Too bad you can't do Raymond," said Claire.

"Yes," said Joe very sincerely. "I think Raymond would have been great."

☎

"I liked it better when there were prefixes. 'Plaza,' 'Gramercy.' Those were the days. Then, when you were dialing, you were really doing something. Is this all right? Am I doing all right?"

"You're doing fine, Lou."

"When I lived in Westwood, I was writing a show called *Ghosttown*. Ever heard of it?"

"I always watched that show."

"A lot of tricks from Topper, but it worked."

"I remember."

"We had a black phone. Phones were black then. Blacks were Negro." He laughed.

"He made a black joke? One, that's disgusting. Two, he's married to a black."

"Shush," Joe told me.

"I guess the phone kind of kept me alive. You know, my wife left me and I was rattling around the house, eating deli.

And I would call my daughters. I have three great daughters, but one didn't have a telephone, she was living at the beach with some losers. Maybe you better cut that part out. No, use it, it's fine."

I turned off the tape machine. "Joe, this is embarrassing."

"No, it isn't."

"Yes, it is."

"I'll cut that part out."

"What part?"

"About the losers." He pressed Play again.

"Sometimes when I'm lonely now, I call information."

"Last week, he dialed Japan," Claire piped up. Her voice sounded far away.

"This interview's about me," said my dad.

"Well, that's about you," she said.

"When you call information, what do you say?"

"Oh, you know, I ask for a number and then I sneak in some chat. 'Bet you've been working hard,' that sort of thing. They go for it." He laughed again.

I pressed Stop. "He has a horrible laugh. It sounds like a snake. Do snakes laugh? Edit it out, okay?"

"Eve, relax." Joe turned it on again.

"Do you have an answering machine?"

"Georgia gave me one for a wedding present. That's Georgia Mozell, my daughter. She's the articles editor of *Harper's Bazaar*. Knows everything, all the latest. But you know, I can't get the hang of it. Too many buttons. Mostly I'm home, anyway, and can answer myself. Otherwise, I'm out. What I don't know can't hurt me, right?"

I clicked the machine off. "I've heard enough."

"Did you know he proposed to your mother on the telephone?" said Joe.

"He did?"

"He called her from a pay phone on the corner of Broadway and Forty-ninth, and when he hung up, he took the subway to Aqueduct and won the exacta."

"I don't think that's true. I don't think my dad went to the races before he moved to Los Angeles."

"Oh, well, it doesn't matter. He said it, I can use it. It's going to be a terrific piece."

☎

It was, and Joe almost didn't marry me as a result. Or maybe it was the opposite. I almost didn't marry him. As soon as the interview aired, my father started phoning.

"I'm a star."

Another call. "I'm a big star."

Another call. "Ten people called me from L.A."

"Twenty-five people called me."

Then Joe phoned to say my father had rung him six times in the last hour alone. "Why did you give him your number?" I asked.

This continued for a week. Then my father went out and bought twenty-five radios, tried to buy a radio station, and had to be hospitalized again to have his lithium levels adjusted. Claire called us at four in the morning. "Get over here and put him away. I do this all day at work, no way I'm doing it at home too." She greeted us at the door drinking a white wine spritzer. It was January 1976. Georgia nicknamed this, his third hospitalization, "his Bicentennial breakdown."

I blew up at Joe because it was all his fault. He should have believed me when I told him my father was nuts. "I can't marry someone who doesn't understand crazy people."

"But you're not crazy. In fact, you're dangerously level-headed."

"Don't insult me. I come from crazy. You have to be careful around crazy."

It was a terrible, stupid fight. We had it on the telephone when he was in Los Angeles and I was still in New York, and we swore never to discuss anything important on the phone again.

In the end we made up and eloped. My wedding was one more family milestone that had to be celebrated on the sly.

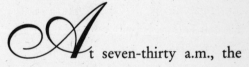

Eight

At seven-thirty a.m., the phone rings. "He's dead," I say to Joe, who stops in the middle of pouring coffee. Ifer looks up from her cereal, which she always eats like a little animal, her mouth right next to the bowl as she shovels the Cheerios in.

"Aren't you going to answer that?" asks Jesse, who's stuffing his lunch into his backpack.

"You answer it," I say.

"Eve, for God's sake." Joe takes the phone in exasperation. "Hello?"

We all watch his face, which stays calmly neutral, just to irritate, I think. "Yes, she's here. Are you calling from the hospital?" He nods yes and we all nod along in unison. He holds out the phone.

Ifer puts her hand in front of her mouth to be prepared to stifle a yelp. "Hello," I say bravely.

"Hello, this is Dr. Omar Kunundar speaking."

"Oh, Dr. Kunundar, hello." It's not the hospital, I mouth to everyone.

"He said he was calling from the hospital," says Joe.

I turn away, walking toward the kitchen door to reduce interference. "Did you get the estimate?"

"I do not follow."

"The estimate to repair your car."

"We almost did this," he says, "but that is not why I call. I hope it is not too early, but already I have surgeries."

"It's fine."

"I was waking up last night and thinking about you. I told you to see your father. When was that? I work so much I lose the days."

"About a week ago."

"Yes, and I was worrying, how did it go? Are you all right? How is your father?"

"He's . . . I want to take this in my study. Would you hold on?" I look over at Joe, Jesse, and Ifer, who are all watching. Suddenly I don't know which one I trust to hang up for me. "Ifer, I'm going to talk on the upstairs phone." I hand her the receiver.

"Who is that?" asks Joe.

Jesse answers. "The dude who hit me."

I run upstairs. "Okay, Ifer," I shout. There's a click.

"Hi, I'm back." I hear myself laugh and it sounds dumb. "I did go to see my father right after I spoke to you, and he was 'home,' just as you promised. I can't thank you enough for making me go."

"And since?"

"Well, no, I haven't been. Too scared. It's silly, isn't it?"

"Not silly." His voice is soothing, resonant. His mother may sound like the tinkling keys of the piano, but he—do I call him Dr. Kunundar? Omar?—evokes the poignant strings of the cello. He understands pain. It informs his words.

"Are you sleeping?" he asks.

"Excuse me?"

"Are you getting a good night's sleep?"

Oh, it was a doctor question. "Not really." I don't tell him about the boy with the fist in his eye who visits me nightly. *When you're dead, you don't know it.* It seems baby-ish to have a demon from childhood that I can't shake. I was frightened of black birds too. Starlings are what they were, but I didn't know that. I thought they would eat me. And I was scared of the dark. I'm a scaredy-cat. I don't say that either. "This is so nice of you to call. I can't believe how considerate you are."

"It is nothing," says Dr. Kunundar.

"My father is leaving UCLA Geriatric/Psychiatric today. He's been there over three weeks. They say he's stabilized, but who knows. He's going back to the Jewish Home for the Aged, where he lives. My sister Madeline is picking him up and taking him there. It's her turn."

He doesn't respond immediately and I realize I am talking a blue streak, telling him more than he has asked for. I also realize I'm sweating and will have to take a shower all over again.

"It is nice to hear. A good sister. She goes with you when you visit?"

"She went once. Usually I go alone."

"Aha, that is why I am worrying." Omar is excited. I imagine his hand thumps flat against his chest and remains there, a beautiful, graceful laser-operating hand, immobilized by concern. "I worry and I don't know what, but then, yes, I find out."

"Well, don't worry about me. Now that I don't·have to visit him anymore at Geriatric/Psychiatric, I'll be fine." That's what I say, but what I'm wondering is, What are you doing a week from Saturday? Are you going to the party for four hundred fifty ear, nose, and throat doctors that I happen to be organizing at the Nixon Library? Will I meet you?

"You say he goes back to the Home for Jewish Aged?"

"Yes. Why?"

"I am looking at an X ray of a nose that needs me very much and I am thinking, you need a mother."

"A mother?"

"Good-bye and do not worry."

"I don't understand. What about the estimate?"

"Yes, that too. I am on the case." He hangs up.

On the case? What case? My father's? My mother's? Mine?

"What did he want?" asks Joe.

I didn't even realize he was standing there. "He wanted to know how I am, that's all. He's nice."

"He wanted to know how you are? Isn't he supposed to tell us how much we owe him to have his car fixed?"

I don't bother to respond. Joe and I are not friendly these days. I will not forgive his lack of sympathy and he is fed up with me for expecting sympathy. We act friendly but that is not the same as being friendly. I end the conversation by opening my date book and checking my appointments. While Maddy returns my father to the Home, I will go to the caterer's. The party at the Nixon Library is ten days away; today we must select the menu.

"Eve?"

I don't look up, but I act friendly. "What, Joe?"

"If you think someone's calling to inform you that your father's dead, you shouldn't tell Jesse to answer the telephone. He's a kid."

"But you insist my father isn't dying."

"He isn't, but you think he is."

These conversations are worthy of the bouncy man. They go around and around. Their only goal is to express anger.

"Are you telling me I'm a bad mother, Joe?"

"Mom, Dad?" Jesse is at the door. It's not one of his accidents that he shows up now. I know this behavior. I did it myself to my parents. He wants to distract us. "Ifer and I are leaving for school," he says.

"Have fun," I say.

"Work hard." Joe musters a smile. Jesse makes a face at him.

I head to the bathroom, using Jesse's presence to make a getaway. "I'm taking a shower."

"I thought you already took a shower," I hear Joe say as I lock the bathroom door.

Starting my day over, standing there with the water beating down on my back, I think about my mother. She started over. So could I. I could leave my unsympathetic husband, my son, his car accidents. Omar was up last night thinking about me. Is he married? When I asked if he had gotten an estimate, he said, "We almost did this." Is "we" he and his mother? He and his wife? Or is "we" just himself, and he has a problem with pronouns? I am almost my mother's age.

"I was forty-five," that was the reason she gave me for dumping us.

I remember her on the twig couch, her wavy hair softer, longer, more relaxed. Her back erect; even her posture expressed pride and no guilt at her new, family-less self. "I was forty-five," she said to me.

Life is finite, that's all she meant.

When I was a teenager, I couldn't grasp this, because death was so much further than arm's reach. But now my father has the dwindles and I can't remember a short wide actress from the fifties. It's late, but not too late, is it? I had better get to the taste-testing. Madge Turner will be waiting. Buddha needs her pill.

I grab a towel and get out of the shower. If I left, I could leave Buddha behind too.

☎

I drive halfway to my office before I realize that's not where I'm supposed to be going. This makes me fifteen minutes late to meet Kim and Madge Turner. It's not a big deal to be late, but it's demoralizing. I have a sense these days that no matter when I start my day, I am behind.

Madge is examining a platter of canapés when I arrive. "Caviar, smoked salmon, mushroom, eggplant." Leon, the chef and owner of Food for Your Fancy, points out each variety in the elaborate way he has of pointing, a very precise cocking of his index finger.

"Hello. I'm sorry I'm late. I hope no one's allergic to cats." I dump Buddha on the floor.

"We forgive you," says Leon. He is wearing white trousers and a smock. His clothing evokes Dr. Omar Kunundar and what he might wear on his rounds. Leon leads me on a tour of hors d'oeuvres, main courses, salads, and desserts.

"Here's my philosophy," I say.

"Yes?" says Leon.

"I'm willing to taste everything, but in general we should stick to food that's recognizable. Guests shouldn't have to ask what they're looking at, so let's not have crêpes with secret things inside. And I don't think people should discover, once something's in their mouth, what it is. I'm practically religious on that subject."

"She is." Madge pats Leon's arm. "Believe me, I know, this is our fifth party together. I have a wonderful idea."

"What?" I say.

"Let's imagine what President Nixon would like to eat."

"Cheeseburgers. His favorite food was a cheeseburger. Charcoal-broiled," says Kim.

"How do you know that?"

"It's in the Presidential Forum Room at the museum. The question is 'What's your favorite food?' and that's what he answers."

"But he's dead."

"It's prerecorded," says Kim. "His favorite movie is *The Sting*."

"You want cheeseburgers for these doctors?" asks Leon.

"No, of course not," I answer. "We'd have to set up grills. What time is it?"

"Are you expected somewhere?" Leon's eyebrows curl with worry.

"No, my father is being moved back to the Home today. I was thinking, my sister has probably picked him up by now."

"I wish I had a sister," says Madge. "I'm just a poor old only child. Oh my goodness, taste this delicious thing."

"Potato Puffs Charlene. I named them for my daughter because she loves potatoes."

I sample some.

"They're fantastic. Will they taste all right cold?"

"No. We'll put them in a chafing dish." On the wall is a list of the food, and Leon checks off Potato Puffs Charlene.

"How many sisters do you have?" asks Madge.

"Two."

"And no brothers." She marvels at one of life's most common miracles, siblings of the same sex. The phone rings.

"Interrupted while dining." Leon makes a tragic face. "Hello. Food for Your Fancy." He holds the phone out to me. "It's for you."

"Hello?"

Heavy breathing.

"Hello?"

Heaving. Choking? Someone trying to catch his breath. "Jesse, were you in an accident again? Ifer?"

"Maddy." The end of her name is a squeak and now she is wailing.

"What's wrong? Is it Dad? Did he die?"

I realize Madge Turner is chewing her canapé in slow motion and her eyes are the size of salad plates.

"They fired me."

"What?"

Maddy sobs some more; then there's quiet.

"How did you know I was here?"

She gulps before answering. "Joe. He gave me the number. It's because I'm pregnant. They're replacing me with the temp."

"I'm sorry. That's terrible."

"They called me on the phone. They told me on the telephone."

"Where are you now? With Dad at UCLA?"

"I can't go there. I'm too upset." She throws in more
sobs. The first may have been genuine, but I swear these are
sound effects. "Suppose I have a miscarriage? The doctor says
I have to stay in bed. If I have a miscarriage, I'm suing them."

"But someone has to go."

"I can't, Evie. My baby could die. Oh, hold a second,
that's my call waiting. Maybe they're phoning to say they
changed their minds."

I address the group. "I may have to leave." Leon puts his
hand over his heart.

"It was the dentist's office," reports Madeline. "I was
supposed to have my teeth cleaned tomorrow but I canceled.
Oh, Evie, this is so sad for my baby. What's going to happen
to my baby?"

"Your baby will be fine."

"Thanks, Evie." Pause. "I'm going to have a baby and
nothing else."

"I'm sure you'll get another job."

"No, I won't. And I'm a good actress, I really am. On
Cheers, when Shelley Long was pregnant, they just showed
her from the breasts up."

"I'd better go now, Maddy. I have to get to the hospital."
As I hang up, I see that Leon is staring desolately at the food.
"Oh, Leon, you have to forgive me."

"Of course, it can't be helped," he says graciously. Nobly. Like a man whose heart's been broken but who only
desires my happiness.

"Thank you."

"What happened to her baby?" asks Madge.

"Nothing. She's just upset and can't move my father, so I have to."

Madge pats my shoulder. "Don't worry about a thing. Kim and I have excellent taste buds."

I sling my purse over my shoulder and run. I am gunning the engine, waiting impatiently for a break in the traffic so I can pull out of my parking space, when there's a knock on the window. It's Madge, holding Buddha. I lean across and unlock the door. Madge carefully lays her on the front seat. "At least you have your kitty with you. They're so comforting."

☎

In the hall, with his wheelchair parked next to the plaque that reads "UCLA Geriatric/Psychiatric," my father looks like a museum exhibit: "Geriatric/Psychiatric Man." He doesn't recognize me and has the sour face of a kid whose mother forgot to pick him up from school.

I apologize to Doris for being late, and I blame Madeline for finking out as I fold his release forms into my purse and take his suitcase. "Hi, Dad."

He doesn't answer.

"How do you feel?"

"He's not talking today, lucky you," Doris says. She unlocks the door to release us.

"Good-bye, Mr. Mozell," Dr. Kelly says brightly. "Don't forget your magazines." She plops a stack of *Georgia*s on his lap.

On the way down in the elevator, he is immobile. He has no reaction to leaving the place or the building, or to being out in the fresh air for the first time in almost a month. Jocko, the very large orderly, comes with us. He crams my father into the backseat of my car. Really, he just stuffs him in, picking him up and scrunching him through the door, and then putting him down on the seat and letting him expand back to normal, although "normal" is surely not the right word. Then Jocko collapses the wheelchair and puts it in the trunk, along with the suitcase and the collection of *Georgia*s.

I drive north on the San Diego Freeway, then west on the Ventura. Fortunately, my father's not only in the back but on the other side from me. It does not seem impossible that, in his unstable mental state, he might strangle me from behind in the style of a gangland revenge murder. I keep an eye on him in the rearview mirror. He shows no interest in anything, and he has hardly enough wits or strength to live up to my fantasy, although every so often he leers as if some erotic vision has passed through his brain. He doesn't react when I pull into the circular driveway in front of the Home.

The Jewish Home for the Aged is a two-story brick building with green-and-white-striped awnings on every window. The awnings are cheerful in the way paintings brighten hospital corridors, which is to say they make absolutely no dent in the institution of it. Behind the double glass doors, which open automatically as if you were entering a supermarket, is a row of old people passing the time. It's not a languid wait. It has nothing to do with mint juleps or lazy summer days in the heat, although it is always hot in the San Fernando Valley. It's more forced—these are strangers trapped in a holding area, waiting for the plane to be announced.

I manage to extract my father from the backseat with the help of a man who ferries patients up and down the halls in a golf cart, and Angie, my father's aide here, who has spotted us from the window and hurried out. They wedge him into his wheelchair.

"Welcome back," says Angie, putting her sweet face an inch from my father's. No reaction again.

I can't decide what to do about Buddha. Even to me, who has little cat sympathy, it seems she has spent too much time today in an automobile. I ultimately crank the windows open for air and stroke her head. The *Georgias* I leave in the trunk. I don't think my father will be doing a lot of reading.

A woman in the chair nearest the door has a walker and an oxygen tank, and tubes running into her nose. She smiles through all the equipment. "Hello, Lou."

"Dad, you remember—" I blank. "I'm sorry, I forgot your name."

"Frances," she says.

"Of course, Frances. How are you?"

"Shut up," says my father, coming to life for the first time today.

Frances flushes bright red, as if she had done something wrong. I feel my stomach start to tumble. My father's going to do something crazy, I know it. I have to get out of here.

I slow down, letting Angie take charge of his wheelchair. Unfortunately, I have his suitcase. I'll just walk into his room, put it down, and split.

I see Angie and my father disappear into his bedroom. Into his "den," that's what it seems like. I speed up. Move quickly now. Do it before you think.

Angie is turning down his bed, chattering about how everyone missed him.

"Get rid of her," he tells me.

"Angie's here to help you, Dad." I put on a fake smile. "Well, I'm late to—"

"I know what she wants," he interrupts, snarling. "You think you're doing it with us?"

"Doing what?" Angie looks up from plumping the pillow.

"Nothing," I say.

"You think I'm into that kinky stuff?"

"I think nothing of the sort, Mr. Mozell. Would you like to get into bed?"

"Not with you." He cocks his head my way. "Kick her out, Lola."

"I'm not Lola." I hear the trembles in my own voice. "I'm not Lola," I shout.

"I like them sassy."

"Sassy? Where the hell did you get that word?"

"Eve?" Angie lays her hand on my arm.

"Oh, I know, that's from *Luck Runs Out*. It's a stupid piece of dialogue that you wrote. Goddamnit, shut up. Lola's a lesbian. She's a lesbian!"

My father starts twitching. Oh God, something weird is coming. Something even sicker. He makes strange sounds— *p, p, p*—his breath is backfiring. His head drops sideways, his arms and legs jerk like those of a lab rat in an electric shock experiment. His eyes roll back.

I flee from the room, Angie behind me. "Help!" Our arms are waving like distress flags. We are evacuating, escaping terror.

"The phone," says Angie. "Dial the phone."

"The phone."

We spin around and rush back in. He's still twitching. I press zero. "I think my father's having a stroke."

"Who is this?"

"Eve Mozell."

"We'll be right there."

Angie and I stay stuck in place, listening for the siren,

although there won't be one, only the clatter of feet in the hall.

"What happened?" A nurse rushes over to my father. As she checks his pulse, two volunteers in striped outfits appear, then another nurse.

"My father's having an attack, a stroke." I move backward, easing my way out.

"It looks like a seizure," says the second nurse. "Wait outside, please." She pushes Angie and me the final foot into the hall.

Various residents emerge from their rooms. Angie and I are soon surrounded by gray heads and a motley collection of fuzzy bathrobes and floppy slippers. "What happened?" asks a man who has one eye covered with a piece of gauze and two crisscrossed pieces of masking tape.

"We were just talking," says Angie. "Just chatting with him." I nod. "And he went off his rocker." I nod furiously.

A nurse exits his room. "We get one of these fits a week," she says. "It's from brain deterioration."

"That's true," says Angie, as if it should comfort.

I collapse on one of the chairs that are placed every few feet along the hall so that anyone who tires can take a time-out.

"I don't think he's in any immediate danger," says the nurse. "We'll just watch him for a while."

"I'm going home. I'm going home, okay?"

"You do that," Angie says. "I'll call you later."

I get in the car and drive onto the freeway. My hands are sweating. I'm leaving big wet stains on the steering wheel. I change lanes quickly. A car horn blasts me. I check over my shoulder and see that I almost hit one of those big cars, one of those crosses between station wagons and jeeps, whatever they're called. Maybe I should phone Omar. I mean Joe. Joe,

Joe, Joe. I grip the wheel tighter. Pay attention. Pay close attention. I turn on the news, not taking my eye off the road. It's the seasoned driver's move—I know exactly where the radio knob is, without looking. "It's seventy-nine degrees in Los Angeles. There was a drive-by shooting on the Ventura Freeway at one this afternoon." We were on the Ventura Freeway then. I could have been the victim. So could my father. Suppose I shoot him? Suppose I walk into his room with a forty-five, press it against his head, and shoot him point-blank? What is a forty-five, anyway? These are words you hear only in the movies—"forty-five" and "point-blank." Suppose I loaded the gun with Dad's bullet? Suppose I took the bullet John Wayne gave him and put it through his head? I suddenly realize what I'm thinking about. You can't think about this. I switch the station. Golden oldies, that's what I need. I need to sing along.

☎

"Your mother had a rough day," Joe says to Jesse.

"Duh?"

"Duh?" Joe repeats threateningly.

Jesse sits up straighter. "I mean, I figured. That's why we're having takeout."

Joe, Jesse, Ifer, and I are sitting at the dining room table, where the food has been hastily thrown. The white Chinese-takeout containers are open next to the brown paper bags they arrived in. The bags stand there upright, empty; I haven't bothered to remove them. Plastic packets of duck sauce, mustard, and soy sauce are strewn around, along with a bag of crispy noodles, a few fortune cookies, and several sets of chopsticks in paper sleeves.

Unlike my mother, I have always prided myself on my cooking. But in the past week we have dined on sandwiches, grilled cheese or tuna, and tonight we are having Chinese food taken straight from the front door to the dining room table. I don't have the energy not to be my mother.

"My father had some sort of fit today when I returned him to the Home. Like an epileptic fit," I explain to Jesse.

"I once saw someone have a fit," says Ifer. "When I was at the supermarket with my mom. It was really creepy." She puts her elbows on the table, props her chin in her hands, and stares at me balefully.

"Did it come out of nowhere?" Joe asks.

"I was talking to him."

"About what?"

I pick up a container and start poking around for a water chestnut. "I don't remember—nothing." Maybe I could bring my father takeout Chinese? Maybe he could choke on a water chestnut and because he's in a wheelchair there's no way anyone could do the Heimlich maneuver on him. "Is death by choking painful?"

"Why do you want to know that?" Joe smiles, immediately sensing that this is not an innocent question. I have no privacy with my secret evil thoughts.

As a way of counterpunching, I get more serious. "I was just worried. He doesn't have his teeth in, so he can't chew."

"Euu," says Ifer.

Jesse runs his fork back and forth across his plate to pick up the last of the soy sauce. He licks the back of his fork. "So, uh, Mom, are you done?"

"Done what?"

"Done talking about this stuff. Ifer and I were thinking of hitting the movies."

"Yes, I'm done."

"You sure? 'Cause if you want to carry on and every-thing, it's okay with me."

"I'm fine, Jesse."

He gets up, and Ifer jumps up right after him.

"Take your plates," says Joe.

Ifer dumps the cat on my lap. "Hold Buddha, Mrs. Marks. She'll help you feel better. Like if you get cramps, she keeps you all warm like a heating pad."

"Thank you."

"Bye," says Jesse.

"Bye," echoes Ifer.

Joe waits until we hear the slam of the front door. "I talked to him," he says, "about being so self-centered."

"I can tell."

The phone rings. Neither of us moves.

"I'm not getting it. I'm not talking to anyone, I don't care who it is, I'm exhausted."

Joe stretches back so his hand reaches from the dining room inside the kitchen to the wall phone. He can't quite pick up the receiver, but manages to flip it off the hook and catch it. "Hello? Oh, hi, Madeline."

"I'd better talk to her," I say.

"Your sister's right here." He hands me the phone.

"Maddy, my God, are you all right? I'm so sorry you lost your part on the show. You must be so upset."

"I'm fine."

"You are?" I am caught up short. "How could you be fine?"

"They're giving me a huge exit scene. Where I get to explode at my boss. I'm really going to have tape now."

"What is tape?"

"Videotape, God! So I can show people how good I am."

There's a beep on the line. "Ohmygosh, that's probably my agent. He's negotiating my settlement, hold on."

I hang up. I sit at the table and resume eating cashew chicken. "I hung up," I tell Joe.

"I see that."

"I don't have to hang on while she leaves me on hold."

"I agree."

The phone rings. I grab it. "Hello?"

"Did you hang up on me?"

"I am sick of call waiting, Madeline. It's completely rude."

"But I just got off for a second."

"Joe and I are eating dinner, what do you want?"

"I need call waiting, Eve. Suppose there's a crisis with my baby, how could they reach me?"

"Who?"

"The baby-sitter."

"Your baby isn't born yet."

"Well, when it is, God."

"Get a second number. Look, if you're going to put me on hold, I'm going to hang up. I hate call waiting. You hear a beep, you say, 'Hold on,' meanwhile the person is sitting there like a dolt while you decide whether the new call is more important than the old one. Do you think I have nothing better to do than hold on? I'm in the middle of this Nixon party. It's in ten days, I'm still dealing with the menu, and the mariachi band canceled. Do you think there's nothing else going on in my life that I have time to hold on while you get your stupid phone calls?"

I slam down the receiver, crash back into my chair, and glare across the table at Joe.

The phone rings.

"I'm not answering."

"Me neither," says Joe.

Dimly I hear the machine pick up in Joe's study. I strain to hear, attempting not to give the least indication of it, just folding my napkin over and over. "Hello, Eve, this is Angie calling—"

I dash for the study, jabbing my side into Joe's desk as I race around it to the answering machine. "I'm here. Wait a second, I'll turn this off."

I try to find the Off button. I can't figure out where it is, somewhere on the side of the machine. I can't read the tiny lettering. I squint. I still can't read. I hit a few buttons. Nothing happens.

"Sorry, Angie, I can't figure out how to turn this thing off. Just talk anyway. How's my father?"

"He's fine."

"Fine?"

Angie sighs. "It's been a very long day. I'm not thinking anymore. Your father was such a sweetheart, I miss him."

"Did he die? I thought he was fine."

"He's not dying. But between the fits—"

"Fits? He only had one."

"So far. And the unpredictability. Oh, I miss your old dad."

"You do?"

She bleats on. "He used to call me all the time from his room. 'Don't be mad at me, Angie,' he'd say, when it was the fifth call and I was about to bust. I've still got some old messages of his. 'Just checking in.' Isn't that sweet? Here's another. 'Georgia won the Pulitzer.' He was so proud of your sister winning the Pulitzer and all. And he never complained about taking his pills. I never knew your father to hide a pill under his tongue." Good for him, I think. Perhaps you would consider pouring an entire bottle of them down his throat.

She rattles on. "But I realize, now that he's back from that Geriatric/Psychiatric place, we don't have the staff to cope with him."

"What?" I squeak.

"Could you hire a private nurse?"

"A private nurse? How much will that cost?"

"Twenty-five dollars an hour."

"Are you kidding?"

She goes on.

I don't hear anything she says. "Excuse me, what?"

"I can hire the nurse for you, if you write the check. You know, honey, you don't have to do it right away. Take the weekend."

"Does his Medicare cover it?"

"No."

"I don't believe this," I say when I return to the dining room.

"What is it now?" Joe asks.

"First of all, Dad needs a private nurse. Second, I need glasses. I can't read anything anymore. I can't read the blasted words on the answering machine."

"Everyone needs glasses after forty. Why should you be any different? I've worn them since I was five." Joe throws his napkin down and walks into the living room.

Why should I be any different? Why should I be any different? Joe sits on the couch, picks up one of his weekly papers, and starts reading. I want to rip the newspaper out of his hand. *Why should I be any different?* That's the whole point, Joe.

I can see the boy with the fist in his eye. He's sitting in the chair across from Joe. He's got his feet propped up on the coffee table. He's making himself at home.

I stare at the back of Joe's paper. Read, that will help.

That will blot out your torturer. "Nursing Home Nurse Guilty of Murder." Maybe Angie will take pity on my father and murder him. "Joe?"

"What, sweetheart?" He puts down the paper and gives me his complete attention.

"I ran out of my father's room. I didn't want to mention it when Jesse and Ifer were around. I freaked."

"I'm sure it was frightening."

"My father almost dies in front of me, and I flee?"

Joe shrugs.

"He had his fit right after I shouted that Lola was a lesbian. Did I give him the fit? Did I almost kill him?"

"Wait a minute." Joe twirls his pen in the little rewind motion he makes to his engineer when he broadcasts. "You told him Lola was a lesbian?"

"Yes."

Joe cracks up. He roars with laughter. He laughs so hard he has to wipe tears from his eyes.

"Joe, stop it, it's not funny. Stop it."

"You can't expect to talk to your father as if he's normal."

"How would you know? You haven't seen him."

"Eve," Joe says quietly, although he has to wait a beat so he doesn't break up again, "I've offered to go before, and I will go with you to visit him tomorrow."

"I'm not going tomorrow." Omar wouldn't laugh. He would listen and then he would say something warming, soothing, calming. "It is good you know a lesbian. I will tell my mother." Something like that. "Good-bye, Joe."

"Where are you going?"

"Nowhere."

I storm upstairs into our bedroom and stop dead, assessing the options. I zap on the TV. I change the channels. Zap,

zap, zap. Finally I hit the news. Show me something or I zap you.

"In California's Palm Desert today, a star high school basketball player collapsed on an outdoor court in hundred-four-degree heat and died."

Maybe I could take my father out for a walk in the sun. Maybe I could walk him to death.

Joe appears in the doorway. "Take it easy, Eve." He doesn't say this sweetly. It's an order.

I move my eyes back, over to the television. This feels exquisitely mean and satisfying, just to move my eyes and not acknowledge his statement even with a turn of my head. I hate you, Joe. I don't say it. We have rules, boundaries. But I hate you.

☎

Angie said to take the weekend. I do. I hole up in my office completing arrangements for the party. I don't speak to Georgia or Madeline or the Jewish Home for the Aged. I take care of flowers—table arrangements of hyacinth and heather, daisy chains for the doorways, and single white roses for the women when they arrive. Kim and I design a program, Madge approves her welcoming speech. I love this part, going down to the wire, when I get to cross things off the list. Each detail is defined, manageable. Why can't everything in life be planned, known, seamlessly executed like this party?

Well, I can try. On Monday I attack these messy family calls as if they were business.

"Maddy, Eve. Dad needs a private nurse or they're going to ship him out. Medicare doesn't cover it, so I'll have his accountant pay the bill off his bank account. He may eventually run out of money, which means your baby won't inherit anything, but unless you have another solution, that's what I'm doing."

"Fine."

"Good-bye."

"Georgia?"

"Eve, it's almost over."

"No, it isn't. The doctor says he could go on like this—"

"I was talking about the anniversary issue. We've almost closed it. I dropped the article on eggplant. It was a tough decision, but you know, the other day I saw a menu that listed eggplant pizza, and I thought, There is entirely too much eggplant in the world. It was a gut reaction, but if I know nothing else, it's that I have to go with my gut."

"Dad needs a private nurse. Would you call his accountant and see how much money he has left in stocks and treasuries? And tell the accountant to expect nursing bills."

"Absolutely, don't worry about it. Anything I can do. My assistant will take care of it. Corinne's a gem. You should have him sign a blank check."

"Why?"

"Then you can withdraw everything from his checking account and we can use it. And in case he does die, we'll have one less account to deal with."

"A blank check?"

"Can you find one?"

"I suppose so."

"Guess who we are putting on the cover of the tenth-anniversary edition of *Georgia*."

"Who?"

"Georgia."

"Who?"

"Me! Isn't that daring? Corinne, pick up the phone."

"Hi."

"Hi, Corinne," I say.

"I just told Eve, and she's speechless."

"That's true."

"Hang up now, Corinne."

"Bye."

"Bye, Corinne."

I keep dialing. Sometimes, when I start I can't stop. The mouth wants to talk. The body wants to feel the snug security of the receiver tucked between the ear and the shoulder. The whole self craves the high that comes from playing the phone. I press those buttons with amazing speed and dexterity, and then I connect. No matter for how long or with whom, talking on the phone quells my anxiety. Although it's arguable that, when the hit is over, when I disconnect, the anxiety returns with greater force. Does the phone actually calm me down or rev me up? I don't know the answer.

"Hello, Madge, this is Eve."

"Wait, before you say anything, I have the most delicious idea. We should name all the food in honor of Richard Nixon. For example, Potato Puffs Charlene should be Potato Puffs Patricia. That will be so original."

"It's a wonderful idea."

"But we'll leave out the painful parts, I think, just dwell on the positive. China, his daughters, his love of music, and his roots."

"Definitely. Madge, do you have the RSVP list handy, because there's a doctor that I was wondering . . . I was wondering if this doctor is on it. His name is Kunundar. K-U-N-U-N-D-A-R."

"Just a second, dear, I'll look, is he a friend?"

"Well . . ."

"You don't need to answer. I'm just being nosy."

"He's an acquaintance."

"Well, he's on the list. Omar."

"He's coming?"

"Well, he's been invited."

"Has he RSVP'd?"

"Thus far, he's nonresponsive, but there are five days left, and I'm sure we'll hear from him. Ear, nose, and throat doctors tend to be reliable. They're more like dentists, really."

"Well, thanks. As soon as you change the names on the menu, fax it to Kim."

"Adrienne, you busy?"

"I'm making tea. And I'm having warm chocolate chip cookies. Hold it."

I hear her refrigerator open and close. I know she has just poured the tea from her pink two-cup pot with the dancing lady on top. She bought it before she met Paul, when she thought she'd never meet her Paul, and she said that the dancing lady was her, all alone having a very good time. I know that right now Adrienne is adding so much milk that the tea turns a light tan. One of Adrienne's gifts is to make everything more comforting, often more fattening.

"Ann Sothern," she says.

"What about her?"

"That's the actress, isn't it?" She takes a moment to sip her tea. "Short, wide, with bangs."

"No, it's not. This one's wimpier. Wifey, in a really fifties way, or is it forties, I'm not sure. Anyway, listen to this: Georgia is putting herself on the cover of her magazine for the tenth-anniversary edition."

"Your sister is insatiable. Egomaniacal."

"Driven. Oh my God, that's it."

"What?"

"The D word. 'Driven.' She's doing an article on it and I couldn't figure out what it was. She is really smart. I mean, everyone is using that word."

"She's not that smart. She's like one of those pigs that hunts truffles. She's always got her nose to the ground and eventually she comes up with something."

"Adrienne, that's mean."

"You know what I'm saying."

"A pig that hunts truffles. Adrienne, my God."

"I'm just saying she's very New York, and in New York everyone thinks they're smarter than everyone else. Why do you suppose I live here? Have you kicked that girl out yet?"

"Who, Ifer? No. You know, she's just like Maddy. I think we're having an intelligent conversation, and then, bang, she mentions Ouija boards or reincarnation. Maddy's always hitting me with 'Take Dad to the sun.' "

Adrienne sighs. "It's like Spanish television. I'm switching from channel to channel, looking for something to watch, and I think I've found a riveting black-and-white forties movie, and the next thing I know, everyone is speaking Spanish. I'm trying to do a cartoon called 'Oops, Spanish Television,' but I haven't nailed it yet. I'd better go. I'll talk to you soon. Say hi to Joe."

"If I talk to him."

"What's that supposed to mean?"

"It doesn't mean anything. He left yesterday for Montana

to spend a week in the woods with a woman who talks to moose. That's all."

"Oh. Okay. Bye."

☎

In my desk drawer are some of my father's blank checks. Angie sent them to me when she cleaned his room before we checked him into UCLA. I slip one in my wallet.

For days I have put off going back to the Home and getting him to sign away his life savings. The ear, nose, and throat party, now a day away, has kept me from going. Also Angie's reports of his rising suddenly out of his wheelchair (when his 'round-the-clock nurse looked the other way) and crashing down. She says this week he rarely talks—a consequence of his seizure, perhaps. Looking after Jesse and Ifer while Joe's in Montana, even seeing Buddha through her final days of pills were excuses I made to myself for not dealing with the check business sooner. But this morning I woke up determined to get it signed and over with.

I come down the stairs at full speed. "Jesse, listen, I'm going to see my father, then I'm stopping at my office and— Why aren't you two ready for school?"

Jesse is at the table stabbing his toast with a fork. Next to him, Ifer, her arms straight down at her sides, her head hung forward, is weeping. Buddha is licking milk out of her cereal bowl. "Get that cat off the table," I say.

"She has to go home," says Jesse.

"Don't make me," wails Ifer. She throws herself at me, wrapping her arms around my neck. "Please don't make me."

I disentangle. "If your mother wants you, then you have to go home. Have you seen my purse? I took my wallet out and now I don't know where my purse is."

Jesse turns his head to the left and then to the right. "I don't see it."

Ifer follows me back upstairs. "Can't you go to court with me and help me divorce my mom?"

"Is she abusive?" I rummage through my closet. Ifer's breath is on my neck.

"Yes, she is so rude. Baby M divorced her mother."

"No, she didn't. That was a boy named Roger or something. I forget his name. Anyway, rude isn't abusive." I look under the bed, then check the bathroom.

"What's abusive?"

"Hitting." I see my purse. "Thank God, here it is. I'm out of here." I rush down the stairs and out the door.

"Suppose I'm pregnant," Ifer yells from the window as I start to drive down the block. This makes me accelerate. Considering this seriously will break the stress barrier. I don't even look back.

I walk into the Home briskly, wave at Angie, who is behind the desk, and don't hesitate until I get to my father's room.

This pause before entering is habit now: habit formed after a lifetime of worrying about what I will find. I wish my being nervous were a consequence of not wanting to see someone I love in an advanced stage of the dwindles. Then entering his room wouldn't seem treacherous, only sad. What drives me isn't love but responsibility. I am the best Girl Scout ever. If only I could get over this fear of the unknown.

"Hi, Dad. Dad?"

He's in his wheelchair, bolted in now with a metal bar across the front, the way people are locked into roller coasters so they can't fall out. He stares at me blankly. I open my purse and pull out the check. "I need you to sign this."

"Is that Eve Mozell?" A woman peers around the door, which, given how I barged in, I have almost slammed into her. She's in a chair, knitting.

"Yes?"

"I am Ogmed Kunundar."

I shove the check back in my purse. "Mrs. Kunundar?"

"Ogmed," she corrects.

"You're the nurse they hired? What an amazing coincidence."

"Oh, no. The nurse is having coffee."

"Then what are you doing here?"

She puts down her knitting and pats the bed. "Sit."

I sit instantly, obediently, as if I were her pet dog.

"Omar is worried. He says you do not have an arm or a shoulder."

"An arm or a shoulder?" I repeat dully.

"For leaning on," says Ogmed. "So I am here."

"You don't even know me."

Ogmed shrugs. "Sometimes I am the Salvation Army."

I am having trouble comprehending this entire development. First he has his mother call. Then he's so concerned he sends her? I remember he said, "You need a mother." Well, yes, but yours? "How did you know I would be here today?" I ask.

"I took a chance." She smiles at her own cleverness.

"Pat," says my father.

"He keeps saying that," Ogmed tells me. She tugs at the yarn that runs out of her lap and down into her purse, which is open on the floor. "Pat," says my father again, staring at Ogmed with a look that could be happy but then again could be something else.

When Maddy and I were little, we used to play a game. I would put my hand over my mouth and say, "Am I smiling or frowning?" She would guess, and when I took my hand away, the face I was making was so odd that she never knew whether she had guessed correctly. That's the kind of face my father is making.

"Pat is my mother's name."

My father starts wheezing. His breath sounds as if it were coming out of bellows. I jump up.

Ogmed watches him carefully, her head cocked to the side.

"Should I get a nurse?"

"Wait," she says.

My father stops wheezing. She resumes knitting, and I plunk myself down again.

"How long have you been here?"

"Not long." She is wearing half-glasses and she peeks over them to answer me.

"It's awfully kind of you to come."

"You mean crazy," says Ogmed.

"No."

"That is what you were thinking." She holds up her knitting to examine it. It is a very large hunk in bright purple. I hope it's not something Omar is expected to wear.

"Is that for Omar?"

"A sweater," she says, nodding. "He is too busy to shop."

"Is he married?"

"I am wishing but nothing is happening."

"Oh." I start to blush. I can feel the heat moving from my neck up. I sort some mail lying on my father's bedside table. An American Express bill. A pamphlet from the League of Women Voters.

My father's head twitches, and every muscle in my body tenses. Don't have another fit, I am begging you. I can't run away hysterically in front of this woman I am never going to be able to call Ogmed. It would be too embarrassing, so please, please, don't have a fit. His head twitches again and then drops forward.

"He's asleep," Ogmed announces.

"Are you sure?"

"Of course."

I feel as if my father has finally done something for me. I feel a tidal wave of gratitude.

"Sit down. Relax yourself," says Ogmed.

There is no alternative, so I do. Ogmed wiggles back in her chair. She must be short, because her feet dangle above the floor. She has the snuggly body of an old-fashioned grandma: just plump enough to be cozy. She's wearing stretch pants in an orange that would be visible three blocks away on a dark night. Her top is a polyester pullover in a tropical print. Neck down, she is straight from Miami, but neck up, she is a Middle Eastern fantasy: a broad face with almost no wrinkles, in the loveliest light brown; thick gray hair pulled back loosely into a long braid; and black eyes that promise age-old wisdom. I want to sit at her feet and sip tea. Sip tea and have her read the leaves.

"May I get you something? They have coffee, tea."

"Shush." She puts her finger to her lips and nods toward my father.

Except for the clicking needles, the room is quiet. Even peaceful. It is unfamiliar to sit this way, it feels almost risky. My family always talks. If we don't talk, we leave. If we don't talk, we hang up.

Still, Ogmed and I stay like this for half an hour, maybe more. My mind wanders. I think about stabbing my father with her knitting needles. I think again about doing him in with his own bullet, now a recurring daydream. Only this time, after I shoot him, I declare to the world that I have done it and I'm glad.

My father's breaths short out now and then. Ogmed looks up, making a clicking sound with her tongue that sounds almost exactly like her knitting needles. He wakes and stares straight ahead at the TV, which is not on. Ogmed clicks her tongue at that too. I watch his eyes water. Are you sad? Frightened? Or are your tear ducts breaking down like everything else? Can you tell me something about what's happening to you? Anything?

I think all these things to avoid thinking about something else: the check in my purse. How in the world can I ask him to sign the check in front of Ogmed? I could say the check is for his phone bill, or maybe back taxes. But why aren't I, the devoted daughter, paying them? Why is the devoted daughter getting her father to sign a blank check?

"We need some money out of my father's bank account," I hear myself say too loudly. My own voice comes at me like a stranger's. "I have to see if he can sign a check."

The needles stop. "You need money?"

I am hating Georgia, hating her for telling me to do this. "No, we need some of my father's cash to pay for his nursing care. Dad, I need you to sign a check so I can send it to Georgia." I put the check on the tray in front of him. I take a pen out of my purse and wrap his fingers around it. "Can you do this?" I ask softly.

He moves his hand, and then it starts shaking, batting back and forth like the needle on a heart monitor showing intense fibrillation. I pull the check out from under the pen, which rips it, and jam the check back in my purse. I wait to hear the needles clicking again before I look up.

Ogmed is bent over double, stuffing the knitting into her purse. The nurse, returned from her hour-long coffee break, is waiting for us to leave.

"May I buy you lunch? It was so kind of you to come. So unnecessary and so kind."

"I would like a cup of tea," she says as she snaps her purse closed and tucks it under her arm. "Good-bye, Mr. Mozell." She bobs her head at him.

"Be sure to call if there are any problems," I inform the nurse for Ogmed's benefit. This is not what I planned to say. I planned to tell her to call Madeline.

"Bye, Dad." I kiss him for Ogmed's benefit too. I touch my lips to his forehead, which doesn't feel like skin. It feels like waxed paper. "Let's go," I say to Ogmed.

We head down the hall, slowly because she doesn't like to move fast, I can tell. "He has the dwindles, that's what they said at UCLA when I asked them what was wrong."

"He's dying," she says.

"That's what they mean, I think. In a year or two."

"Now."

"What?"

"Anyone can tell," she says impatiently.

"I thought—" I can't say any more.

Ogmed slides her arm under mine and guides me. I feel my chest start to split. She squeezes my arm. "Look at that," she whispers as we walk by a woman who is reading the newspaper. Or rather, the paper is open, wide open, her hands grasp the pages firmly, but she is sound asleep. Her head has fallen forward like a dead weight. It makes a dent in the top of the L.A. *Times.* My eyes start to blur as Ogmed steers me past the woman, past Angie, and out the door.

"Which way?" she asks.

I point at the deli on the corner where my father and I used to lunch.

Ogmed accelerates, and now I am just her sidecar. We get to the restaurant.

"Two, please, by the window," says Ogmed, keeping a firm grip on me. She lets me off at one side of the booth. Again, obediently, I sit.

The waitress is not Debbie, thank God, but another who has endured four years of my father's obnoxious flirting—the entire time he has been housed at the old folks' home and brought here regularly for an afternoon outing. "How's your dad?" she asks.

Now I am weeping buckets.

Ogmed opens her purse, fishes around, and pulls out a tissue.

"I'm sorry, it's just that I knew he was dying—" The D word comes out in a choke and I'm flooding the table. And sweating too. My shirt is sopping wet. "I said he was, but everyone else said—"

Ogmed pats my hand, which starts another flood. "We will have two cups of tea and two tuna fish sandwiches. You should eat," she adds. This practically makes me wail.

"You like tuna fish?"

I nod.

"Good."

I hunt for a dry spot on the tissue. Ogmed produces another from her purse and offers it.

"You see, he's always been such a nightmare and—" I can't get any further.

Ogmed reaches over and smooths my hair. Again and

again, she moves her hand across my brow and over my head. I sit back, out of her reach. If she touches me once more, I swear I will cry and never stop.

"So," says Ogmed, as if I were not Niagara Falls. "So tell me about yourself. Are you married?"

I nod.

"How many children?"

"Just Jesse, the driver. He's sixteen." I mop my eyes.

"And what about the rest of your family?"

"Two sisters. Georgia and Madeline. I'm in the middle." Now I have no trouble speaking. The thought of Georgia and Maddy dries me up.

"Georgia is the one that needs the money?"

"Oh no, she doesn't need money. It's that my father has to have 'round-the-clock nursing or they'll kick him out, and it's very expensive."

"I will take care of this."

"What?"

Ogmed unsnaps her purse, hunts around under her knitting, and pulls out a portable phone. She taps in a number. "This is Mrs. Kunundar. I have to speak to my son.

"Omar, I am here with your friend Eve. She is fine. Yes, we went to her father. He is dying, but she is very lucky. It is not a good idea for her to pay for the repair. One of your noses will pay for three cars and that should be the end of it. I will tell her." She presses End, snaps the portable phone closed, and puts it back in her purse.

"Now you don't have to worry."

"But I don't mind paying for the repair. It's my son's fault."

"Fault is never the point. As far as I am concerned, it is settled and you should tell your husband."

I should tell Joe? How will I explain this to Joe?

She sits back and sips her tea. The waitress puts the sandwiches on the table.

"Why am I lucky? Why did you tell Omar that I am lucky?"

She says this as if it were completely obvious: "Because you are here."

☎

"Kim, I just saw my father and I don't think I'm coming in."

"What's wrong? Where are you?"

"In the car. I'm exhausted. I'm going home to take a nap. Could you go over to the Nixon Library and run through the party schedule with Madge Turner? Make sure the food stations are all located correctly, double-check the time schedule for the speeches, the food, the performances."

"No problem, I can do it."

"Did you confirm the Citrus Singers? What about the flowers? They should be there tomorrow by three. Leon too. Call him. Remind him the party starts at seven-thirty."

"Eve, stop, it's fine, don't worry about it."

On the car radio, I vaguely register a news item. A young girl, lost for three days in the Sierras, has been found. "She's safe," her father's voice breaks, and I can hear in the background a little eight-year-old, "Daddy, Daddy, Daddy."

"Are you there?" asks Kim.

"Take care of things, okay?" I push End, which disconnects us, then push Auto Dial and zero-two.

"Corinne, it's Eve, would you put Georgia on?"

"Hello, darling." I hear her upbeat voice. "We're done. We just closed the issue. Maybe I am the world's eighth wonder. Then again, maybe not."

"I can't believe you asked me to do that."

"What?"

"Make him sign the check. That was disgusting. He's dying."

"Who said he's dying?"

"Anyone can tell."

"Who said it? Did the doctor say it?"

"I'm not asking him to sign anything else."

"Take it easy. You didn't have to do it. Why do you always think you have to do what people tell you to?"

"It's my fault? Are you saying it's my fault?"

"What I'm saying is, it's not mine. Hold on a second."

I push End. End, end, end.

I go into the house quickly and quietly. I can see Ifer's and Jesse's backpacks and books spread all over the living room. Did they ever get to school today? Who knows? Just hurry. Get upstairs fast.

"Mom?"

Not fast enough. "What?"

Jesse and Ifer come into the hall and gaze up at me on the stairs. Ifer is still in her boxer shorts and T-shirt. "Can we talk now?" asks Jesse.

"Are you pregnant, Ifer?"

"No." She has the decency not to meet my eye.

"Good. Now leave me alone."

I go into my bedroom and slam the door. There's a knock immediately. "What?" I say in my nastiest voice.

"Dad called."

"He did? Did you tell him where I was?"

"I told him you were visiting your father."

I whip open the door. "You mean your grandfather!"

"Okay, my grandfather. God, don't have a cow, Mom."

"Say it again."

"My grandfather." Jesse starts backing down the stairs.

"I didn't go there." I am amazed to hear this lie fly out of my mouth.

"You didn't. I thought you—" He stops. "God, your eyes are all red."

"That's what I looked like when Matt dumped me," says Ifer. "I wouldn't even go out."

"I have a headache." I close the door.

I start rummaging in my purse, scrounging for a Benadryl, an Actifed, something that will knock me out. It's like the bottom of a garbage heap, this purse. I locate a naked Certs, a few Tic Tacs, some dirty pennies. I catch a glimpse of myself in the mirror across the room. I look like a blotchy little ferret, digging madly. But then I find it. An antihistamine that will put me to sleep and clear up my sinuses, which, God knows, need it. I swallow it dry and throw myself on the bed.

Why did I lie to Jesse? Why do I feel guilty? I didn't invite Ogmed to visit. Should I feel guilty because, while having a fantasy about a man, I end up involved with his mother?

I move over on the bed sideways, leaving room for Joe as if he were here. I wrap my arms around the pillow. Joe does not need to know.

"Mom?" I hear Jesse's voice through the door.

"What?"

"Don't get mad at me for asking, but the mechanic called. My car's fixed. Can we go over later?"

The car. I have to tell Joe about the car.

"Mom?"

"I don't think so. Not today. I don't feel well. I'm going to sleep."

☎

The phone rings. What time is it? What day? I look at the clock, which glows in the dark. Nine. I slept six hours. The phone keeps ringing. It's Joe. For sure, it's Joe, calling back. I have to tell him about the car.

I force my eyes wide open. I shake my head as if to settle the mess inside. I use my cheeriest voice. "Hello?"

"Eve, it's Angie."

"Yes?"

"Your father . . . Well, we thought he was being a clam."

"Yes?"

"But I poked him."

"And?"

"It seems he's in a coma."

☎

I am racing from one room to another. "Where's my purse? Would you help me look, would you please help me look? Oh God, I'm carrying it." I open the closet. What am I doing here? What do I need? A jacket, right, I need a jacket. "Jesse," I yell, "are you ready?"

"I'm right here," he says quietly. I almost collide with him coming out of his bedroom.

"Excuse me, Mrs. Marks," says Ifer, as they follow me down the stairs, "but is he dead? It's okay if he is, I just have to prepare myself if I'm going to see him dead."

"You are not going to see him at all." I open the door and virtually march down the front walk to the car.

"Excuse me, Mrs. Marks, but—"

I spin around. "Jesse's grandfather is dying now, Ifer—"

"I know, but—"

"What?"

"You're getting into the wrong car."

"Whose car is this?"

"I don't know," says Jesse. "It's just a car that's parked on the street. Mom, I think it would be better if you let me drive." He puts his hand out for the keys.

I open my purse and start hunting around. "I can't find them." I burst into tears. "I can't find anything anymore."

"It's understandable," says Ifer, taking my purse and handing me Buddha. "Your daddy's dying."

"You're very upset today," says Jesse.

"No." I cry harder. "I'm like this every day."

Ifer hands Jesse the keys, takes the cat, and returns my purse.

"I want this cat out of the house," I weep.

"Okay," says Ifer agreeably. She gets into the backseat with the cat.

"I don't want to ride with the cat."

"Mom," says Jesse. "You are really bonkers. I think you should get in the car."

We ride along in silence. "Don't talk," I say after a few minutes.

"Could I ask one tiny thing?" Ifer leans over the front seat so her chin is resting on my shoulder.

"No."

"Is he in a coma?"

"I think so, yes." There is a pause.

"Could I say one more thing?"

"No."

"Maybe we should talk to him. Tell him it's okay to die and everything. Well, not me, because I don't know him, but maybe you." She rolls her head to the side so she is peeking up at me. "I wish I knew him, 'cause he was Jesse's grandpa."

"He used to be really nice."

"When?" asks Jesse.

"I don't know. Just sometimes. Like when I was getting over this love affair with this stupid guy that I thought I might marry. He said, In marriage, you can exist without love, but never without like."

"Wow," says Ifer. For emphasis, she throws herself against the back of the seat. " 'Never without like.' That's cool."

"Where's your father, Ifer?"

"He lives in San Francisco. I visit him like for holidays and stuff. My good old dad," she intones. "He's my best friend."

I start crying again.

"That's a McDonald's commercial," she adds. " 'My good old dad, he's my best friend.' You know, you should probably burn sage in his room. Sprinkle it around his bed. To get rid of evil spirits. Kasmians do that."

I turn around. "Ifer, I swear to God, if you say one more word, I'm throwing you out the window."

Ifer screams.

Jesse smashes into the car in front of us.

"It's not my fault."

That's the first thing I hear. Then, through the wind-shield, I see a man slam out of his car and start shouting. "You shit. You stupid shit."

Jesse leaps out. "It's your fault," he shouts back.

Ifer pushes the seat forward with me in it so she can squeeze out too. "It is your fault, Mister, I saw it all," she claims.

I start checking my body to verify that I'm still in one piece. Then I look out at Jesse and Ifer yelling at the man. He's pointing to his car, which I notice is brand-new. It doesn't even have plates. In the rectangle where the license plate belongs, it says "Wilshire Lexus."

Jesse has left his door wide open, in the middle of Pico Boulevard. "Hey, close the door." He doesn't hear. He's going to have another accident. He's rear-ended someone and now our door is going to be knocked off too. I lean across the seat and pull the door closed. Then I get out.

"We're taking my mother to the hospital," Jesse is saying. "My grandpa's dying."

"There's a stop sign right here." The man points. The sign is partially hidden by a palm tree.

"Huh, when did that get there?"

"It's always been there."

"It has not!"

"I never saw it," says Ifer.

I inspect the cars. Our grill is destroyed. There's no damage to the other car, not even a dent in the bumper. "There's no damage," I say.

"There might be inside," says the man. "It could have internal injuries."

"There's no way a car has internal injuries if it has no external injuries. It's not a person." I start crying again. It comes as a total shock to me. Tears are streaming down my face, and yet I'm speaking normally. I would be absolutely certain that I'm not crying, except there are so many tears I can taste them.

"My mom is very upset," says Jesse. He puts his arm around me.

The man takes a beat to glare at us, to make us feel really low. Then he gets in his car and drives away.

"What a jerk," says Jesse.

"You rear-ended him. It's your fault."

"I didn't know he was going to stop. Jeez, how did I know? That stop sign's never been there before."

"Just forget it and let's go."

We get back in the car. "Wait," says Ifer.

"What now?"

"Is Buddha in front with you?"

"No."

"Where's Buddha?" She starts bawling.

☎

"Adrienne, are you awake?"

"Oh God, your father died."

"No. He's unconscious but stabilized. They're keeping an eye on his kidneys. I talked to the doctor on the phone and that's what he said. 'I'm keeping an eye on his kidneys,' as if his kidneys might disappear when the doctor wasn't looking. Like Buddha."

"Who?"

"Ifer's cat. I spent the entire night searching for it. I never reached the hospital, and the cat was under the car the whole time. Thank God, because the last thing I want is to attend a cat funeral."

"Eve."

"What?"

"You're not making much sense."

"That's because I haven't been to sleep. It's four-thirty in the morning, which makes it seven-thirty in New York, so I assumed you'd be awake."

"Yeah. Paul and I are going running. Where's Joe?"

"Still in Montana with the moose lady. I can't fall asleep. I know the minute I do, the phone will ring and he'll be dead."

"But you said he's stabilized."

"We're not talking rational here, Adrienne."

"I know, I'm sorry."

"I can't even locate Georgia, and I spoke to her this afternoon. She'd closed the issue. Where is she? We should discuss extraordinary measures, not that we'll take any, he's hardly got a brain, but Ogmed was right, he's dying. Georgia should come out."

"She's on her way to Paris."

"What? Are you serious?"

"Who's Ogmed?"

"How do you know about Ogmed?"

"You just mentioned her."

"I did? She's just someone I know. How do you know Georgia's going to Paris?"

"I had a meeting with her a few days ago, and she told me she was going there as soon as the anniversary issue closed."

"You two had a meeting? I thought you couldn't stand Georgia."

"Actually she's pretty smart."

"Why'd you have a meeting?"

"She saw my cartoon 'Memory Helper.' Do you remember it? That's not a joke."

"No, I really don't."

"It was done like an advertisement for a telephone service: 'Can't remember the name of your best friend's mother? Dial Memory Helper.' "

"Can't remember the name of a short, blonde, wide movie star with bangs?"

"I put that in."

"You did? You didn't ask me if you could."

"I never ask. What were you going to do with it?"

"That's not the point. Forget it. It's no big deal. So why's Georgia in Paris?"

"She said she was going for a short vacation, and when she gets back we'll talk about my working regularly—"

"What?"

"A monthly cartoon for her magazine . . . and we'll all have dinner—me, Paul, what's her boyfriend's name, that shrink?"

I don't answer.

"Eve?"

Some big emotion has rolled in from somewhere, a yawning, huge wave of sadness, and if I try to speak, it will flatten me.

"Eve, are you upset that I might work for Georgia? . . . Eve?"

"I was just . . . I was trying to remember his name. Stephen—that's it." The more I talk, the easier it becomes. "I haven't even met him, neither has Madeline. So you're all having dinner?"

"I'm sure she'll forget about it."

"When is she planning to come out here, did she say that? Is she ever planning to come out here?"

"I don't know."

"Oh . . . Well, it's great you're going to work together. I mean, that's fantastic, Adrienne. Congratulations."

"It's not for sure yet."

"Still, it's great."

"We'll see. Who's Ogmed?"

"Just someone who's been really there for me while this has been going on with my father. She's been really supportive and really helpful."

"What kind of a name is that?"

"I have no idea. I've got to go to sleep. I've got this big event at the Nixon Library."

"Today? But you're beat. Your father's dying."

"I have to go."

"Eve, Kim can take care of it. She's been your assistant forever."

"There's no way I can't show up. And if I don't get some sleep, I'll look terrible."

"What do you care? It's just a bunch of ear, nose, and throat doctors."

"Right."

"Let me know how it goes."

"What?"

"Your dad, what else? Is there something else?"

"No, of course there's nothing else."

I hang up. I lie there. The phone is lying right next to me. Of course, it's not, really. It's on the night table, but I feel like we're in bed together. I roll over on my side and stare at it.

Now I turn onto my stomach and inch up the mattress to the top so I can peek down at the telephone cord, snaking its way along the wall behind the bed to where it hooks into the little gray phone box. I reach down behind the bed. It feels daring. It feels practically revolutionary. I squeeze the plastic doohickey on the end of the phone cord. It comes right out.

I get up and pull on my robe. I walk into my study to kill the telephone there, then downstairs to unplug the living room phone and Joe's rotary model. I deactivate the kitchen phone by prying it off the wall with a screwdriver.

Back to my bedroom. I snuggle under the covers. I lie there in the quiet that is not going to be shattered by the ring of the telephone, where there will be no news unless I want to hear it. I can feel my body sink into the mattress. It's possible I'm relaxing. It's possible, but the feeling's not familiar so I can't be sure.

Nine

*W*hen Jesse was little, Georgia

sent him a toy touch-tone executive telephone. A battery

inside made it light up in the dark, and in addition to Speaker

Phone and Redial, it had two Hold buttons. It was more

elaborate than our real phones. Joe was using a black rotary-

dial model for aesthetic reasons.

We had been married almost eight years and were living in

West Los Angeles. Unlike my childhood neighborhood of winding hilly streets, where we lived was flat, blocks laid on a boring horizontal-vertical grid. But Joe and I loved our house. It was old, Spanish style, with thick stucco walls, tile floors, curved arches, and cool rooms. We frequented flea markets for old rugs, pine furniture, and slipcovered couches and chairs where one could either feel the springs or sink so low that getting up and out required firm commitment. We owned nothing without heart, like matching smart uphol-stered items or wall-to-wall carpeting. A woman could never go loco here, I assured myself, the way my mother did.

In the backyard, we had a palm tree where a parrot lived. Every morning Jesse would run outside and squawk at the parrot, and from high up in the tree, the parrot would squawk back. This was Jesse's favorite thing to do until the telephone came, a week before his fifth birthday.

I remember because it was the day Joe's first grant came through.

"Only fifteen thousand?" Georgia had said puzzled, when I called whooping and cheering, after parking Jesse in front of the TV to watch the Smurfs.

"But you don't understand," I explained. "It's a travel grant from the NEA. Joe can do his interviews all over the country now. National Public Radio is picking up his show."

I called Maddy and then Adrienne to complain about Georgia's reaction, hung up, and went to meet Joe, who had arrived home with champagne.

"They all say congratulations," I announced as he popped the cork. I covered my eyes. "You never know where these corks will fly, especially now when we are ecstatic. It would be just like one of them to hit one of us in the eye."

"You probably think rice is dangerous too," said Joe.

"It can get stuck in your ear."

"Exactly. You think the world is full of newlyweds who had to cancel their honeymoons because they had rice in their ears." He kissed me, taking his long, slow time. The first time he had given me a kiss this light and sweet and tender, under a streetlamp on Fifth Avenue, I knew I was in love. He was taking so much care for a single kiss, so much care for me.

The phone rang.

We stopped kissing and stared at it. "Who needs this," he said, picking it up. "Hello?" He handed over the receiver. "Some people always call when you're really happy or really busy," he said, by way of telling me who it was.

"Hi, Dad."

"If I have to hear one more goddamn thing about Raymond . . ." my father said.

"Ha. I knew you were talking about me." Claire suddenly materialized on another extension.

"Get off the phone," he barked at her.

"Do you want me to handle him?" Joe asked.

I shook my head. "Dad, calm down. I'm not going to talk to you guys if you're going to fight."

"Tell the lady to get off," my father said.

"I live here," said Claire. I could hear her pull herself up in that alcoholic way—that move in which a person suddenly stands straighter, gets regal, I suppose plays sober.

Joe bent down, lowering his head so it was right in front of mine and I couldn't miss it. "I can take care of this for you."

I waved him away. "Don't you think you could be a little more tolerant, Dad?"

"Your dad's a drug addict," said Claire.

"Well, sometimes you drink too much."

"Just when I'm with him. He's a hack, anyway. You're a hack, Lou. Raymond was an artist. An artist and a saint."

At that moment the doorbell rang and Joe went to answer it. I carried the phone into the front hallway so I could see who was there—the UPS man. Joe offered him some champagne.

"Your daughter never calls you," Claire told my father.

"Claire, he calls me all the time. That's why I don't call him."

"Not you," she said. "The editor in chief."

Which is what Georgia was now. It had happened the year before. Editor in chief of *Harper's Bazaar* at thirty-six. "This is some sort of record," she had proclaimed. "Although with all these yuppies around, people are being promoted younger and younger, so perhaps it's not a record."

"They put Georgia in *People* magazine this week," said my father.

" 'They put Georgia in *People* magazine this week,' " Claire imitated him.

"You two really should see a marriage counselor. You're not communicating."

Claire hung up.

"She's gone," said my father.

"Right."

"I wonder where she went."

"See, Dad, listen, you are hooked. You like having these arguments."

"Did you see Georgia in *People*?"

"Yes, for the fifteenth time."

"That's some office she has. I called her and told her I knew she was a success when I saw her plants. She's got one that hits the ceiling. Bet she doesn't have to water it. Bet they do it for her."

"I really think you and Claire need help."

"Her kid's a giant," said my dad.

"So? What's that got to do with anything? She's a successful model."

"I should never have left your mother."

"Dad, she left you."

Joe reached over my shoulder and took the phone. "Hi, Lou, it's Joe. . . . Yeah. I'm sorry you're having problems."

He handed me the UPS box, and paced with the telephone, making comforting sounds. "Mmmm, uh-huh." This went on for a while. "Sure, talk to you soon." He hung up, then looked over at me with a grin so wide you could swim laps across it. "I took care of it," he said proudly.

"That was weird."

"I'll say." Joe downed the rest of his champagne and poured himself some more.

"I mean it was weird that you took the phone out of my hand. I was dealing with him."

"Eve, honey, he's calling ten times a week to complain about Claire. Believe me, you're not dealing with him." Joe started hunting through the cabinets. "We need something to go with this champagne. We need"—he laughs—"remember Cheetos?"

"Cheetos still exist."

"They are an amazing color," he said, shoving bottles and cans aside, looking for something to eat. Joe even went through cabinets in an exuberant manner. "Who's the box from?" he asked.

I read the label. "It's from Georgia, for Jesse. Joe, suppose we get a separate phone and tell the new number to everyone we know but my father. Then we won't have to take his calls."

"And what do we tell Jesse? This is a number your grandfather calls on and we don't answer it? Bingo." He pulled out a package of Goldfish crackers, ripped it open, and tossed a few from his palm into his mouth. "Look, what's the big deal. He's a pain in the neck, that's all. A pain in the neck but harmless."

"Right."

"Do you want more champagne?"

"No, I don't think so." I wandered out into the living room. Joe followed me.

"What's wrong?"

"I don't know." I plopped down on the couch, feeling suddenly gloomy. "I think it was weird of you to do that."

"But I thought you'd like it."

"I did, but . . ."

"What?"

"I did."

☎

The next Saturday, Joe and I spent the morning decorating for Jesse's party. Joe taped "Happy Birthday" signs all over the house—across the entryway, on the doors, above the fireplace. They were more than "Happy Birthday" signs, they were happy-family proclamations.

I had not worked for three years after Jesse was born, but I now had a part-time job planning promotions and parties at L.A. Events. This meant I could get a discount on helium balloons. In celebration of Joe's good news and Jesse's birthday, I went crazy: fifty of them were nudging the living room ceiling, all with long ribbons attached.

While Joe and I buzzed around decorating, Jesse sat on the floor playing with his new toy telephone.

"I think someone's here, Jesse." Jesse ignored me, pressing numbers on the phone, then a button to make it ring. "Hello, this is Jesse Marks speaking," he said.

"He has the phone gene," said Joe as Maddy let herself in, floating gently into the room, moving along like a rippling wave. Her long hair was pulled back into a braid, and she had adopted an ethereal walk. This all signified something new, but what? She had one arm out behind her, and it turned out that her index finger was linked to the index finger of a man whom she pulled in after her. Was he linked to someone else, was this a daisy chain? No, it stopped there, with this man who was wearing a leather vest and no shirt on under it. There was curly black hair on his head, arms, and chest, and he was built oddly, with a big burly top and a narrow waist and bottom. His shoulders were so wide you could shelve books on them. "Carlo, meet my family," said Maddy. Carlo flipped his free hand up, kept it there like a stop sign, and then flipped it down again.

"She's dating a silent wonder," I heard myself preparing to tell Georgia.

"Hi, Carlo, how are you doing?" said Joe. Carlo gave him the thumbs-up.

Maddy grabbed Jesse and swung him around, "Hey, birthday boy." Her clothes were different too. For months, ever since she had seen the movie *Flashdance,* she'd been wearing sweatshirts with scissor-cut necklines that dropped down off one naked shoulder, and she had developed this habit of rubbing her shoulder against her cheek. "Very fawn-like," Joe had observed. But today she wore a peasant dress, an itty-bitty flowered print down to her ankles, which billowed now and then as she moved along rhythmically, one might say spiritually. Perhaps she had discovered God.

Guests started arriving—mostly parents and kids from

Jesse's pre-kindergarten class. The parents introduced themselves as someone's mom or dad, and they stood around talking while the children rushed together and collided like players turned loose on a football field. "I'm really pleased to meet you, I've heard a lot about Jesse." I kept hearing some version of that over and over. Then Minnie Mouse appeared. I had hired her, sight unseen, on the suggestion of my boss at L.A. Events. She was a cute girl wearing a Mouseketeer hat, tights that turned her legs into barber poles, high heels three sizes too big, a leotard, and a short felt skirt. She didn't look like Minnie Mouse, more like something that leapt out of a cake at Mickey Mouse's bachelor party. "Who's the leader of the club?" she asked. "You," screamed the kids. Except Jesse, who was fighting over the toy telephone with a boy named Dakota.

"Do you need help with anything?" asked Maddy, following me into the kitchen.

I pointed to a stack of napkins with G.I. Joe on them. "The party hats are over there. Put one at each place." I slid two pizzas into the oven to heat.

"Are these apples washed?" She took one out of a bowl.

"Yes."

She bit into it, took the piece she had bitten from between her teeth, and examined it. "You're serving pizza and chocolate cake?"

"That's what I'm doing."

Maddy popped the piece back in her mouth and chewed.

"Is there something wrong with what I'm serving?"

"No."

"Good."

"It's just so completely unhealthy."

"What's so unhealthy about pizza?"

"Processed cheese." She opened the refrigerator and

gazed into it. "I swear, Eve, you're the only person I know who still eats white bread."

"Did you see the thing on Georgia in *People*?"

"First I bought it. Then Dad sent me a copy. Then he sent me another copy. All he does is call up and talk about Georgia."

"I know. Doesn't it drive you nuts? He always picks a day when I've done nothing but schlepp Jesse from one place to another. I think he has antennae for when I feel especially drippy." I nodded toward the dining room. "Don't forget the table."

"Oh, right." Maddy closed the refrigerator, took the paper napkins and hats, and froze.

"What's wrong?"

"I just remembered something. This is really terrible."

"What?"

"Well, Carlo has this friend who's a fashion photographer—"

"Yes?"

"And he heard that Georgia— Oh God, this is so upsetting?"

"What, Maddy?"

"She could lose her job."

"But why? Why would Georgia lose her job? She just got it last year."

"Ad revenue is way down." Maddy dwelled on the word "way."

"Oh, dear."

Maddy and I were silent a second, already psychologically at Georgia's job funeral, grieving our heads off. Maddy absentmindedly tried on a birthday hat and snapped the elastic strap over and over. The beat provided a funereal accompaniment to our thoughts.

"Should we say something to her? Does she know about it?" I asked.

Maddy shrugged.

"God, she gets fired right after she's in *People.* How embarrassing."

"I wouldn't be in *People* magazine," said Maddy, pulling the hat off and smoothing her hair. "Well, I might be, when I become famous and need to publicize something, like myself. And I would be on Johnny Carson but, like, not . . ." She twirled her long braid around and around her index finger while she thought, but she couldn't come up with any TV shows she wouldn't be caught dead on.

"Famous as what?" I heard crying in the next room. Then screaming. Unmistakably Jesse.

"I've decided to become an actress," I heard as I rushed out.

Jesse was clutching his telephone to his chest. Dakota was crying, and his mother was kissing his forehead. "Jesse hit him with the receiver," she said almost apologetically.

"You're not allowed to hit." I tugged the phone out of Jesse's arms and presented it to Dakota. "Say you're sorry."

"I'm sorry," Jesse mumbled.

"Did you hear what I said?" Maddy asked.

"I heard." I picked Jesse up. "You want to be an actress? I'm surprised. You came in with a sort of earthy, peasant aroma."

"Aroma?"

"I mean style. I wasn't expecting—"

She interrupted. "I look centered, that's all."

"But aren't you old to become an actress?" I pulled down a balloon for Jesse to hold. "Dakota will play with the telephone for a while and you will play with the balloon. When do you want to open your presents?"

"Now." He wiggled, trying to get out of my grasp.

"I don't see how you can say that," said Maddy.

"Why? You're almost twenty-eight. That gives you only twelve years, and you haven't even taken a class yet. Isn't forty the end of it for actresses?" I set Jesse down. "Now, behave, okay?"

"Okay?" Maddy groaned. "Eve, for God's sake, don't ask his permission."

"I do that too," said Dakota's mom, as she went by, carrying Dakota and the phone.

"Didn't Georgia run a piece called 'Five Careers You Can't Have After Forty, and Five You Can,' and wasn't actress a can't?"

"I wouldn't know, I read *Vogue*. I'm not surprised they're firing her if she runs articles like that. Carlo's twenty-five and he says I look much younger than him." I glanced over at Carlo, who was sitting on the couch in the middle of jabbering five-year-olds, reading *California* magazine. "I can pass for twenty-three. No one needs to know if you don't tell them."

"Who would I tell? I don't know anyone."

"That's for sure," said Maddy, looking around the room.

"I think Rachel's dad is a producer. He's the tall one in the sweats. Come on, I'll introduce you."

We waded through the guests, Maddy doing her lilting walk and bestowing on each and every one a beauteous, if mirthless, smile. I had to speak to several people on the way —a circumstance she dealt with politely, though she poked me in the waist when I chatted too long. "Alan, hi," I said finally. "I'd like you to meet my sister, Madeline—"

"Madeline Lee," interrupted Maddy. She extended her hand and widened her smile. To go with her new career, new boyfriend, new clothes, new walk, and maybe even new firm handshake, she had a new last name.

I left them, Maddy tugging on her braid, engaged in an intense conversation about life change.

"Come on, everyone," I called. "It's time for Jesse to open his presents."

As I put Jesse in an armchair with the gifts stacked around him, I noticed that Joe was talking to Minnie Mouse about what it was like to walk in gigantic shoes. "Joe, I need help here." The doorbell rang again. "Would you please get that?" I called to Katie's mom.

"Hand me the cards when you open the presents," I whispered to Jesse. He obediently passed one over. "This is from Dakota," I announced.

"Me." Dakota jabbed the air with his small fist. Behind him, I saw my father lurch into the living room.

The party stopped. Everyone looked at the wild man.

His hair, which was now gray and getting sparse, stood straight up, and his eyes were popping. He looked as if he'd been shocked—his hair spiked, his eyes boggled, and like this they had remained ever since. He held a dirty blue TWA bag, and jammed into the lapel pocket of his rumpled sports jacket was a plane ticket.

I caught Maddy's eye across the room. "Hi, Dad," I said. "Jesse, look who's here. Your grandpa!"

"Who?" said Jesse.

I saw a woman hold her hand in front of her face, and then the smell hit me too. Scotch.

My father batted at the ribbons hanging in front of him. "I ran away," he announced.

Joe took him by the arm, coaxing. "Come on, Lou."

My father dug in, not moving. "Looks like D Day," he said, tilting his face up at the balloons.

Joe pulled his arm. My father yanked it away.

"This is my son's birthday party," Joe said firmly. "We're going into the kitchen."

"You first." My father grinned.

Joe headed that way. My father swayed after him.

Jesse ripped open a present. "Look what you got!" I sold the excitement of it in a mommy birthday voice, and everyone at the party started functioning again. "Thanks," Jesse said to Dakota, looking at the Hot Wheels, then throwing the cars down without taking them out of the plastic. He grabbed another present. The doorbell rang again. "Maddy, would you get that?"

She moved over to my side. "It's probably Claire," she whispered.

We stood cemented. "Carlo," she said finally, "would you get the door?"

Carlo dutifully put down the magazine, climbed over some children, and went to the door. I read another card. "This is from Rachel."

"It's a Cabbage Patch doll," Rachel shouted, waving her own as an exhibit.

All the parents were watching Carlo disappear into the hall. "Do you want us to leave?" asked Katie's mom. I shook my head.

"It's the cabdriver," yelled Carlo, without even sticking his head back in sight. "He wants his money."

"Do you have money?" I asked Maddy.

"Me?" she squawked. "I'm an out-of-work actress."

"I'll take care of it," said Katie's mom.

"Thank you." I called to everyone, "Would you excuse me for a minute?" and went into the kitchen.

My father was standing in the center of the room with his arms across his chest and his mouth in a pout.

"I'm not giving you a drink, Lou, so forget it," Joe was saying.

"Claire's a bitch, we're getting divorced."

"I don't give a damn," I said.

"Take it easy," said Joe.

"How dare you? How dare you come to my house drunk? This is Jesse's birthday."

"I'm calling her up."

He walked past Joe boldly, bravely. Now he didn't just have the bullet, he was John Wayne himself, daring Joe, the bad guy, to do something like shoot. If Maddy turned out to have acting talent, this would surely be where she got it.

My father turned his back to us while he dialed. "Claire! Answer the fucking phone, Claire!" he shouted. Behind him, through the door, I could see a slice of the living room, all heads craned this way. Jesse started crying. Maddy picked him up.

Joe took the receiver from my father. "Sit down, Lou, and shut up."

"No, get out." I started pushing my father, hitting him on the shoulders, knocking him backward. "Get out and don't ever come back."

I could feel my forehead tighten and my jaw lock, some strange paralysis setting in. I was squeezing every feeling into a tight little wad. I reached around him, pulled the back door open, and pushed him out. He stumbled backward down the steps and landed on his ass.

"Don't ever come back to our house. Ever."

"I saw you talking to the mouse," he told Joe.

"What?" said Joe.

"I know what you're up to."

"Out of here," I screamed.

He pulled himself up, holding on to the ivy hedge. The ivy broke, and he seized the wire fence behind. He managed to stand, but rocked like a capsized boat that had flipped back upright. "Your mother was right about you," he sneered. " 'Throw that one back.' That's what she said."

"She was right about you too," I shouted. "Get lost, get lost."

Joe was pulling me into the house. He shut the door.

"What happened?" Maddy stood there carrying Jesse.

I put out my arms and he went into them.

"What?"

I just shook my head.

"I'll take care of the party," said Joe. He went back into the living room.

"What did Dad do?" asked Maddy. I shook my head again and turned so I was facing the wall. I wanted to scream. I wanted to howl. But I just hugged Jesse tighter and tighter and started making those faces you make to stop your face from doing what it wants, which is to break into a million wet pieces. "I hate him. I hate him so much." I turned around. "Madeline, I'm never speaking to him again. I'm never letting him set foot in my house. If he calls, I'm hanging up."

Maddy nodded.

"I'm not kidding."

She nodded some more.

"Oh God, I feel awful."

Maddy stood at the counter, biting her lower lip and looking wilted, slumping, her long peasant dress sagging into a pup tent. "Aroo," she said.

"Right, aroo." I put Jesse down. "Go find your father, sweetie." He ran off.

"At least you have Joe," she said.

"I know."

She picked up the birthday napkins, which still hadn't made it to the table. "I'll set it for you, okay? I'm sorry, I forgot before." But she didn't move.

"I'm fine," I said. "Really."

"What's wrong with our family?"

"Don't say that. Please don't say that. We're fine." I put my arm around her. She handed me a birthday napkin to wipe my eyes.

"Claire! Answer the fucking phone, Claire!" Maddy and I peered through the kitchen doorway. Jesse was sitting on the living room floor in the middle of his party, playing with his executive telephone. He hung up, pressed the Ring button, and when it rang, answered. "Claire!" he shouted. "Answer the fucking phone, Claire!"

☎

The next morning I woke up yelling at my father. Not out loud, just in my head. All day I was in instant replay. My father sprawled backward, me at the kitchen door, but this time I screamed hundreds of wounding lies: that I saw my mother every day, that I loved Tom Winston, that we had Thanksgiving there and Christmas, that Mom loved Jesse and he loved her. One fantasy even had me yelling that her dogs, probably long dead, had sleepovers with Jesse whenever my mom and Tom went camping. I told him Claire was too good for him. I told him I never wanted to see him again. I told him that especially, over and over and over.

I called Adrienne six times before I reached her. She had begun jogging, a strange development for someone who preferred the coziness of four walls, her drafting table, the TV, and a cup of tea. Adrienne in running shoes. It was hard to envision. But she'd met a man. She had jogged past him every morning at six. He'd been running too, but had stopped for a cigarette break at the West Village park right near her apartment. After the first day they started waving at each other. Finally she stopped to say hi. "The last of the big-time smokers," she reported with dismay, although she immediately sold a cartoon with that title, showing a man trailing butts across a map of the United States. Paul was a sportswriter. So far he hadn't done anything off-putting like wear his running shorts on his head, but they'd spent only one night together, and she apologized for not being home when I needed her. Which was the sweetest thing. She said it was sad I lived three thousand miles away—she couldn't come over and cook for me. She said she was going to do a cartoon called "Rendezvous," which would be scenes of men and women meeting all over New York City—at the Central Park reservoir, under the arch in Washington Square Park, on the torch of the Statue of Liberty. Meeting Paul had made her prolific, and if she worked fast enough, maybe her drawing could be a *New Yorker* Valentine's Day cover. She also said maybe it had already been a cover, some other artist's, it sounded familiar. And speaking of magazines, she said, there was an interview with Richard Nixon, a huge interview, the month before in *Esquire.* "Mark today's date," she said. "January 19, 1984: Your father's in exile and Nixon's back."

I didn't tell Georgia until a few days later, and I didn't call her, she called me.

"I heard it all from our sister, Madeline Lee," she said. "Don't tell me to speak to him again, because I won't."

"Eve, darling, you don't have to speak to him if you don't want to."

"Joe hates him even more than I do. Joe said that his behavior was unforgivable."

"You don't have to speak to our father."

"Thanks."

"He made it back to New York, in case you were worried. And they *are* getting divorced. Claire's moved out."

"I told you, I don't care. Remember when I was in that car accident, soon after I moved here to live with Joe? For the first few days afterward the world felt so dangerous that I took only teeny-tiny steps wherever I went. That's what I feel like now. Like Dad came to my house and ran me over."

There was a long pause.

"How dramatic," said Georgia. "Well, forget about him, I mean it. Do you want to hear my news?"

"What?"

"I was fired."

"Fired?"

"Yes."

"God, I'm sorry. I thought *Harper's Bazaar* was doing so well, I mean, I know your ad revenue was down, but—"

Georgia jumped on me. "Who said that?"

"I don't know. I read it or Joe knew or something."

"Everyone's ad revenue is down, that's no big deal."

"Oh."

"*Harper's Bazaar* is irrelevant, anyway. I'd been sneaking relevance into it, but I had to sneak all the time."

"That must have been hard on you."

"Believe me, you have no idea."

"Well, why don't you come out here and visit?"

Dead silence.

"Or why don't you go to Jamaica or wherever?"

"Martinique?"

"Right, Martinique, somewhere like that. You've never had any time to yourself, you work so hard. I mean, it's like a sudden death, the death of your job, you have to grieve."

"I'm starting my own magazine."

"What? How can you do that?"

"I have backers. It will probably take me a year to get it going, but I'm calling it *Georgia*."

"You're calling it *Georgia*? As in Georgia Mozell?"

"Yes."

I got off immediately to call Maddy, so I could be the first to tell her that Georgia was naming a magazine after herself. But I didn't call my father. I didn't speak to him again for seven years.

Once he called me. "Don't hang up," he said, and I hung up. He asked Georgia to intervene and she refused.

Every so often I told someone that I didn't speak to my father. I announced it in a blasé manner. I didn't add that I had no contact with my mother either. Being on the outs with both of them seemed extreme, as if the problem were mine, as if I were neurotic. It was too complicated to explain that my mother wasn't a mother, which meant I couldn't reject her. There was simply an absence of something between us, that's what I told myself. My father *was* a father: a horrid, distorted version in a funhouse mirror. "I don't speak to my father," I declared, often to provoke someone who had confessed to a minor resentment of his own: that, for instance, his father had sent his brother an airplane ticket to visit but had expected him to pay for his own. "I don't speak to him," I would needle, hoping to cause the other person to do likewise.

"Suppose he dies?" I'd invariably be asked. "Aren't you worried he's going to die?"

"If I knew he was going to die, I would speak to him." I liked saying that. I liked the cold-bloodedness of it. For seven years I was as relaxed as I was capable of being. For seven years the phone never rang at an inconvenient moment.

☎

Seven years later. Spring 1991.

"Hi, Eve, it's me. You won't believe this. Dad just called and told me Georgia won the Pulitzer."

"The Pulitzer? Maddy, that's incredible."

"Yeah."

"My God."

"I guess she's going to be more successful than ever."

"I guess so. Well, that's great. That's just fantastic. Did you talk to her?"

"I put in a call, but she was in a meeting."

"We should send flowers," I said.

"Hold on, that's my call waiting. . . . It was Dad again, telling me the same thing. That's the third call. You're so lucky you don't speak to him. What were you saying?"

"That we should send flowers. When did you get call waiting?"

"I've had it for months."

"Months?"

"Everyone has it. Haven't you noticed, you never get a busy signal anymore? The busy signal is practically obsolete. God, Eve, what planet are you on? Look, would you order the flowers? I'll pay you back."

. . .

"Georgia Mozell's office."

"Is Georgia there? This is her sister Eve."

"She's in a meeting."

"Tell her congratulations. Tell her to please call me the minute the meeting is over."

"Will do."

"Hey, Mom."

"Jesse, where are you? I thought you were coming home after school."

"Matt, Jennifer, and I are hanging out at his house. We're watching *Monty Python and the Holy Grail.*"

"Again? How many times is that?"

" 'Bring out your dead. Bring out your dead.' 'Here's one.' 'I'm not dead.' "

"What are you talking about?"

"That's from Monty Python, where he's got this cart with all these dead guys."

"Your aunt won the Pulitzer."

" 'I blow my nose on you. I fart in your general direction.' That's from Monty Python too. What did she win?"

"Never mind. Be home by five."

"Hi, honey."

"Joe, where are you?"

"In the Denver airport. I've just finished up. I'll be home in three hours."

"Georgia won the Pulitzer."

"What? For what? Something in that magazine?"

"I guess so."

"You've got to be kidding. That doesn't make sense."

"Well, she got it. Dad called Madeline."

"My God."

"It seems ridiculous that she got one and you didn't. I mean, what you do is so much more original."

"They don't give radio people Pulitzers."

"Well, they should."

"I didn't think they gave them to magazines either."

"Still, it's great for her."

"Absolutely. It's great. They're announcing my plane. I have to go."

"I love you."

"Hello, I'm calling from California. I'd like to order flowers. How much do I have to spend to get a lot?"

"At least one hundred dollars."

"One hundred dollars? Uh, okay. Beautiful spring flowers. It's lilac season. Do you have them?"

"For lilacs you need to spend one hundred twenty-five."

"Forget the lilacs. Send the flowers to Georgia Mozell at—"

"We know. We've sent her flowers before."

"Oh. Thank you. Can they be delivered tomorrow morning?"

"No problem."

"The card should read, 'Congratulations and love, Eve— E-V-E—Joe—J-O-E—and Madeline—M-A-D-E-L-I-N-E.' Here's my credit card . . ."

. . .

"Hello, Eve."

"Georgia, hi, this is so exciting. Fantastic. Congratulations."

"For what?"

"I heard you won the Pulitzer."

"Who said that?"

"Dad. He called Madeline."

"That's what he told her?"

"Yeah."

"I told him I was thinking of hiring Roxanne Pulitzer to write a sex column. But then I decided not to. It's tacky, it's really not *Georgia*. It was one of those four-o'clock-in-the-morning ideas. What are we going to do about him? He can't live alone anymore."

"He can't live alone because he got Roxanne Pulitzer confused with the Pulitzer Prize? He probably just has bad hearing complicated by not listening."

"The police picked him up twice in the last month. Once he was wandering down the middle of Fifth Avenue in his boxer shorts. Another time he wandered into an art gallery on Madison Avenue where they had some sculptures made of beer cans. He took one, popped the top, and drank it. They wanted to charge him twelve thousand dollars for ruining this great piece of art. Thank God I am famous, or we never would have gotten out of it, and I still keep expecting the event to turn up in some column."

"Why didn't you tell me?"

"You're not speaking to him, remember? So I thought you didn't need to know."

"That's very nice. Thank you."

"You're welcome. I think we have to put him in a home. He's seventy-seven now. He needs a controlled environment. I think I can get him into the Jewish Home in L.A."

"Here? Where I am? You're sending him back to where I am?" My voice scaled high enough to break glass.

"Not exactly. It's in the valley. It's in a different area code from you. Eve, it's really hard to get old people into good homes." Her voice turned sincere, even heartfelt. She was no longer the director of transportation, preparing to ship cargo to a preferred storage location. Now she was the champion of old people. Now she was virtually running for office on the plank "Save Our Elderly." "Do you know what most homes are like?" she asked achingly.

"No."

"Well, I do, believe me, and Stephen's father—"

"Who's Stephen?"

"That psychotherapist I hired to write a column, 'New Solutions to Old Problems.' His father lived there."

"New Solutions to Old Problems?"

"I know it sounds boring. I may have to change the title, but Stephen is brilliant."

"Are you involved with him?"

"What does that have to do with it?"

"I wondered why you didn't tell me about him. Are you in love?"

"I like him very much."

"You're in love, I can hear it in your voice."

"Really." The word did not have its usual edge. There may even have been a blush in it. "Stephen gives the Home a lot of money, it's one of the nicest things about him."

"Do we have to put Dad there?"

"He can't take care of himself. He's calling me twelve times a day. Of course, I rarely talk to him. My assistant should be awarded the Purple Heart. I'm sure I can convince him to go. You know, in the end he's a pushover."

"I think just with you. Most people are."

"Yes." Georgia sighed deeply at the burden of being impossible to refuse. "It will be the best thing."

"Are you sure?"

"I really am. He'll have a life, which is more than he has now. Nobody sees him, he has no friends. You remember how happy he was at Bloomingdale's?"

"How do you know? You never visited."

"You told me, darling. I figure it will take a month or two to arrange it, and I'll ship him out. Someone has to take him there."

"Madeline can."

"Hasn't she started that soap where she plays a secretary —or is it an assistant? Secretaries are never called secretaries anymore—that soap that she has to be at every single day?"

"Oh God, I'm going to have to speak to him again."

"Well, it's not as if you haven't had seven good years."

"I feel sick. I'm getting off."

"Eve?"

"What? Honestly, I feel completely nauseous. I have to go lie down."

"Did you purchase that Armani jacket I told you about?"

"No, but Chantell has called three times. Joe keeps saying, 'Chantell's a person?' He wants to know if people get those names before they become Armani saleswomen or after. He's thinking of doing a funny interview with several of them. Do you know any other ones with silly names?"

"You can joke about this if you want, Eve, but you have your own business now. When you want to impress people, you must always wear Armani and you must compliment men on their ties. That's something not every women's magazine will tell you, but *Georgia* will. We're not afraid to sound stupid if it's smart."

"Thanks, Georgia."

"So you'll pick Dad up?"

"I really have to get off. I feel terrible."

"Hello. I ordered some flowers for my sister, Georgia Mozell. To be delivered today?"

"Yes."

"Is it too late to cancel them?"

"I'm afraid so."

"Well, okay. Thank you."

☎

Joe refused to go to the airport. "Furthermore," he said, "Lou Mozell is never setting foot in my house again." The statement had an antiquated quality and reminded me of something an old-time movie father might have said. One of the dads from *Meet Me in St. Louis* or *Life with Father.*

"You can forgive him but I never will," Joe also said, which was more extreme than anything that crossed the lips of those movie dads. "I'll talk to him on the phone if I answer," said Joe. "That's as far as I'll go."

"Joe refuses to see him," I announced proudly to Georgia when she gave me the arrival time. "I'm taking Jesse to the airport instead."

"Why?" she asked. "I hope you're not foolish enough to think our father will pay attention to him."

"I didn't say that, did I?"

"No. Never mind." Georgia didn't say she was sorry, but she softened her tone. "He's older. I'm warning you, he's older."

"He's older," I told Jesse as we stood at the arrival gate.

"Than what, Mom? I don't even remember him."

I had a cramp in my stomach and a stabbing pain between my eyes. My legs were weak; even my arms felt peculiar. "A case of the dreads" was what Adrienne used to call my state of body and mind before I saw my father. How familiar these feelings were, maybe even comfortable, like a long-lost friend of whom you might say, in amazement, "We picked up just where we left off."

"What did you say, Jesse?"

"I said, 'I don't even remember him.' When we get home, I'm sleeping at Matt's."

"Fine. Look, Jesse, I can't concentrate. The thought of seeing your grandfather makes me crazy."

Jesse, who was attempting to check his reflection in a four-inch strip of chrome that separated the airport window and wall, shifted his attention over to me. "So why are you seeing him?"

"Your aunts have watched over him for seven years. It's my turn again."

"Well, if you're dreading this, you should do what I do at school."

"What's that?"

"Count down. Just think like, 'Okay, fifty-five minutes to go, fifty-four minutes to go.' How long is this going to take, anyway?"

"Between getting his luggage and getting him settled, I'd say two hours."

"God, I'm never going to get to Matt's."

At the first sight of my father, I didn't recognize him. I was expecting Dracula, or someone equally deadly. I had accumulated enough anger and fear over seven years to justify that vision, and instead saw an old man moving at his own slow speed, his only speed, and being bumped around by other passengers. He was shorter than before. The stewardess who shepherded him out had to lean down to talk to him.

He wore no sports jacket—nothing that would have given him a sense of presence or adulthood. His trousers were too long. They sat like hats on his Reeboks, and his shirt was so cardboard stiff, even after being on a shlumpy little guy for a five-hour flight, that it maintained a shape of its own. "Ever since Claire left, he buys only fabric made in a test tube," I recalled Georgia saying. Although it didn't look as if he'd bought these clothes at all. They looked donated.

He could still walk without falling forward, and he was alert. His eyes darted, searching for me, who else? But he seemed like someone who spent his days on a park bench feeding pigeons, not my crazy drinking dad who'd smashed his nose with a tennis racquet.

I waved, signaling I was here.

"Hey, Evie." My dad smiled his familiar crooked smile, the one that meant to be a whole smile but got sidetracked by tears, which always lurked.

"Hi, Dad. This is Jesse. Do you believe how big he is?"

"Hey, Evie, it's you," he said again. His eyes overflowed.

He pulled a handkerchief out of his pants pocket. A white pressed handkerchief. It was as amazing as if he'd pulled a rabbit out of a hat. It caused me to have an unaccountable wave of goodwill.

"Don't cry, Dad, please. You always cry." I patted him gingerly on the back, and for this minor act of kindness I felt I deserved a medal. One hour and fifty-eight minutes to go.

He wiped his eyes without unfolding the handkerchief, just patted that square against one eye and then the other. "Aren't you going to kiss me?" he asked plaintively, sliding the handkerchief into his pocket, astonishing me again. I'd seen him do it a million times—take that handkerchief out, wipe his eyes, and slide it back. It was like teeth: your whole face can age but your teeth remain the same. Georgia had once pointed this out to me—a person can have ancient, sagging, spotted skin, bags to his toes, creases as deep as the Grand Canyon, and retain a Colgate smile. Well, my dilapidated father kept a clean white handkerchief that he could still slip coolly into his pocket.

I pecked him on the cheek and nodded to Jesse. He did the same.

"How was the trip? Was the plane crowded? What movie did you see?" I was too nervous to wait for answers. "I think we want to go this way."

"I'm going wherever you're going. That's all I know," said my father.

"Well, I'm taking the escalator."

My father balked at the top, staring down at the moving steps. I took his arm. One hour and fifty-three minutes to go, I thought.

All the way down, I babbled. "They're all ready for you. A woman named Angie. Listen to this, she's worked at the Home for twenty years. She said she'll be checking in herself soon." I laughed and then realized from Jesse's look that what I had said wasn't funny. My father didn't pay attention, anyway. He was focused on the bottom of the escalator. He took his step off too soon, then almost tipped backward as the moving steps abruptly stopped.

"Whoa there," said Jesse, catching my father's arm with both hands and helping me pull him upright. Whoa there? I had never heard Jesse use words like that. It was language for old people. He'd spouted them spontaneously, the way people fall into "Cootchy-coo" when faced with a baby.

As we drove out of the airport and onto the San Diego

Freeway, I asked my father, "What do you think of Jesse? Doesn't he look handsome?"

"I'm not old," said my father, ignoring the question.

"You're not young. You're seventy-seven."

"I don't belong in one of those places."

"You might like it. You'll have lots of company. Your life hasn't been too full lately, has it? I mean, what do you do with yourself?"

"I eat grilled cheese sandwiches. And sometimes I screw the lady at the Chinese restaurant."

"Dad, for God's sake, Jesse's in the backseat."

"So what? I'm twelve," Jesse piped up.

"Don't take me there, Evie."

"You have to go."

"Why?" asked Jesse.

"Be quiet, Jesse. I think you'll like it there."

"Your sister's a piece of work. Try saying no to Georgia. She could run the Israeli army."

"You're lucky that you have Georgia," I said. "Georgia's great."

"Yeah." His lips started their usual quiver and twitch. I pushed the button on the tape deck. *Gypsy.* No one can cry when Ethel Merman is blasting.

I saw my father's mouth move. I turned the music down. "What is it?"

"Is Ella Fitzgerald alive?"

"Yes," I said.

He nodded. I turned the tape back up. One hour and fifteen minutes to go.

When we walked into the Home, it was about five-thirty, which turned out to be dinnertime. The big open room behind the lobby was the dining room, and there were four gray heads at every table. My father stopped short, like some old raccoon who's no dope: he knows danger when he sees it. He started retreating, backing into Jesse, who yelped.

"Hello, Mr. Mozell, I'm your aide. I'm Angie." The perfect woman for the job, round and warm, a muffin, popped around the front desk and put her hand out. "I'm so pleased to meet you."

"I'm not saying likewise."

"That's what he answered?" Joe said later, when Jesse and I got home and immediately crashed in his study.

"Don't tell me you're impressed."

"No. But he's still got his marbles."

"His marbles are banging around in his head. It's like they're in a pinball machine. Every so often a marble hits one of those things that lights up, but usually they just careen randomly from one side of his head to the other."

"Gosh, Mom."

"Don't criticize me."

"Mom, you're calling the man who gave you life a pinball machine."

"You don't understand."

We sat there, Joe absentmindedly hitting buttons on his tape machine, making a kind of rhythmic music out of Stop and Rewind.

"So he's in and he's fine," Joe said finally.

"I don't know if he's fine. We left him sitting in his room on this single bed. Just sitting there with his feet on the floor."

"It was like a jail cell," said Jesse.

"Hardly. Almost an entire wall was glass, and the wall-paper was—"

"Cheerful?" Joe supplied the word.

"Exactly. Flowers."

Jesse stuck his finger down his throat.

"We unpacked his bullet and put it on top of his bureau where he could see it."

Jesse clutched his stomach and gagged.

"That's enough, Jesse. My father has his own bathroom, and his own telephone, unfortunately."

"Creep city," said Jesse.

"Well, do you want him living here?" I snapped.

"Here! He didn't even say hello to me." Jesse jumped up. "I'm going to Matt's."

"Who's taking you?"

"His mom. I'll wait outside. Want this open or closed?"

"Closed," said Joe.

"Okay." Jesse shut the door. We heard his chant down the hall. " 'Bring out your dead. Bring out your dead.' 'Here's one.' 'I'm not dead.' "

"Truer words . . ." said Joe, as the phone rang.

I picked up. "Hello."

"Hey, Evie," said my father. "Hey, Evie, I'm back."

☎

The first time Jesse and I left him at the Jewish Home for the Aged, I was so grateful to be sprung that I promised to visit every week. By the time we reached our car in the lot, I wondered how in the world I'd said that, and mentally adjusted the promise to once a month. I actually visited at about six-week intervals. Always I headed there with the same thought: In one hour and a half it will be over. I counted down, right through greeting him, eating lunch at the corner deli, where he flirted with the waitress, and taking him back to the Home. For the next four years, this was our routine.

"He winked at her with cole slaw hanging off his chin." I

reported the details to Georgia or Madeline. The waitresses started backing away as soon as we entered. I even saw one of them push another to take care of us, and she freaked: "No way." My father didn't notice. He told them over and over about Georgia, while they had smiles pinned on, and then about the bullet, about *Ghosttown,* about Maddy. "I've got one daughter who's a big editor and another who's a big actress." Then he would point at me. "Don't know what she does, but she's a big hit too."

"Congratulations," the waitress would usually say to me.

"Thank you." Thirty minutes to go.

Maddy said she wouldn't be caught dead taking him anywhere. She would bring him a schnecken, a cup of coffee, and a recent videotape of her show. They would watch it together on the big TV in the lounge, my father waving over anyone who happened by. "It's really fun for him, and I don't have to talk," Maddy explained.

Whenever I went to pick him up, there was a row of residents sitting at the entrance. Frances, who had a walker and oxygen pipes, was my favorite. I always wished I was visiting her because she asked me how I was. "How are you, dear?" She said it in the sweetest way. As I was answering, my father would growl, "Let's get out of here." He always ordered the same thing at the deli: a corned beef sandwich and a Coca-Cola. One day, when he was holding his glass in one hand and his sandwich in the other, I noticed that his hands were trembling, the Coke and sandwich shaking like maracas. I couldn't help myself, I put my hands out to steady his. It was the first time I had touched him voluntarily since he'd come back into my life, and the first time since Jesse's fifth birthday that I'd felt compassion. It was a gut reaction, that's all. Nothing personal. Anyone would have had it if faced with an eighty-year-old man who was practically spasmodic. But the moment I touched him, I felt a frisson: in a blink, I will be on his side of the table. Merry Christmas. And a Happy New Year.

I let go of him, let go with a spasm myself, as if I'd stuck my finger in a socket, and put my hands under the table, hidden, where they could hold on to each other.

Whenever I took my father out, I worried that I would smell him. I tried not to stand too close or take deep breaths. There got to be tufts of hair in his ears and more and more cuts on his chin until finally Angie took his razor away and began shaving him. His nose and ears grew larger, dwarfing the rest of his face. And his thinned hair seemed to get coarser. It stuck up around his head in points, until Angie began grooming him. Then, with his hair parted neatly and what remained of it smoothed down, he looked like the oldest person ever to attend Sunday school.

"He took out his teeth in the middle of lunch and then put them back in," I told Georgia. "I didn't know he had dentures."

"There's an article in this," said Georgia.

"In dentures?"

"No, in surprises."

"I hate surprises."

"Obviously. Why else would you name your company No Surprises? You know, Stephen says that there is one thing, like an attitude or a quality, about every person that defines him. A person could have an entire analysis simply talking about that one particular thing. I'm going to have Stephen do his next column on this. Can he interview you? Because I think with you that one thing is surprises."

"I don't want to be in the magazine."

"Why?"

"I just don't."

"All right. But you'd enjoy talking about yourself. Poor Dad. He does sound disgusting."

"I hate to touch him."

"Eve, all you have to do is have lunch with him. Some people bathe their aging parents."

"I would rather die first."

Sometime during his fourth year at the Home, shortly after he'd turned eighty-one, I noticed that my father began to slant when he walked, like a person blown forward by the wind. He trotted along, his feet trying to keep pace with the part that preceded him, but since they could never catch up, he trotted faster and faster. Would he pitch forward? He needed security. He needed people in front carrying a net, clowns perhaps. One day, walking the short distance from the front door of the Home to where my car was parked, he stopped, wobbled like a bowling pin deciding whether to go down, and asked plaintively if I would bring the car to him. "Sure," I said. Forty-four minutes to go.

At the deli, there was a new waitress who didn't know enough to dread the sight of us. She was standing by the counter intently marking a *Sassy* magazine with a pencil. As soon as we sat down, she slapped it closed, stuck the pencil behind her ear, and hurried over. "I was taking a test. 'How assertive are you?' Not very." She giggled.

"Who *are* you?" asked my dad.

"Debbie." She flicked her fingers against her name tag. "And I'm nineteen today. Want to wish me Happy Birthday?"

"Happy Birthday," I said.

"Thanks."

My father got this grouchy look: his lips rolled up as if someone had stuck little cotton pads under them, his shoulders hunched, and his eyes got squinty. If he had been taking the waitress's assertiveness test, he would have scored off the charts. We both immediately switched our attention to him.

"Bet you don't know who my best friend was," he said.

"Who?" asked Debbie. "You mean someone I know?"

"John Wayne. I wrote three movies for him and he gave me his revolver. Took his six-shooter right out of his holster and handed it to me."

"Who's John Wayne?" she asked.

My father jerked his water glass, dousing her.

I jumped up. "I'm sorry, I'm sorry." I scrambled around picking ice off the floor. "I think my father's upset today." Crazy, I wanted to add. A lunatic, but I couldn't. I actually felt loyal.

Debbie stood there startled, the water dripping off her chin.

"I'm really sorry this happened." I stuffed some napkins into her hand so she could dry herself off. I didn't look around the restaurant; in fact everything faded out except my father, sitting dumbly as if this whole business had nothing to do with him. "Come on, Dad, we're leaving."

"Huh? Did we eat?" He took a slice of pickled cabbage out of a little bowl on the table, put it in his mouth, and crunched.

"No, we didn't eat, get up." I used my bossiest voice, grasped his arm and pulled. His body rose reluctantly. I could feel every pound like dead weight. "Out, we're leaving." I pointed him toward the door, and thank God, he trotted his crazy slanted way in that direction, clutching a remaining bit of pickled cabbage in his hand.

A week later, I got a call from Angie that something was wrong with him.

"Something more, you mean," I joked.

Angie didn't laugh. She said he'd punched the man who

had the room next to his. No one knew why. His gait was so unsteady they'd put him in a wheelchair. "And he doesn't know who I am," she added. "He needs to be evaluated."

I called my sisters. "They're sending him to UCLA. To the geriatric/psychiatric ward. He's, oh God, what's that word when you don't know who you are or where you are?"

"Disoriented," said Georgia.

"Right, he's disoriented. He's going into the loony bin again."

Ten

"Where are you?"

"Across the street from some restaurant called Patty's Pie Place."

"What happened to your car phone?"

"I left it at home on purpose."

"On the day of the party?"

"Kim, tell me how I get to the Nixon Library from here. I took a wrong turn."

"John Gerity's having a fit. Leon says the microwave isn't working, and he blew a fuse trying to plug in his grill."

"Just tell me how to get there, Kim."

☎

A sign is posted at the entrance to the parking lot: "Private Party Tonight." How did I miss it? How did I drive right by the Nixon Library and fail to notice it, as well as the gigantic geyser shooting out of the reflecting pond?

Although it is late afternoon and the party doesn't start until seven-thirty, I am already dressed and coiffed, and carrying a tote with all sorts of touch-up equipment inside. I have even brought stain remover, not for furniture but for my clothes. Trying to cover every base. Who knows? Some plum sauce from Leon's Great Wall of China dumplings might spill on me. I have to look my best for Madge, or in case someone else wants to hire me. That's what I told myself when I packed a tote with every manner of beauty equipment, and tossed it into the trunk of my car with the smashed grill.

I walk across the lot fast, about as fast as I can go in high heels and still look vaguely dignified. Through the glass doors, I can see Kim. She is not sitting down, even though there is a chair right in front of her. She leans over it to reach the table, and is loading boutique shopping bags with the speed and hysteria I associate with people turned loose in supermarkets who have five minutes to grab as much as they can. She throws in some party favors, like cologne, a large yellow envelope containing vital information—the program for the evening, a floor plan of the Library, a brochure on the Pasadena Ear, Nose & Throat Institute, and so on—and finally a white rose with a little plastic water holder slipped onto its stem. She drops the bag into one of the large wicker baskets at her feet.

"Is everything under control?"

"Please fire me," says Kim.

"I'll fire you tomorrow."

Kim blows upward in a futile attempt to get the hair out of her eyes, while her hands, on automatic pilot, continue to stuff. "Your skirt's unzipped."

"Oh my God." I zip it, but—"It's caught. It's caught on my blouse."

She comes around the table and starts tugging at the zipper. "Hold your stomach in, how's your father?"

I just wave my hand in front of my face. I don't want to deal with this, not now, I am saying.

"Madge is on her way," says Kim, "but she wants you to call her in her car. There, it's fixed." She zips my skirt closed. "You can use the gift shop phone."

"Where's the RSVP list?" I say this with the same urgency with which I might ask whether she happened to see some show on television the night before.

"In my briefcase. In the back, in the offices."

"Would you get it, please?"

"I'd better finish filling these bags first."

"Kim, I want that list."

"Why? Is something wrong?"

"Just get me the list. Now."

"Sure, fine."

"And ask Leon for a tablecloth. This table is the first thing people see when they arrive, and it looks terrible."

"Ms. Mozell?"

I swing around.

"John Gerity." He offers to shake hands the way a toy soldier might, arm crooked at the elbow, hand rigid.

This man is lean, brisk, and crisp. He wastes neither words nor expression. His mouth returns to rest position immediately after speaking. His clothes are spiffy. Undoubtedly he does not wrinkle his khaki pants even when he sits.

"I hear your mariachi band is wonderful," I say.

I am rewarded with a grim smile, which disappears almost before I see it. "I am the Citrus Singers."

"Oh, of course, I'm sorry. I'll be right with you." He follows me to the gift shop.

"Hello, Madge."

"Eve, dear." I can hear freeway sounds in the background.

"Is anything wrong?"

"I didn't sleep all night."

"Me neither," I say, thinking of how I wandered around dark L.A. streets, calling, "Buddha, Buddha." Then lay in bed too wiped out to read, too wired to sleep, until I finally yanked the phone cords.

"These parties are so agitating, aren't they? Do you think we made a mistake not having name tags?"

"No, I don't."

"But name tags are such a comfort. Then there's never a moment when you can't remember a name."

"That would be an amazing experience, but it's too late to do anything now."

"I have tags in the car."

"Madge, please."

"I know. Forget I said it. I'm such a worrywart. How's your father?"

"He's . . . dying."

Gerity looks over from the bookshelf where he's pretending to browse. "We don't know when," I add, then hear myself say brightly, "Death has its own timetable."

"That is so profound," says Madge. "I have to remember that. When my father died, I thought, 'Well, Madge Turner, you're an orphan now.' "

"How old were you?"

"Fifty-two. The terrible part is this. Once your parents die"—she lowers her voice to a whisper, although she is all alone in her car—"there's nothing between you and death." Regular voice again: "Is your mother alive?"

I don't hesitate. "Not really."

Madge doesn't notice anything ironic. "Then you're going to be an orphan too."

"I guess so. I'd better get off. I have to deal with the Citrus Singers."

"All right, dear. I'll see you soon. I'm only a few avocado trees away."

I hang up. "Kim told me you're upset," I say to Gerity. "What's the problem?"

"I'll show you."

As we walk through the museum, we are joined by an employee named Victoria, wearing a Republican-blue blazer. "I'm here to help, just ask me," she declares. We pass fruit and vegetable receipts from the Nixon family store, Nixon's public speaking medal from college, the station wagon he drove when he ran for Congress. Every campaign button, every aspect of his life is documented. On television sets from various decades, Nixon is giving the speeches he gave then. "Do you think Julie and Tricia like this?" I ask.

"Certainly," says Gerity.

"Who wouldn't," says Victoria. "Here their daddy lives forever."

We stop at the Living Legends Room, where there are statues of de Gaulle, Golda Meir, Chou En-lai. There is a sign that tells us to press a legend and hear what President Nixon thought. Gerity puts his hand on a picture of de Gaulle. We hear Nixon's voice.

"I would say he is almost gentle."

And what memorable words will I remember? "Your sister's a bitch. I'm her father, I can say it."

"You see the problem." Gerity's lips purse in, then pucker out, as if he were using them to push off from one end of a swimming pool to the other. "You see the problem," he repeats.

I do.

"If someone presses a button and Nixon speaks, it will interfere with our singing and clogging."

"We have a bullet at least. That's not a lot, but it's something," I say.

"Are you referring to the World War Two Colt forty-five revolver and six silver bullets that Elvis Presley gave the President?" asks Victoria.

"Yes," I lie.

She smiles. "Good, because right in front is a perfect place to sing and clog."

We are heading toward the Colt when Kim runs up with the RSVP list. "We're moving the Citrus Singers across from the revolver," I tell her. I start flipping the pages, scanning the list. H, I, J, K. Kalawitz, Keefe, Kerlin.

Victoria's beeper goes off. She listens to her walkie-talkie. "You have another call," she says.

"Oh God, he's dead."

"Yes," she says sadly. "He's buried in the back with Pat."

I pick up a wall phone. "Hello?"

There's static. Then a man says, "Well, what the hell, did Mitchell know to any degree what was going on?"

"Mitchell? Who's this?"

Victoria takes the receiver from my hand. "That's not a real phone. That phone plays the President's smoking-gun call with Haldeman. Throwing these events makes me scrambled too."

Old telephone calls, perfectly preserved? This is a museum of horrors.

As I take her portable phone, I keep reading the RSVP list. Klein, Kolter, Kraven. It helps if I concentrate on the list while I answer the phone. It keeps me from worrying about what's waiting for me on the other end. "Hello?"

"It's Madge again."

"Aren't you here yet?"

"My, yes, I'm in the atrium. I didn't want to walk all the way over to you, so I phoned."

Krupp, Kubalik, and then I find his name. I find what I am hoping for. "Madge?"

"Yes, dear."

"I think we do want name tags."

I see Kim looking at me. Her mouth falls open. She fans herself with her hand. "We don't have time, we can't possibly—"

"How marvelous," says Madge. "I'll snatch them right out of my trunk."

I start back to the atrium. "I'll help you fill them out," I say.

"There's no way we can do hundreds of—" Kim is chasing after me.

I whirl around. "We'll all help." A stop sign. Unlike Jesse, she observes it.

☎

Two hours later the name tags are done, and the first doctors are drifting in and over to the table where Kim and Victoria sit with the tags and checklist. Having freshened up using all my beauty supplies, I hover around behind, straining to catch the names, but then John Gerity demands that the Citrus Singers be served dinner and Leon rushes up to protest that there is not enough food. Besides coping with this, I notice that the doctors are now coming in hordes, too many, too fast to keep track of.

Perhaps Omar is fat. Perhaps he is three feet tall and has to stand on a chair to work his lasers.

I have to get a look at the checklist. I have to see if he has slipped by. "You need a break," I tell Kim.

But her gaze drifts. Off my face and over my shoulder. A dreamy look washes over her and her lips part, almost involuntarily. I turn.

"I must give you my name," he says.

I elbow Kim out of the way—almost knock her off her chair actually—grab a pencil and hold it poised, preparing to check off the name I already know. I can hear my own heart beat. I can hear it so loud it might be coming out of stereo speakers. Can he hear it too? Is every ear, nose, and throat doctor going to start marching around the Nixon Library to the beat of my deranged heart? "Yes, please, what is it?"

And now that he has heard my voice, he knows me too. Now he will say "Eve," in that velvety way.

"I am Dr. Kunundar. Omar."

Okay, he didn't know me, but he didn't know I was

going to be here. I scan the list pretending I don't know he's on it.

I hand over his name tag and he smiles. The temperature rises thirty degrees.

Did I say what he looks like?

He has the exact height required for nonchalant elegance. His skin is a smooth, mellow coffee-cream, his hair thick and raven black. I won't get into his cheekbones or the decisiveness of his jaw, but his deep brown eyes have black pools suitable for drowning in. And he has the dashing mustache of a gambler who carries only silver dollars for change and plays for very high stakes. But he is not a gambler, he is a thief. He is the highwayman who comes riding, riding, riding. And I am at the old inn door.

He is even alone. How is this possible?

"Kim, would you take over?" I say this as if I have worked for hours.

I follow him at a distance. A discreet distance, at least at first.

"He's going to order vodka, straight up," I tell myself as he goes to the bar. One with a name—Absolut, or that other one. "Tomato juice," he says. I move up next to him.

I see the Citrus Singers start dancing to "California, Here I Come." If Joe were here, he would be plying them with questions. What attracted you to clogging? Is it your family sport? Do wooden shoes hurt your toes? If you live in an apartment, does the clogging bug your neighbors?

"May I get you something?"

"Excuse me?" He actually spoke to me and I didn't hear.

"May I get you something?"

"I am Eve Mozell. The woman whose son hit you."

"No!" It is the astonishment of my dreams.

"I organized this. This is what I do for a living."

"It is fate," he says solemnly.

"I am married."

I blurt this and want to die, but he laughs. "Then it is my tragedy. But you must talk to me."

He looks around, but there is nowhere to sit. The couches in front of the TV showing the Nixon–Kennedy debates are filled. He takes my arm. "Wait, what may I get you?"

"White wine."

"Of course." He says this as if white wine suits me and only me. As if he has learned something deeply telling. The bartender hands it to him; he presents it to me. Then he steers me down the hall. Moves me expertly through the crowd. His competence overwhelms. I begin to envy his patients. I begin to wish for nose surgery.

"Here." He stops at the "Ask the President" room. We go in, past the computers with buttons for selecting questions, to the rows of seats in front of a big screen where Nixon's videotaped answers appear. This high-tech place is not where we should be, of course. We should be outside near a weeping willow tree under a full moon. I doubt there is a weeping willow in Yorba Linda, although there is surely a moon. Even Yorba Linda gets to have the moon.

Dr. Omar Kunundar pilots me to two seats at the end of the front row, as private a location as possible, and waits until I sit before he does. He fastens his brown eyes on me. "How are you?" It is the most meaningful question I have ever been asked.

"I'm very sad." It is a relief to say and a relief to feel for the first time that I am in no danger from this feeling. It will not wash me out to sea.

He nods understandingly. "You love your father very much."

"No, I don't. How could I? How could I possibly?"

"That is a very deep question," says Omar.

We contemplate it.

Finally he sighs, a sigh that implies a thorough search with tragic consequences.

"What?" I ask.

"You think love is something healthy. That is the problem."

"Well, of course, isn't it?"

"You think how you love your husband or your son, that is love. This other thing, what could it be? How could you love this—"

"Nutcase?"

"A very good word. I will never forget it."

"This selfish nutcase," I say fiercely.

"Yes, this selfish nutcase. The uproar man."

"Uproar?"

Omar smiles, and his eyes crinkle with kindness. These little lines of care evince hours spent at the bedsides of patients, explaining their X rays, their blocked sinuses, their deviated septums. "This is why I leave Persia," he says. "The Ayatollah loves uproar. Everyone must be upset all the time. He eats this. It is his bacon with eggs. Your father has a bad case of uproar, but not as bad as the Ayatollah."

"Nixon loved uproar too."

"Then how perfect that we are here." He raises his glass of tomato juice. "To your sadness."

"To my sadness." We clink. We celebrate my grief. We toast it as if it were an achievement.

Omar does not take his eyes off me, even while we drink.

"How is your father now?"

"He was back in the Home, but now he's in Tomorrowland."

"Excuse me?"

"He's been moved to a hospital, on a floor with all old people. I spoke to the doctor this morning. He said my father's kidneys are failing and he's not conscious. I just called it Tomorrowland because it's where we'll all end up . . . if we're lucky."

"I do not understand."

"I mean, if we live a long time, we get to die there."

"Yes," says Omar, "it is a queer reward. When I was a resident, I worked on a floor like the one that has your father, and every day I made an imagination that I was visiting an ancient civilization. All these—" He lifts his hands helplessly, the word has escaped him.

"Relics?" I say.

"How did you see that is what I don't know?"

I shrug modestly.

"Relics." His tongue rolls the *r* over and beds it. "Living relics." He seduces the *r* again and continues on as if the conquest is meaningless. "They are concealing secrets and knowledge, that is what I think. What can your father tell you?"

"His regrets." I laugh, and Omar looks at me curiously. "I'm sorry. His life must be one big regret—all those hospitalizations for drinking or craziness, barely a thought in his head that didn't pop out of it. You know, when I think about death I often say something obvious. Regrets, that's so conventional. I want him to have regrets, that's what I want."

"You want him to be sorry for his cruelty," Omar says without judgment.

"No, not really. If he were sorry it would be too much feeling poured in my direction. He was more like a flood than a father."

"You must think hard. What do you want?"

We sit in companionable silence.

"Something so I'm not afraid of death," I offer.

"Ah, you want wisdom and comfort."

"What I never had in life."

"Yes, it is hard to have that from a 'nutcase.'" He laughs at the word. "But it is not the end yet. Maybe you will be surprised."

"I hope not." I say this so sincerely that he is startled.

"Eve." He taps my nose. "I think it is the opposite of death that you are scared of."

This causes me to feel peculiar. What he says. His sweetness. The tap on my nose that seems to be lingering even though his hand is back in his lap.

I look at the screen, where the question now reads, "You met Elvis Presley. How would you describe him?" And Nixon, preserved on tape looking hale and hearty when he is in fact buried in the back with Pat, answers, "Some say, because he used drugs, he could not be an example to young people, but they overlook the fact that he never used illegal drugs, only drugs prescribed by his physician."

Joe would love this room, I think. All these questions with their nutty answers. It would put him away.

I spring up. "I think I'd better make sure everything's going all right."

"I am sorry to hear that." Omar smiles again, and I feel dizzy. I grip the back of the seat for balance.

"I'm here for work."

He gets up. "Yes, I too have business. I suppose I must scatter."

"You mean mix."

"Yes, mix."

I put out my hand. "It was so nice to meet you. And your mother is a wonderful person. Say hello to her for me." We shake but he does not let go.

"You are a warm person," he says.

"Thank you."

"Why do I think this warmth is something you got from your father?" He kisses my hand. "Good-bye, Eve."

And he disappears. If there had been a mist, it would have enveloped him, but instead he is swallowed up by a bunch of clog dancers who are taking their dinner break.

☎

"Well?" Kim demands as we wait for Leon to stow the last of his cooking equipment in his truck.

"It was a success."

"Not the party, that's not what I mean. The doctor you were talking to. Who was he? What did he want?"

"I think he was here only for me. Someone sent him." I don't wait for her to ask "Who?" since I have no answer. "Thanks, Kim, you were great, as usual. Thanks for everything. I'll see you Monday."

"But Eve—"

"Bye, Kim." I run to my car. "Thanks again," I cry, but a wind has come up and it blows the words back at me. I can tell this because Kim starts toward her car and doesn't look back. No one can hear me. I am alone in a parking lot in Yorba Linda. I am tempted to shout, "Omar." I will shout his name and let the wind carry it to the stars, where it belongs. "Omar," I venture quietly.

When I pull into the driveway, all the lights in the house are on. "Eve, is that you?" Joe calls from the bedroom window, then throws open the front door. "Eve."

"What are you doing back? Did you finish with the moose? Did my father die?"

"No. My God, I was worried." He wraps me in his arms. "You're home," he whispers. "You know that, don't you?"

I lay my head on his shoulder by way of an answer, finding the nook between his neck and shoulder that has always been my resting place.

"I couldn't reach you, so I got on a plane," says Joe. "Why did you unplug the phone?"

"I didn't want to be surprised. My father's spent my whole life surprising me, and I'm going to find out he's dead only when I want to."

"That makes perfect sense." Joe lets go just long enough to admire me and my wisdom, then folds me in again. The phone rings.

"You plugged it in?"

"I'm sorry," says Joe.

"Well, he must be dead. What else could it be at one in the morning?"

"The phone's ringing," Jesse yells from somewhere upstairs.

"We hear it," shouts Joe.

"I'll get it," I say.

"No, I will," says Joe. "You'll hear the news from me. That will make it easier."

Meanwhile the phone continues to ring. "It's the ringing I've always hated. The suddenness of it," I tell him.

"The surprise," says Joe. "But sometimes it's good news."

"True." We are in the living room now, heading toward the telephone on the little round side table. The sound is especially dreadful and insistent. To accompany it, the phone ought to vibrate, the way it does in a cartoon, the receiver shaking right out of the holder, demanding, "Answer me."

"I'll get it," I insist. "I can handle it. It's not a problem." I take the receiver out of Joe's hand, and realize, as I do so, that what I have said is nearly true. "Hello?"

"This is Jennifer's mother."

Wrong number, I mouth to Joe. "What number are you calling?" I ask.

"Isn't this the Marks home?"

"Yes."

"I would like to speak to Jennifer."

"Oh my God, you mean Ifer."

"I mean Jennifer. I told her to move back home tonight and she hasn't appeared. Would you send my daughter home now?"

"Gladly." I hang up. "Ifer's mother wants her home."

The news sinks in. Just the thought of Ifer's imminent departure, and the house feels like ours again. We should run from room to room leaping for joy. "She's really a sweetheart," I say to Joe. "I'll miss her."

"Me too," says Joe, who is already out of the living room and halfway up the stairs. "Ifer," he calls.

Ifer and Jesse stick their heads over the banister.

"Sad news," I say.

"Your mother wants you home," says Joe. "And she wants Buddha too. Don't forget Buddha."

Ifer groans.

"You'd better get going. Right now. Jesse, you can take my car." Joe tosses the keys to him.

Ifer comes limply down the stairs, barefoot, with Buddha in her arms and her dirty canvas backpack slung over her shoulder. With each step, her foot lands more heavily. Her sentence is finally being executed: she is no less than on her way to the gas chamber. "Spiritually she's not my mother," she wails. "If you kick me out, I'll be an orphan."

"No, you won't." I give her a brisk kiss on the cheek. "An orphan is someone in England whose parents died in World War Two. Or a poor child in a Dickens book who turns out to be rich in the end. That's what an orphan is."

"Not technically, Mom." And undoubtedly Jesse has more to say about this, but Joe closes the door.

"Come on, sweetheart." He starts upstairs.

"Joe."

"What?"

"I have to see my father."

"We'll go tomorrow."

"No. Tomorrow may be too late."

☎

The hospital is deserted. Our footsteps in the corridors, the ding of the elevator doors when they open sound jarring and frightful. "It feels like we're waking the dead," Joe says as we get off the elevator. On the wall are groups of room numbers with arrows pointing in all directions. Trying to deduce the location of my father's room feels monumentally difficult.

"I know this is stupid, coming at this hour," I tell Joe, "but I want to talk to him."

"It's not stupid. Well, maybe it is," Joe amends. "He's unconscious, isn't he?"

"With failing kidneys."

I hook my arm through Joe's, latching on to the only available security as we approach my father's room. His door is shut. "What's that quiz show where you choose door number one, door number two, or door number three?"

"*The Price Is Right*," says Joe. "I think."

"So what's behind the door? My father in a coma, or a washer-dryer?"

"A television," says Joe. "I can hear it. And if he's in a coma, who's watching it?"

Ogmed. Who else?

Joe goes over to the nurses' station, where one nurse sits, her head down on the desk on folded arms. "Excuse me?" he says.

She lifts her head and rubs her bloodshot eyes.

"We're here to see Lou Mozell."

"I'm just covering," she says. "The floor nurse is on break."

"Fine, but I believe my wife's father is unconscious, and we're wondering who's in there with him."

She shrugs. "Some woman."

OhmyGod, it *is* Ogmed. Who else would be here? She must have called the Home to check on him, heard the news, and driven over. The Salvation Army, that's what she called herself.

"Joe?" I take his arm.

"What?"

"I have to talk to you."

I look around wildly for someplace private, but in fact the whole hall is private. "You know that doctor whose car Jess hit?"

"Yeah."

"Well, remember I told you his mother called?"

"You didn't tell me that."

"I didn't? Well, she did. I guess she handles stuff for him like a secretary, so I happened to mention that I was going to the hospital, and she got upset about Dad and came to see him. She sat in his room and knitted and then she said we didn't have to pay for the repair because she felt sorry for me."

I search Joe's face for a reaction while he thinks about this.

"How strange," he says finally.

"I'll say."

"We don't have to pay? This is the only thing your father's ever done for us." He starts laughing. "Who is she? Where'd she come from?"

"Persia."

"You mean Iran. Iranians always say they're from Persia because they think everyone hates Iran." His brow knots with thought. He runs his hand again and again through the shag of hair that insists on falling over his forehead. Then he shakes his head as if to jog his thinking loose. I recognize the process. It's unmistakable. "An old woman—is she old?"

"I guess."

"An old woman sits at the deathbed of a man she doesn't know?" Now the hairs on the back of his neck are tingling. "What was she knitting?"

"Something purple."

"I'd like to do a story on her."

"I don't think so, Joe, and please don't ask her, because she's in there."

"You think that woman—"

"Ogmed."

"You think Ogmed is in your father's hospital room now? At two in the morning?"

"Yes."

"You're nuts, Eve." He walks over to the door and pushes it open.

"Shush," says Maddy, not moving her eyes off the television.

She is sitting in the chair next to my father's bed, so they are both facing a small television, the kind with a tape deck built in, that she has placed on the windowsill. Her back is arched, so her pregnant belly, which is still nearly flat, protrudes as much as possible. "Shush," she says again.

I realize she's watching her soap.

It's her final exit scene. "Dad, look," she whispers.

My father lies on his back with his eyes wide open. His dentures are sitting on his adjustable bed tray. He has one tooth of his own remaining, a holdout, the last soldier in the Alamo. It's on the bottom, smack in the center. I can see it because his lower lip hangs down loosely.

"I've just gotten back from vacation and I'm feeling great," Maddy explains, as on TV she strides into her boss's office with a present, a cactus from her trip to Santa Fe.

"I don't think I can accept it," the boss says.

The Maddy in the room tenses with excitement as on TV she swerves around, back and forth from boss to temp, a sexy young woman, then takes some time to put two and two together. "Oh, I get it. You couldn't make it with me, so you're making it with her."

On the TV, Madeline seizes the telephone, rips out the cord, and heaves the phone at her boss, who ducks. It shatters the glass on his framed law school diploma. She stomps out of the office.

Madeline flicks off the tape by remote control and looks

to our father for validation. He breathes. "I wanted you to see what I can do," she says softly.

"Do you really think he was watching?"

Maddy tosses her head. "It's possible."

"He wasn't even looking at the television. He's facing that way, but he's on his back, his eyes are aimed at the ceiling."

"Would you be quiet, he can hear you." Maddy goes to the doorway and stands there, waiting.

I join her, and together, as if we are about to slug it out, we step into the hall.

Madeline throws the first punch. "Just because he's unconscious and all his vital signs have crashed, you think—"

"His vital signs have crashed? You mean he could die at any minute? When did this happen?"

"Tonight." She pushes her hair around. "That's why you're here, isn't it? You didn't come to see my tape, that's for sure." She walks back in.

"I like your acting," says Joe as Maddy disconnects the TV and starts to fold the cord.

She ignores him. "Didn't they call you?"

"They probably couldn't reach us. Our phones were unplugged."

Maddy parks herself in the chair again, holding the arms as she sits to let herself down gently, I assume so she doesn't jar the baby.

"Can I talk to Dad alone?"

"How can you talk to him," she says sarcastically, "if he's unconscious?" She pats his hand. "Sorry, Dad."

"All I said, Maddy, was that he wasn't looking at the television, but maybe he can hear. Maybe he'll wake up when I talk to him. You never know."

"Fine, Eve, whatever." She hoists herself up, using the chair arms again for assistance, and flounces out.

Joe squeezes my shoulder. "I'm going to try to reach Georgia. It's nine hours later in Paris. There's a phone down the hall."

So now it's just me, Dad, and death hanging out together. I try to feel its presence. I imagine it floating above the bed, a shadow of my father, all negative image, until, boom, it drops. But I feel nothing. I have heard and read of inspiring death-room scenes, family clasping hands around a bed, providing a hammock of comfort that allows the dying person to let go, if the person wants to, which is also something I can't grasp. Death and peace. How can you feel peaceful if you don't feel anything? The idea that peace comes with death is one more false comfort for the living. No, there is no spiritual feeling in this room. I look at my father closely, aware that for most of my adult life I have tried not to. He has a mustache suddenly. I suppose the nurse couldn't manage to shave the hairs beneath his nose and left them. Or maybe she amuses herself by putting mustaches on dying men the way kids draw mustaches and beards on people in magazine photographs.

"Dad?" I throw the word out into the air. It feels ridiculous, like throwing a pass with no receiver.

I walk around the bed, working up energy, trying to imagine I'm Ifer the Kasmian, who believes in spirits and magic, so what I'm doing doesn't seem foolish. "Dad, if we had such a special relationship, you owe me."

I lean in close, my voice in his ear. I am minimizing the chance that my words will have no impact, that they will disappear on their way to his brain the way almost everything else I've said over the years has. "I'm not mad at you." My God, that's so stingy. "I've loved you, even though . . ."

No, no qualifications. "Are you afraid?" Blink. Do something. "Give me some solace, please."

I want to jump on his bed and pound him. Help me, you self-centered loony. You doled out insights before. You provided moments of guidance even if they vanished like Brigadoon almost the second they occurred. I constructed a father from them, used them to justify a lifetime of devotion.

I stare at him fiercely, trying to will something out of him, trying to force a final act of generosity. It can't be too late.

☎

We have been here now for several days off and on. My father's blood pressure teases, playing a game with us. It drops down—"Any minute now," the nurse announces— then rebounds inexplicably. When it's low, my father takes rasping labored breaths, and his chest strains with every intake, as if there were weights holding it down. Madeline and I have designated chairs, much as we had them at the family dinner table. She always sits on the left side of the bed, one hand resting on her tummy. I sit on the right. We are the only two people stupid enough to try to get from an unconscious man the wisdom and comfort that we could never get from him when he was conscious. You'd think that would be a bond. Or in the face of death, that our irritation with each other would appear insignificant. But we speak only when necessary, each appalled by the insensitivity of the other. Joe is the only bridge, getting us coffee and sandwiches when he is not working or looking after Jesse. We have been here enough to have opinions about the cafeteria food, to recommend the tuna, which I am eating now, and avoid the chicken salad. We have this knowledge but no one to pass it on to.

I hear unfamiliar noise in the hall. Unfamiliar because, while not loud, it isn't restrained. When I go home at night, Joe points out that I have taken to speaking in hushed tones. "Your hospital voice," he calls it. But this chatty and gay conversation I overhear could be from a cocktail party. I exchange a rare look with Maddy, then walk out.

A crowd of nurses—in fact, I didn't know there were so many working here—yak loudly as they move in a huddle, each carrying a magazine. They wave them, read them, clutch them to their chests. Georgia emerges from the crowd. She has flown nonstop from Paris and, even so, surrounded by white uniforms and clumpy white shoes, appears the perfect rose in the center of the bouquet. Her linen suit is only slightly creased. A double strand of pearls, long of course. Her black hair shiny and sharp. A slash of red lipstick.

"Here." She whips into a leather bag and presents me with the tenth-anniversary edition of *Georgia*. "Hot off the press."

On the cover, against a shiny metallic background, Georgia is seated in a high-tech desk chair. She is positioned exactly like Rodin's *The Thinker*, except that she is not naked but sports a snazzy black suit. "What I wear to work but better." Georgia, reading my mind, examines herself over my shoulder. In the photo, just like *The Thinker*, she rests her elbow on her knee and her chin against the back of her hand. Only instead of looking pensive, she is winking at us. "I wanted it to say, 'I'm serious, but you know what, I'm fun too.' "

"You look great," I say.

"Thanks." She kisses me on both cheeks, a habit picked up after less than a week in France. "How's he doing?"

"He could go at any minute." I cup my hand over my mouth so only she can hear. "I'm not speaking to Maddy. Do you believe she showed Dad a tape of her—"

"Shush." Georgia is looking over my shoulder. "Hi, Madeline, darling." She kisses her on both cheeks too. "How's the baby?"

"Fine. Thank you for asking." Maddy looks pointedly at me.

"Stephen couldn't come," says Georgia.

"It doesn't matter," I say. "We don't know him."

"I'm crazy to have you meet him, but he had to get back to his patients."

"It's okay. You've only been together four years."

Georgia lets out a big laugh, then clamps her mouth closed, turning wistful. She links one arm through mine, the other through Maddy's, and shifts her sad face back and forth between us.

"May I have your autograph?" Madeline breaks away to sign as the nurse hands her magazine and pen past Maddy to Georgia.

"What's that?" asks Maddy.

"The tenth-anniversary edition," I tell her.

Georgia signs a splashy signature above her winking head. "I love *Georgia*," the nurse is confiding. "I always read your message first: 'From the Editor.'"

"Me too," says another.

"You know," says Georgia, "we did a readers' survey because we wanted *Georgia* to contain what you were really interested in, and we discovered that my greeting was the most popular thing in the magazine, isn't that amazing?"

A sniffling nurse offers around a box of tissues. "If you read her message this month, you're going to need one," she warns.

"Thank you, I need one," says Georgia, pulling out a tissue. "I'm going to see my father now."

With Madeline leading the way, Georgia leaves the group of nurses comparing her autographs and admiring her photo, and walks into our father's room. I trail after, flipping open my copy of the magazine. It seems to fall naturally to the "From the Editor" page. Georgia probably has it precreased so this happens.

She walks slowly around his bed, taking in his every angle. "Oh my goodness," she whispers, "where is he? I can't even find him in that body."

"I know what you mean." Maddy grimaces.

I start reading aloud: " 'This was the hardest challenge of my life: to put out our tenth-anniversary edition while my father's life was slipping away. Anyone who's lost a parent knows how wrenching it is to see her mother's or father's life ebb. Every day there was less and less of the daddy I loved, but upset as I was, I forged on—'

"How dare you write this," I hiss at Georgia. "You didn't see his life ebb, I did."

"So did I," says Maddy.

"Barely."

"Don't be so noble, Eve. You like that role too much," says Georgia.

"I just end up with it because I don't get any help."

"I resent that," Maddy sneers.

We are attacking each other across the bed—Georgia on one side, me on the other, Madeline at the foot. We trade barbs over this fading hunk of flesh that is my father. It feels as if we are at some bizarre family get-together. Thanksgiving, perhaps, and we are arguing across the turkey.

"Let me refresh your memory," says Georgia in a stage

whisper. "I looked after him all those years when you weren't speaking to him."

"You didn't. Your assistant did. Besides, it's not hard on you."

"That's not my fault."

"It's not Eve's fault either," says Maddy. "Dad picked on her especially."

"She wanted it," says Georgia.

"I did not." I abandon all pretense of quiet. I have to deny this really loudly because I know the tiniest bit of it is true. I didn't welcome the curse of his attention, but was flattered even as I railed against it. Being his confidante and caretaker was a way of standing out, of being in the middle and not being squashed. My crazy father was a trophy in a competition among Georgia, Madeline, and me. Maybe I was the only sister actually vying, maybe I was the only one foolish and needy enough.

At that moment, my father shudders, and his breathing stops altogether. We all hold our breaths, a spontaneous sympathetic response.

A nurse peeks in. "I'm really sorry to interrupt, but my dad died too and, well, reading this helps me a lot."

"I think you'd better examine my father," I say testily.

As she walks to the bed, he takes another convulsive breath, we all jump, and then the covers start moving up and down regularly again.

The nurse takes his pulse. One eye is closed, and she pushes up the lid, flashes a light in, then lets the lid drop down like a window shade.

"Can he hear what we say?" asks Georgia.

"Probably not," says the nurse. "I don't think there's too much upstairs now."

"You're wrong," says Maddy.

Three hours later, there are no new incidents. Joe has paid a visit and left again, to get Jesse dinner. He gives me back my copy of *Georgia*, which he was thumbing through, and I drop it in the wastebasket. Georgia pretends not to notice. She has borrowed a third chair from an empty patient room, and sits with her feet propped up on the edge of the bed. Since none of us is on speaking terms, no one talks. My father is taking his last breaths in a room of angry daughters. Serves him right.

"Who does Dad look like?" Georgia says suddenly.

I can't resist. "Richard Nixon."

"He used to, but no more. His hair's so neatly parted and combed, and it's white. The color has really left him already, hasn't it?"

"What about that weird mustache?" says Maddy, indolently stroking her stomach.

"I know who he looks like—that man who wrote detective stories. Who is it? He went with Lillian Hellman. Oh God, another name bites the dust."

"Dashiell Hammett?" says Georgia.

"Right." I sit up, pulling at my blouse to neaten it, a feeble attempt at getting a grip. "For weeks Adrienne and I have been torturing ourselves trying to think of this short blonde actress from the fifties or maybe the forties, I'm not sure."

"Donna Reed?" says Georgia.

"No."

"Is it the actress who plays the woman who becomes a famous trash writer in the movie about two friends? What's that movie called?" Georgia says. "Not *Two Friends*, but something like that. I think her name's Millicent, or maybe that's her name in the movie."

"Is that the same movie where the other friend is a serious writer?" I ask.

"Yes."

"It's not her."

"Jill Clayburgh," says Maddy. "Isn't she from the fifties?"

"Hardly. And she doesn't fit one physical description I gave."

"Oh."

"I think this one's name starts with an *l.*"

"Short blonde actress . . ." Georgia muses.

"Played wimps, and she's kind of wide." We all stare at each other as our minds experience simultaneous hard-disk failure.

I clasp my hands and raise them high. "Oh, please tell me and give me peace of mind."

"June Allyson."

I look at Georgia and Madeline. "What?"

"I didn't say anything," says Georgia.

"Me neither," says Maddy.

"Then who said that? Dad?" I jump up. "Dad!" I stand over his bed, freaked. "Dad, you said that, didn't you? You said 'June Allyson.' "

"Who's June Allyson?" asks Maddy.

"Dad? Nurse, nurse!" I am screaming.

Georgia sprints out the door. "We need a nurse," she shouts, "right now."

The nurse bustles by her into the room. "He's coming around, I swear, he's coming around." Maddy grasps my hand.

"Mr. Mozell," the nurse bellows in his ear.

"He just said 'June Allyson,' " I explain. "Oh, thank you, Dad. Thank you. It *is* June Allyson."

"That doesn't start with an *l*," says Maddy.

"I know, but it almost does. Anyway, that's who it is. She's in all these movies where the guy dies in a plane crash and there's this scene where she doesn't know he's dead and—"

Georgia clutches my arm. The nurse is checking my father's pulse. She puts the stethoscope in her ears and listens to his heart. She pulls the stethoscope off.

We stand immobilized, waiting for her to tell us what we know.

Down the hall, in the distance, I hear a phone. It rings and rings and rings. Why doesn't someone pick it up, why doesn't someone answer? I look at Georgia and Madeline. "The phone. No one's answering the telephone."

Georgia puts her arm around me. Maddy buries her head in my shoulder. My eyes are blurry now. "It's never going to be him again."

"That will be a comfort," says Georgia. She is crying too.

☎

It's past eleven, Joe and Jesse have gone to bed, but my sisters and I hang on, sprawled in the living room. I am on the floor on my back, perhaps in some semiconscious mimic of a dead man. Georgia is stretched across the couch, her arm flung up across her forehead in classic damsel-in-distress mode, except that she is never distressed, only flamboyant. Maddy slouches in an armchair, a Chinese-takeout container balanced on her stomach. It is very cozy being too tired to talk much, and besides, I don't want the night to end. When will we get together again? Will we commune on the phone as often, now that we share no burden?

"Why doesn't your lipstick wear off?" I ask Georgia.

"A special brand. I'll send you some, but not red." She lifts her head to scrutinize me. "I think you want plum." Her head drops down again.

"Where do you think Dad is now?"

"In a refrigerator," says Maddy. "At the mortuary in a gigantic refrigerator." She blows her nose into a paper napkin. "My baby's never going to have a grandpa."

"Stephen says the thing about losing a father—"

I butt in. "We don't want to hear what Stephen thinks. If we don't know him—"

"No, listen." Georgia sits up. She takes a moment to shake off the dizziness from switching to vertical so rapidly, before making her pronouncement. "Stephen says that once your father is dead, there's no more hope. It's now set in stone: For better or for worse, that's the father we got."

"Well, what's sadder? Who he was or who he wasn't?"

"My baby's never going to have a grandpa," Maddy moans again, now digging into the takeout container and coming up with a cold sparerib. She views it sadly.

"It's like he was a house, and when you walked into the living room, sometimes you'd find what there was supposed to be in a living room and sometimes you'd find what should be in a kitchen. And when you walked into the bedroom—"

"No," says Georgia, "you never walked into the bedroom."

"Was he kinky always?"

"Who knows," says Maddy. •

" 'You can exist without love, but never without like.' Dad said that to me after I broke up with the horrible Philip."

"You know," says Georgia, "even if you have no photographic talent, if you take a million pictures, one of them is bound to come out great."

"I guess so."

Georgia unscrews her earrings, giving each an affectionate gaze before laying them on the table. "Stephen gave these to me."

"I hope he'll be a good uncle," says Maddy.

"Anyway," says Georgia, "Dad was wrong. Lots of couples exist without love. Isn't hate just as binding?"

"Maybe, but I think he was right. He meant that you can exist happily without love if you really like the person. Anyway, thank God, this isn't my problem—I love and like Joe."

"So why do you care?" asks Georgia.

"Because it's—" I look at her puzzled.

"A moment of clarity," suggests Georgia.

"Yes. And kindness."

"Do you think one of us should tell Mom?" asks Maddy, aimlessly conducting an orchestra with her sparerib bone.

"You mean, do we think you should tell Mom?" I say. "Does she care?"

"Probably not," says Maddy. "But it seems only proper that if your father dies, your mother should be informed."

Georgia hoots. "In case she was thinking of going back with him. And what about telling Claire, wherever she is?"

I sit up now too, hugging my legs to my chest to keep out the cold. I can almost hear his voice, "Hey, Evie. Hey, it's my Evie." I miss him. I actually miss him. I hate to think he's in a refrigerator. I've seen it in the movies, where they slide the bodies in and out on trays. "Do you think he has a tag on his toe?"

"No," says Georgia, "they don't put on toe tags. Or maybe they do." She smiles. "That might be something I don't know."

Madeline tosses her sparerib back in the box and looks around glumly. "Where's his bullet, anyway?"

"I don't know. I think it's still in his room at the Home. I'm sure that's where it is."

"I want it," says Georgia.

"Well, so do I."

"I want it too," says Maddy. "I brought it up."

Georgia stands, dusting off and straightening her shirt. "We'll choose, all right?"

She takes off in the direction of the kitchen. We hear her rummaging around, opening closets and cabinets. Maddy makes the cuckoo sign, circling her finger next to her ear. I giggle. We are girls again.

"Where's your broom?" shouts Georgia.

"For what?"

"Straws. Never mind, I'll use toothpicks."

She reappears, gleeful. "Come on, let's go. Short one wins." She offers them up.

Jay Gullixson

About the Author

DELIA EPHRON has written many books for adults and children, and has worked as a screenwriter. She began her writing career as a journalist for *New York* magazine. Her work has also been published in *The New York Times Magazine*, *The New York Times Book Review*, *Esquire*, *Vogue*, and other publications. She lives in Los Angeles with her husband, writer and producer Jerome Kass.